# Wolf Tales 9

Also by Kate Douglas:

*Wolf Tales*

"Chanku Rising" in *Sexy Beast*

*Wolf Tales II*

"Camille's Dawn" in *Wild Nights*

*Wolf Tales III*

"Chanku Fallen" in *Sexy Beast II*

*Wolf Tales IV*

"Chanku Journey" in *Sexy Beast III*

*Wolf Tales V*

"Chanku Destiny" in *Sexy Beast IV*

*Wolf Tales VI*

"Chanku Wild" in *Sexy Beast V*

*Wolf Tales VII*

"Chanku Honor" in *Sexy Beast VI*

*Wolf Tales VIII*

"Chanku Challenge" in *Sexy Beast VII*

# Wolf Tales 9

KATE DOUGLAS

APHRODISIA
KENSINGTON PUBLISHING CORP.
http://www.kensingtonbooks.com

APHRODISIA BOOKS are published by

Kensington Publishing Corp.
119 West 40$^{th}$ Street
New York, NY 10018



All Kensington Titles, Imprints, and Distributed Lines are available at special quantity discounts for bulk purchases for sales promotions, premiums, fund-raising, and educational or institutional use.

Special book excerpts or customized printings can also be created to fit specific needs. For details, write or phone the office of the Kensington special sales manager: Kensington Publishing Corp., 119 West 40$^{th}$ Street, New York, NY 10018, attn: Special Sales Department, Phone: 1-800-221-2647.



ISBN-13: 978-0-7582-2695-2
ISBN-10: 0-7582-2695-0

First Kensington Trade Paperback Printing: January 2010

10 9 8 7 6 5 4 3 2 1

Printed in the United States of America

# Dedication

This series has taken me places I never expected to go, but it's a journey I freely admit I haven't made entirely under my own power. I've had the support of my agent, Jessica Faust of BookEnds LLC, who moves beyond any superlatives I can possibly conjure up—I consider her my friend, my mentor and my advisor—as well as a fantastic agent, one whose instincts are always right on target. My editor, Audrey LaFehr, gives me the kind of freedom many writers only dream of. Without her amazing support, Wolf Tales would not exist, and I can never thank her enough for the opportunities she and Kensington Publishing continue to give to me.

My thanks, as always, to my generous and talented beta readers: Karen Woods, Ann Jacobs, Sheri Fogarty, Camille Anthony, and Rose Toubbeh. These wonderful women find my mistakes and keep me on track. Their impressive skills combined with some truly wicked humor make the entire process of creating each new book in a continuing series a lot more fun than it probably should be. A special thanks to Rose for her expert suggestions regarding the California prison system—any mistakes in the story are my own, but Mik and AJ's time in Folsom made a lot more sense after Rose pointed out quite a few things I needed to know.

To my readers—I can't thank you enough. Many of you have become my friends and confidants over the years. Your support is a powerful incentive every day when I sit down to write.

Last of all, to my husband. There really are no words—and "thank you" doesn't even come close.

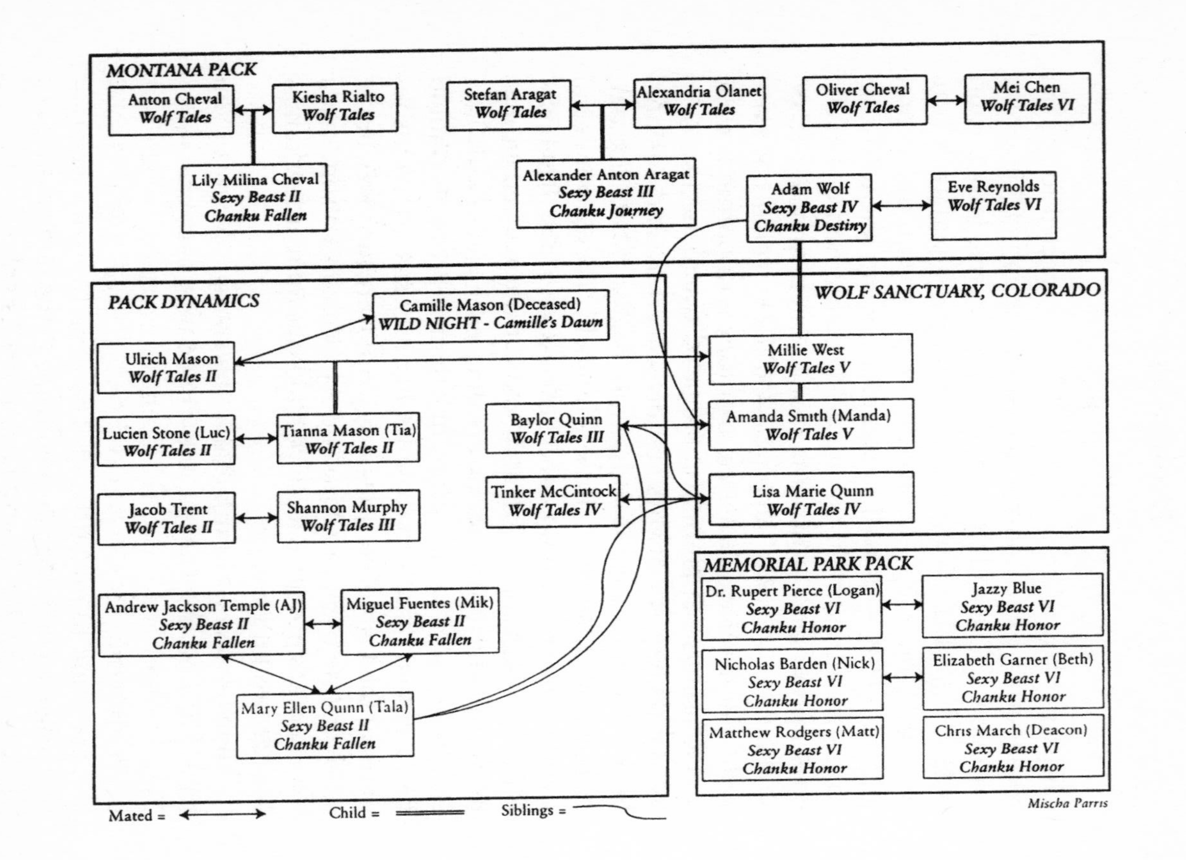

MONTANA PACK
Anton Cheval
Wolf Tales
Kiesha Rialto
Wolf Tales
Lily Milina Cheval
Sexy Beast II
Chanku Fallen
Stefan Aragat
Wolf Tales
Alexandria Olanet
Wolf Tales
Alexander Anton Aragat
Sexy Beast III
Chanku Journey
Oliver Cheval
Wolf Tales
Mei Chen
Wolf Tales VI
Adam Wolf
Sexy Beast IV
Chanku Destiny
Eve Reynolds
Wolf Tales VI
PACK DYNAMICS
Camille Mason (Deceased)
WILD NIGHT - Camille's Dawn
Ulrich Mason
Wolf Tales II
Lucien Stone (Luc)
Wolf Tales II
Tianna Mason (Tia)
Wolf Tales II
Jacob Trent
Wolf Tales II
Shannon Murphy
Wolf Tales III
Baylor Quinn
Wolf Tales III
Tinker McCintock
Wolf Tales IV
Andrew Jackson Temple (AJ)
Sexy Beast II
Chanku Fallen
Miguel Fuentes (Mik)
Sexy Beast II
Chanku Fallen
Mary Ellen Quinn (Tala)
Sexy Beast II
Chanku Fallen
WOLF SANCTUARY, COLORADO
Millie West
Wolf Tales V
Amanda Smith (Manda)
Wolf Tales V
Lisa Marie Quinn
Wolf Tales IV
MEMORIAL PARK PACK
Dr. Rupert Pierce (Logan)
Sexy Beast VI
Chanku Honor
Jazzy Blue
Sexy Beast VI
Chanku Honor
Nicholas Barden (Nick)
Sexy Beast VI
Chanku Honor
Elizabeth Garner (Beth)
Sexy Beast VI
Chanku Honor
Matthew Rodgers (Matt)
Sexy Beast VI
Chanku Honor
Chris March (Deacon)
Sexy Beast VI
Chanku Honor
Mischa Parris
Mated =
Child =
Siblings =

# Chapter 1

A flash of silver streaked the Pacific as the gibbous moon slipped beneath the horizon. Darkness settled around them. Tia Mason Stone shivered and wrapped her arms around her naked body. Her enhanced Chanku vision gave her the ability to see in the almost total darkness as her husband and bonded mate, Lucien Stone, stashed the duffle bag filled with their clothing beneath a fallen tree.

He stood up, straightened, and stretched his arms over his head. Then he smiled, reached for Tia and pulled her into a warm embrace. His body was big and solid, and his muscles rippled in all the right places. The thick mat of hair covering his chest tickled her erect nipples and brushed the side of her cheek when she hugged him back.

She couldn't stop the soft sigh that escaped her lips. Was this really the right choice? Times were not safe and all their lives were at risk.

Luc nuzzled the side of her neck and planted a soft kiss below her ear. He'd been eavesdropping on her thoughts again.

"I love you. You love me. And face it, sweetheart, I'm not getting any younger."

Sometimes, Tia almost wished that the choice to make babies wasn't entirely up to her. Most Chanku females felt empowered by their ability to chose when to release an egg for procreation. Not Tia. She was terrified. So many things could go wrong . . . but that was life, wasn't it?

Luc was right. He was fifteen years older than she was, and it wasn't fair to make him wait any longer. They'd been bonded mates for a year now, and married for almost three months. He'd been hinting about babies ever since her father had told Tia she was destined to have two daughters—little girls with her mother's sass and brass.

Luc really wanted those baby girls. One at a time, of course, but she knew he was ready for fatherhood.

Just as she was almost certain she was ready to become a mother.

Tonight Tia's heat was upon her. If she conceived now, her baby would come in the spring. The timing was right. Shoving her fears aside, Tia shifted. Luc met her, nose to nose in the wild darkness on the western slopes of Mt. Tamalpais. Tia yipped, snapped at his shoulder, and took off at a full run.

She'd mate with him on the mountain tonight, and damn it all, she'd release an egg, but he was gonna have to work for it.

The night was magic and Luc could have raced through the darkness forever. The pressures of running Pack Dynamics meant they rarely had a chance to run together on the mountain. Cautious trips through Golden Gate Park were the closest he'd been to anything remotely forested in ages, but tonight was special.

Tonight they intended to conceive their first child. He'd be damned if any child of Luc and Tia Stone's would get her start from a furtive mating behind stunted shrubs in a city park, with both of them afraid someone could come upon them at any time.

He'd much rather be high in the mountains at their cabin near Mt. Lassen, but there'd been one job after another and he'd not been able to break away. Plus, Tia's students needed her more than most—all of them had special needs, and it was difficult to find a decent substitute who could give them the same loving attention as his wife.

*His wife.* So few of the Chanku actually went through with a legal marriage. The mating bond, after all, was for life. But the minute Luc had slipped a ring on Tia's finger—a ring she rarely wore because she knew she'd lose it when she shifted—he'd felt a connection even deeper than their mating bond. A connection that somehow validated all the terrible things that had gone on before.

To think that this beautiful woman, one of the only pure-blood shapeshifters he knew of, had a heart big enough to forgive him. After all, he'd been the one who fired the bullet that killed her mother. It might have been an honest mistake, an act carried out in the line of duty as a dedicated San Francisco cop, but it was still a terrible tragedy. One he would never truly be free of.

Camille, Tia's mother, had prophesized the birth of two little girls. Maybe, just maybe, those little girls would somehow take away the guilt that, despite Camille's forgiveness from beyond the grave, was still an ever-present shadow in Luc's heart. Two little girls to atone for the loss of one spectacular woman—the woman who had given birth to his amazing wife.

Tia's scent inflamed him. The musky odor of her heat, and the knowledge this would be so much more than a mating simply for pleasure. His body was hard and ready, his arousal a living, breathing force driving him, giving speed to his legs and power to the chase.

He caught her, finally, in a small glen on the far side of the mountain. The lights of San Francisco cast a golden luster across the dry grass and gave the beautiful bitch awaiting him an unearthly radiance. Her eyes glowed with green fire in the reflected light and her sharp canines shimmered like ivory.

She growled softly when he mounted her, but she didn't pull away. He felt himself grow hard and strong, knew from the change in her scent and the sudden catch in her breath that she'd done it—Tia had released an egg for fertilization.

Before she had a chance to change her mind, Luc thrust forward with a powerful lunge of his hips. His long cock slipped through her softened vulva and he drove deep and hard, finding the mouth of her womb on his first thrust.

He felt the swollen knot in his wolven cock expand. Her vaginal muscles clamped down hard, holding him inside as his body responded to her scent.

The beast in him took charge.

Her mind was as suffused with lust as his, her thoughts no longer coherent with human logic but instead a swirl of sense and sound, of bestial desire and uncontrollable passion. Her forelegs collapsed beneath his weight and his powerful thrusts. She went down, but Luc was still locked deep inside and he felt the steady pulse in his balls, the hot jets of his seed.

Seed that would find the egg she'd released. A single spermatozoa that would bind with that one tiny cell and create a child. Their child. A combination, he prayed the Goddess, of all the best Luc had to offer, of every perfect quality that made up his wife.

Panting, he rested his head on her shoulder and waited for the knot to subside. Usually, when they mated as wolves, the two of them would shift and hold each other in their human form, but tonight he wanted this sense of continuity, of who and what they truly were.

Tonight, they were wolves, mating beneath the stars of a late summer sky, both of them fully aware and praying there would be a child in the spring.

Finally his flaccid cock slipped free of Tia's warm and loving body. Luc shifted. So did Tia. He wrapped his arms around the pliant body of the woman beside him and rolled to his back, taking her with him.

She gazed down at him with tears in her eyes and an inexplicable look of sadness on her face.

"Tia?" He brushed the thick blond curls back from her amber eyes. Touched the single tear rolling over her caramel skin. Her mind was locked to him, her barriers high and strong.

She tried to smile and her face crumpled. Sobbing, she pressed her face against his chest. "Oh, Luc. I'm not sure, but . . . what have I done, Luc? I'm so sorry."

*Almost nine months later . . .*

Shannon Murphy set the telephone aside and grinned at her packmate, Manda Smith. "Interested in a trip to Montana?"

Manda raised her head from the button she was sewing on one of her mate's shirts. "Why? Is there a problem? Is Adam okay? Does Anton need us?"

"Nope." Shaking her head, Shannon couldn't have wiped the grin off her face if she'd tried. "For once, it's all good. Tia's decided to have the baby at Anton's new clinic. Now that we have our own doctor, she figures she'd be safer there than in a regular hospital."

"Wonderful! I want to be there. Do you think we can talk the guys into going?" Manda tied off the button and put her sewing kit away.

"If we can't, you and I are going without them." Shannon laughed and pointed her finger at Manda's nose. "I'm not about to go without you, so don't even think of staying home. Tia was my very best friend from the time I was a little girl. She's the reason I have Jake. There's no way I'm going to miss something this important."

"Miss what?" Baylor Quinn wandered into the room,

leaned over and planted a kiss on the back of Manda's neck. "Where are we going?"

"I imagine we're going to Montana." Jacob Trent stepped out of the bedroom with his laptop under his arm. "I just heard from Luc. They're on their way to Montana. Tinker and Lisa are sharing the driving. Mik, AJ, and Tala are already up there and Tia's convinced the baby will be here by the weekend."

Shannon stood up and reached for Manda's hand. "That doesn't give us much time." She slanted a big grin at Jake. "Especially if we're going to take the bikes."

"Hot damn!" Jake high-fived Baylor. "Well, bro . . . it definitely looks like we're going to Montana."

Ulrich Mason set the portable phone on the table and grinned at his mate. Millie was going to have a fit, but there was no way he'd miss this particular gathering.

He steepled his fingers beneath his chin and took a deep breath. "Millie, m'love, I think it's time we give the youngsters a chance to show us what they've learned."

Millie glanced up from her painting and blinked. He loved the way she got so totally engrossed in her art that the world disappeared. "What?" She frowned. "What have they learned?"

Ulrich laughed. "Hopefully how to run the sanctuary in your absence. We're headed to Montana."

Frowning once more, Millie dipped her brushes in a jar of clean water and wiped them off with a damp rag. She stared at the brushes in her hand instead of Ric. "You know how much I hate to leave . . ."

"It's time." Ulrich stood up and walked across the deck. He glanced at Millie's easel, at the beautiful watercolor of a dark wolf poised at the forest's edge. She'd caught Ric perfectly, right down to his grizzled muzzle and the arrogant turn of his broad wolven head. He thought he made a fine looking wolf, especially as seen through Millie's eyes. "That one's going to fetch a pretty penny in the gift shop."

Millie's smile lit up her face. "Do you think?" She turned away and studied her painting. "I was actually thinking of giving this one to Tia and Luc. They've asked for a painting of you, and . . ."

"Perfect." He covered her shoulders with his big hands, turned her around and kissed her on the nose. "We'll deliver it in person. In Montana."

"Montana? I don't understand . . . isn't the baby about due? Tia can't be going to Montana."

"She's almost there. Tia wants Logan to deliver the baby with Adam assisting, and she wants us there when it's born." He leaned close, touched his forehead to Millie's, and opened his thoughts, his memories of Tia as a child. He couldn't help but wonder if this was fair—sharing memories of his daughter's childhood with a woman whose own children had been taken from her at birth.

Would Millie understand? Or would this hurt her . . . he never wanted to bring her pain, but he couldn't *not* go. "She's my only daughter, Millie. She wants me there for the birth of our grandchild. I have to go, but I can't go without you." He kissed her, whispering against her lips, "It's a chance to see Adam . . . and Tia said Manda and Bay are on their way."

Millie laughed and kissed him back. "You fight dirty, Mr. Mason. Real, real dirty. Yes, the kids are perfectly capable of running the sanctuary, but don't you think they'll feel left out, staying behind? I know they miss Logan and Jazzy."

"True, but they barely know Tia and Luc. I'm pulling rank this time, Millie. Matt, Deacon, and Daci and Beth and Nick need to know that we trust them to watch over this place, and I need to be with my daughter . . . and you, my dear, need to be with me."

Millie leaned back in his embrace and gave him a wide-eyed, innocent look. "You left me once before, when you took off on that rescue and stuck me with poor Matt."

Ulrich threw his head back and laughed. "Poor Matt? It took almost a month to wipe the shit-eatin' grin off poor Matt's mug. I think you practically killed the boy."

Millie grinned, and he scented her arousal. He'd been in her memories and knew exactly how his mate and that perfectly gorgeous young man had spent their time while he was away. The visuals made him hot whenever he thought of the two of them together. The few times he'd been with Matt, he'd slipped into the younger man's memories as well, and Millie was always there, front and center.

Matt might be with Deacon and Daci now, but that one night with Millie had changed the boy. Millie's innocent and loving nature had given Matt a newfound confidence, a more powerful sense of self-awareness, an ability to finally tap into the qualities that made him such a fine young man. Ric felt a sense of pride whenever he was around Matt, as if he'd had something to do with the young alpha emerging from a kid they'd all tabbed as hopelessly beta.

"You did have something to do with it, you fool." Millie was actually laughing at him now. "You set us up." She jabbed Ric in the chest with her finger.

He grabbed her finger and nibbled on it. "Are you complaining?"

Shaking her head, Millie pulled her finger free. "Not at all. I'm just wondering when you intend to set us up again."

He wrapped his arms around Millie and pulled her close. "I imagine that can be arranged. However, you might get Deacon and Daci along for the ride."

"I'm not complaining." She raised her head for another kiss.

Ric sensed someone coming at the same time Millie pulled away. Both of them turned toward the pathway that connected Millie's cabin with the two where the younger Chanku lived.

"Speak of the devil . . . " Ulrich chuckled and raised his hand to wave at Matt.

Millie jabbed him in the ribs and Ric pinched her bottom as they turned to greet Matt. Both of them were laughing when he stopped at the foot of the steps to the deck.

"Did I interrupt something?"

"No."

"Yes."

Millie glared at Ric and burst into giggles. "In your dreams, Ric."

He shrugged and grinned at Matt. "You can't blame a guy for trying. What's up?"

"I just got a call from Logan. Tia's on her way to Montana to have her baby at the clinic. Logan was checking to see if we could watch the sanctuary so you and Millie could be there when the baby comes. I told him it wasn't a problem, that the five of us could handle things here. I hope that's okay?"

"Better than okay." Ric glanced at Millie. She still looked undecided. He ignored the stubborn tilt to her chin and turned to Matt. "In fact, I'd like to leave in a couple hours if we're going to get there in time, but I need to take care of a few things in town, first. Do you mind keeping Millie company while I'm gone? I hate to leave her alone."

He sensed Millie's shock and Matt's surprise, but he kissed Millie fast and stepped away. He passed Matt on his way down the steps before either Matt or Millie could say a word. He was still grinning like an idiot when he backed the jeep out of the narrow drive and headed toward town.

Millie could hardly look Matt in the eye. She was going to kill Ric. Eviscerate him, at the very least. Slowly, and very, very painfully. How could he possibly think a juvenile stunt like—

"Millie?"

Her head snapped around and she glared at Matt. His eyes went wide and she reined in her anger with Ric. It wasn't Matt's fault that her mate kept throwing her at the poor kid. "I'm sorry, Matt. What?"

He flashed her one of his absolutely drop-dead gorgeous, sexy smiles and nodded in the direction Ric had just gone. "How long do you think before he's back?"

"At least an hour . . . maybe more."

Matt shrugged. "Beth and Nick are checking the compounds. Deacon and Daci are cleaning pens near the parking lot and said they'd be gone for a couple hours. I finished up the work in the office. I'm sort of by myself, and if Ric's gone, how about . . . "

Millie sighed and shook her head. "You know he set us up, don't you?"

Matt took the steps two at a time and grabbed Millie's hand. "Of course I do, and I owe him big time. C'mon, Millie. I've missed you."

He looked her up and down with such blatant and carnal intent she felt her sex swell and dampen, merely from the naked desire in his gaze. How could this absolutely gorgeous young man want her, a woman old enough to be his mother?

And how could the man she loved above all others be so generous, so willing to encourage what, in spite of accepted Chanku morality, Millie could only think of as an illicit affair?

Who was she to argue? Matt held his hand out. Millie placed her palm in his, and when he tugged her through the open door to her cabin, she followed.

She couldn't have stopped grinning if she'd tried, though when Matt shut the door and closed the two of them inside the cool, dark room, she trembled. Would she ever get over her hang-ups? Her sense that this was somehow wrong, that it would anger Ric to know she fantasized about sex with a younger man?

Was that part of the attraction? The feeling that somehow she was doing something illicit, something truly bad, after forcing herself to be such a "good girl" for so many years?

Matt's big hands cupped the sides of her face. "Quit analyzing, Millie. Ric and I have talked about this. He told me he wants us together on occasion. He wants you to have the chance to discover all those parts of Millie West that you've buried for your whole life, and he wants me to gain a little more confidence with women."

"With me, Matt?" She turned and kissed his palm. It was rough and callused. A man's hand, though she thought of him as a boy. A beautiful boy who, with his packmates, worked very hard to take some of the responsibilities of the wolf sanctuary off her shoulders. She raised her chin and smiled at him. "I find that hard to believe. How could sex with a woman like me give you confidence?"

He laughed, but there was a delightfully strained tone to the sound. "You're kidding, right?" He shook his head and reached for the hem of her shirt. "You're gorgeous. You're the most generous lover I've ever known, and you never make me feel like I'm totally inept."

He tugged the shirt over her head and tossed it on the couch. Then he reached for the front hook of her bra, but he kept talking. "It's like with Daci. I know she loves me, but when I'm with her, I'm with Deacon, too. I love both of them, but sometimes when we're all tangled up and screwing our brains out, I'm thinking of you, of the night we spent, just the two of us. You made me feel so special, like I could do anything after that night we had together, Millie."

He separated the clasp and lifted the bra away from her

breasts. Slowly, he nudged the straps over her shoulders. A draft of cool air brushed her nipples and they ruched into tight buds. Millie licked her lips to keep from moaning.

And Matt kept talking. "I'd never had any self-confidence with women. Not ever, but you responded to everything I did. You showed me where to touch, how to touch . . ." He laughed and tossed her bra on the couch beside her shirt. Then he reached for the snap on her jeans.

"That was so amazing. Nothing seemed to shock you, but at the same time, you acted like it was your first time, like I was teaching you, even though I knew it was the other way around. You taught me so much that night, Millie. I've thought of you ever since. I know you're Ric's and that you love Ric, but I wanted a chance to do this again. To touch you again when it's just the two of us. Just you and me."

He tugged her jeans over her hips and her panties went with the soft denim. She was barefoot, and it was so easy to lift one foot and then the other so Matt could help her out of her jeans, but that left her naked while he was still fully dressed.

Why did that make her even hotter? What was it about wearing nothing but the admiring gaze of a gorgeous young man while he stood there in worn jeans and a T-shirt, that turned her on so much? Her vaginal muscles clenched in a slow, heated rhythm and moisture gathered between her legs, all while Matt stared at her like he could eat her for dinner.

All lanky young man that he was, so tall he towered over her, he leaned close and wrapped his perfect lips around her erect nipple. Then he sucked, drawing just that one bit of her inside his mouth. She felt the flat of his tongue pressing her nipple against the roof of his mouth, felt the suction drawing the blood to the tip. All the muscles in her pelvic area clenched in response.

His lips curved up around her breast and he released

her nipple and slowly knelt before her. She was trembling, and she didn't know why, couldn't remember when she hadn't trembled, when she hadn't felt this horrible need for his mouth and tongue between her legs.

As if he read her mind, Matt cupped her bottom in his big hands and pulled her close against his mouth. She spread her legs wider to hold her balance, but when his lips met her labia, when his tongue circled her clit, she cried out and clutched his shoulders.

He licked and sucked, and his tongue speared deep. She wanted more, wanted the full length of that young man's cock filling her, wanted the heat and the life of him deep inside, but all he did was tease her with his tongue. He nibbled and licked and sucked as if he'd not been with a woman in months. His fingers kneaded her buttocks and his mouth ravaged her sex.

The climax slammed into Millie without a hint of warning.

One moment she was trembling with frustrated desire, the next she was screaming. Her legs buckled. He held her upright, hands clasping her butt, his mouth between her thighs, still licking, still lapping up her cream like a big cat.

Only he wasn't a cat. He was Matt, and he stood up and swung Millie into his arms and carried her to the small guest room as if she were nothing more than a child. She was glad he hadn't taken her to the bed she shared with Ric. Glad that he was sensitive enough to her confused sense of loyalty to the man she loved, the one who wanted her to have sex with this boy . . . no. Matt was most definitely not a boy. Not with a chest like the one he'd just bared. Not with a penis swollen to proportions that rivaled Ric's.

There was nothing boyish about Matt. Nothing but his smile, and that was so sexy it made her womb clench and her body grow anxious and needy.

He slipped out of his clothing. When he came to her on

the bed, she merely lifted her knees, spread her legs and silently invited him in. Instead, Matt sat back on his heels and stared at her. She shivered beneath the intense heat of his gaze. The lips of her sex parted, inviting him in on their own. A cool draft of air tickled her damp vulva, and still he studied her.

Millie plucked at her nipples, silently inviting him. His cock twitched when she touched herself and pre-cum leaked from the tip of his broad glans. He hadn't said a word since he'd undressed her. Not a single word, and his thoughts were blocked to her.

Somehow the silence, the sense of isolation it created, made the anticipation of this joining even more exciting.

Matt ran a finger from her left knee to her inner thigh and she arched her hips to his touch. He trailed his fingertip higher, across her mons, down the inside of her right thigh. Then he touched her clit, so gently she barely felt the contact before he slipped just his middle finger deep inside her vagina.

Her muscles contracted involuntarily, tightening around his finger with its bony knuckles, holding him. He slipped free, leaned over and kissed her. His lips were soft and full and still slick from her cream.

Curious, she traced his lips with her tongue. For some reason she tasted different on Matt's mouth than Ric's. Why? No matter. It was all good.

Matt carefully rolled her over until she lay on her stomach. He palmed her buttocks and she wondered if he would take her there instead. She didn't care, so long as he filled her somewhere, now. She had no secrets from Matt. There wasn't a part of her body he'd not tasted or entered or touched during their amazing night together.

He reached down and lifted her hips, raising her up on her knees until her face rested on her folded arms and her butt was in the air. He ran his finger from her clit to her tailbone, and it felt so good she shuddered, on the edge of orgasm again, merely from one stroking finger.

"Millie, I could look at you all day, touch you forever, but I need you now. Is it okay?"

She bit back a giggle. Now he asked? "If you don't, I'm never speaking to you again."

He laughed. "I take it that's an affirmative."

She wiggled her butt, and for some reason she didn't feel like a woman in her fifties. No, she felt like a young girl with a very sexy young man, and it was wonderful.

Matt pressed the broad head of his cock against her vaginal opening. Slowly he separated her labia and slipped inside. Her muscles clenched, tightening around his thick shaft, stretching to allow him entrance. Slowly, so carefully, he filled her. She heard his soft sigh when he was finally all the way inside.

When he began to move, slowly thrusting his hips forward, and just as slowly retreating, her muscles rippled and clenched, tightening around his erection. He trailed his fingers over her flank and found her clit. Rubbing in slow circles with just the tip of one finger, he took her once again to the edge of the precipice, but this time he held her there, slowly and thoroughly loving her as if she were made of spun glass.

She needed more. Wanted more. Finally, almost desperately, Millie opened her thoughts in that intimate connection she usually saved for Ric. Opened to find a man who was not her mate, but who loved her with the same passion, the same consideration and attention. She linked with Matt and found him waiting, poised on the edge of perfection, clinging to whatever control he could find until Millie was ready to join him in the plunge from the top.

Thoroughly delighted, she pressed back on his next penetration and took him deep inside. His fingers trapped her clit and on his next thrust he squeezed. Screaming,

Millie set herself free. Her body shuddered, her heart tried to pound free of her chest. Caught in a mental loop between Matt's orgasm and her own, she flew.

Tumbling through sensation as if it were a space unto itself, Millie's mind filled with erotic images as Matt saw her—her body was sleek and smooth, her muscles firm, her breasts perfect.

And there beside her in his mind, Millie saw Daci and Deacon, Beth and Nick and even Ric. All of them, sharing a place in his heart. No more, no less. All of them Matt's family, his pack, the ones he loved.

His arms collapsed and the two of them fell to the bed. Matt's cock still pulsed within her and his chest expanded against her back with each deep breath he took. She loved Ric. She would always love Ric, but times like this with Matt were a special gift to be savored, and savor them she would.

Without guilt. There was no need for guilt, only appreciation for Matt, and heartfelt thanks to the generous and giving man who claimed her as his mate.

Ric stepped through the front door into the cabin. He heard Millie in the bedroom, and wondered if Matt had gone. Wondered if he'd even stayed. Millie still had her issues with sex outside of their mating bond, but Ric had to believe she'd get over them eventually.

He walked down the hallway and dumped a pile of bags on the bed. Millie stepped out of the bathroom. She was freshly showered and wearing a soft cotton pantsuit, something comfortable and appropriate for travel.

"Ric! What did you buy?" She opened the first bag and giggled. "Pink? And two of everything? Ric, we do not know for sure if she's having a girl, and we definitely don't know if she's carrying twins. Tia's been very secretive about that." She put one hand on her hip and frowned. "Unless, of course, you know something I don't know?"

He shook his head. "Only what Camille told me. Would you argue with a ghost?"

"Well, I hope you've got receipts in case the ghost screwed up and Tia has one little boy."

Ric reached for his travel bag on the top shelf of the closet. "Are you ready to go? Are the kids okay with the details so you can leave your wolves without fretting all the way to Montana?"

Millie turned and flashed him a smile. "Matt and I discussed everything. They should be just fine."

"I see. So, you were talking the whole time I was gone?" He wiggled his eyebrows and dove into her thoughts, but Millie had a barrier up that rivaled the Great Wall of China.

She grabbed her suitcase and a handful of the baby gifts he'd picked up in town, and then she headed toward the door without answering him. In the doorway, Millie turned around, raised one eyebrow, and said, "Matt and I thoroughly communicated everything we needed to, and that, my dear, is all I'm going to say."

He could still hear her laughter as she went out the front door. Ric found his shaving kit and tossed it, along with plenty of clothes, into the soft travel bag and zipped it shut. It was a long drive to Montana. He'd get the details sooner or later.

And if they were good enough, which he knew they would be, he and Millie could always find a nice place to stop along the way.

Preferably one with a big, comfortable bed.

Whistling, Ric grabbed his bag and followed Millie to the car.

# Chapter 2

Tia looked between her knees at the absolutely beautiful man who was staring much too intently at her pussy—for all the wrong reasons, as far as her worthless libido was concerned.

A not-so-pleasant thought came to mind. "Logan, do you realize I've been as big as a whale ever since I've known you?"

Doctor Logan Pierce raised his head and smiled at her, and damn it all if she didn't feel a spike of arousal that was totally out of place, considering the position she was in—both feet in the stirrups, her big butt hanging off the edge of an examining table and her boobs so huge they flopped into her armpits.

There was absolutely nothing glamorous—or sexy—about a woman almost nine months pregnant.

Logan shook his head. Obviously she'd been broadcasting. "You're still beautiful, Tia. Breathtakingly beautiful. You're also about two centimeters dilated, so active labor could start at any time." He straightened and held out a hand to help her sit up. "But without a doubt, I find you so beautiful that it's extremely difficult for me to remain entirely professional. Trust me on this . . . there is absolutely nothing sexier or more appealing than a pregnant woman. I can't wait until Jazzy feels ready for babies."

Tia grunted as she sat up. She looked down at her heavy breasts resting on top of her huge belly. "Babies, plural, being the operative word here."

Logan handed Tia's clothes to her. "Luc knows, of course, but you haven't told anyone else?"

She shook her head. "I just couldn't. It's so embarrassing, to think I popped out two eggs when I only planned on one."

He laughed, but at least it was sympathetic laughter. She hoped. "Don't be so sure it's all your fault. The sonogram wasn't as clear as I'd hoped, but it appears there's just one placenta and two amniotic sacks, which means a single egg was fertilized and then divided. No matter . . . you're carrying two perfect little girls who can't wait to be born. I can sense them. Their mental signatures are strong and healthy."

He went to the sink to wash his hands, but he turned to look over his shoulder and winked at Tia. "I've heard about your mother's promise to your dad, that you'd have two little girls like her." He raised one eyebrow, and there was a noticeable twinkle in his amber eyes. "Did you ever consider the fact that, just maybe, you had absolutely nothing to do with the number of eggs—or babies? That your mom might have had her hand in this?"

Slowly Tia shook her head. She'd never considered . . . but no. That was just too weird. Her mother had been dead since Tia was six years old. But Anton *had* brought Camille back for that one night. She couldn't possibly have . . . no. Could she? "You don't really think . . . ?"

Logan shrugged. "You never know. Stranger things have happened, but you certainly shouldn't feel stupid for creating a life. Not with babies as beautiful as you and Luc are sure to have. Celebrate, Tia. You're young, you're healthy, you've got a man who loves you more than anything. What more could you want?"

Tia laughed and fastened her serviceable cotton bra, the only one she'd found that could support the massive breasts she'd somehow developed to go along with her expanding belly. "If you want the truth, Doc, I want my body back, and I want to get laid. Not necessarily in that order."

Logan burst out laughing as he turned away from the sink to dry his hands on a paper towel. "It'll all happen. Not necessarily in that order. You're smart to abstain for now. You want those two little girls to have all the time they need before they make their appearance."

He wadded up the damp towel and made a perfect shot into the trash, but there was a rueful expression on his face. "Definitely smart to abstain. If you'll recall," he said drily, "I spent last night with your husband. He topped, and I can honestly say from my own sexually satisfying, yet rather painful experience, the way that man's hung, I doubt your girls have left any room for him right now."

They were both laughing when they walked out of the perfectly appointed clinic. Luc met them outside the door. Tia glanced at Logan, once again he raised an eyebrow and that set them both off again. Luc's head swiveled from Tia to Logan, back to Tia, and he shrugged.

Tia grabbed both his hands, stretched up on her toes and kissed him. Her gravid belly rubbed against his hard, flat one, and she felt their babies move. Luc obviously felt them as well, and he smiled against her lips. "I love you," he whispered, nibbling at her full lower lip. "You are so beautiful this way, your body ripe with my babies . . . Tia, you take my breath away."

A powerful sense of peace settled over her.

She'd been so afraid when she insisted they come to Montana. Had she made the right decision? Was this really where she wanted to have her babies, in a tiny little clinic stuck back in the woods on the western slope of the Rocky Mountains?

Yes. Most definitely yes. Her father and Millie were on their way. Shannon, Jake, Manda, and Bay should be rolling in some time tomorrow. Mik, AJ, Tala, Tinker, and Eve were here, along with the entire Montana pack. Everyone she loved would be with her to offer support.

She had a doctor who understood the ways of Chanku, who could actually communicate with her babies. She had Adam Wolf, a man who fixed things, in case anything, Goddess forbid, went wrong.

She had the most important man in her life—she had Luc.

What better than her husband and a real doctor here at Anton Cheval's perfect little clinic? Add to that, an entire pack of people who loved her.

Tia's fears drained away. The sense of peace grew even more profound. It was all good.

The four from Maine had arrived a couple of hours earlier and were taking a well-needed rest when Millie and Ulrich slowly pulled into the driveway between the main house and Oliver and Mei's cottage. Anton waited alone on the deck to greet them. Though he'd known they were drawing close long before their vehicle actually turned off the main road onto the long private drive to the house, he'd not said anything to the others.

The evening was cool and everyone had either taken off on a run or gone inside to get out of the chill air. He loved it when his house was filled to the brim with those he considered family. After so many years alone or with only Oliver as company, he'd had more than his fill of solitude.

There were times though, like this moment, when he took the opportunity to stand alone in the darkness, to give thanks for the good things that had come to him. To thank the Goddess for such an amazing life.

In the background, he heard adult voices and the squeals of both Lily and Alex, their childish jabbering and bright laughter a joy he'd never expected at this stage in his life. Both babies had just started walking in the past few days and suddenly everything in his home had been rearranged to accommodate the mobile monsters, as Stefan had dubbed the two.

He and Stefan still occasionally got together for a morning glass of cognac, a chance to laugh and lament that their lives would never be the same.

As if either of them truly wanted those lives back again. He still ached when he remembered how alone he'd felt, how bleak his future had looked before Xandi and Stefan, and then his greatest blessing, Keisha, had come into his life.

Children were their future, not merely for the Chanku, but for each of them. They offered the promise of forever.

A promise Ulrich Mason was about to receive. Only a dozen years older than himself, Ric was going to be a grandfather. Anton chuckled softly. And to think he was still hoping for more babies, Goddess—and Keisha—willing.

Age was such a nebulous thing for Chanku. So far, none of them appeared to have aged since their first shift, which made Anton question their potential longevity. Did Chanku grow old? He didn't know, but now that he had his clinic and the lab, and his very own, highly trained doctor in Logan Pierce, Anton was determined to find out.

He raised his hand in greeting as Millie and Ric climbed stiffly out of the car. "Hey, Grandpa. How was the trip?"

Ric's head shot up. "She hasn't had the baby yet, has she?"

Anton was already trotting down the stairs. "No. Not yet, though she's having those weird contractions . . . Braxton-Hicks? Whatever they're called, her belly gets hard as a rock. A very large rock. Make that a boulder." He laughed. "She's reached the point where she looks miserable, but she's not complaining. To any of us, anyway. Luc may have a different take on the matter. I tell you, though, the females are definitely the tougher sex."

Millie threw her arms around him and hugged. "I heard that. It's good when a man actually admits the truth."

"Millie, it's great to see you." He gave her a quick kiss, and grabbed the filled tote bag she held. Millie turned around and showed him a great looking rear end as she dug in the backseat for more of the colorful cloth bags.

"Here." She looped the handles from a half dozen totes over his wrist. "You can take some of these, too." She rolled her eyes in Ric's direction. "Grampa went shopping."

"Dad! You're here!" Tia waddled down the steps with Luc at her side.

Ric's eyes went wide. He looked at Millie and grinned. "What did I say?" Then he held out his arms and drew Tia into a tight hug. "Ah, baby . . . looks like your mama got her way. Again. I knew you were carrying twins."

"Dad! No one knows!" She shot a furtive glance at Anton. When he burst into laughter, she frowned. "What?"

It took him a minute to get things under control. "Dear, dear Tianna, this is not meant as an insult because you are absolutely gorgeous, but you are huge. It's quite obvious there's more than one baby in there. Don't you think everyone's guessed by now?"

Tia glared at him. "I have no pride left. None. Luc? Take me inside, please." Then she got the giggles and totally blew the imperious façade.

Millie slipped an arm around Tia's waist. "Sweetie, I had twins and you have my sympathy. You *will* get your figure back. I promise."

Everyone glanced at Millie's slim figure. She struck a pose, stuck out her tongue and grabbed Tia's hand. "The serfs can bring the luggage. We've got catching up to do."

Anton watched the two women walk slowly up the stairs. He turned to Ric and caught his friend smiling at his mate and his only child with tears coursing down his cheeks. Anton thought of all the years Ric had been alone since the death of his first wife, the years when he'd been afraid to tell Tia of her birthright, the tough cases he'd had with Pack Dynamics when there'd been no one to come home to, no one to share his life with—not the good times or the bad times.

Now Ric had Millie. He had Tia and Luc and two little girls on the way . . . girls with Camille's sass and brass if her spirit had anything at all to do with this. Anton hugged Ric around the neck and pulled him close. Ric sniffed and took a deep breath.

Luc patted his father-in-law on the back, and grinned.

Ric shook his head and punched Luc in the shoulder. "Luc, you bastard . . . I can't believe what you did to my little girl."

Luc grinned, shrugged and picked up Ric's bag without saying a word. Laughing quietly, Ric and Anton grabbed the rest of the luggage and the totes filled with baby gifts, and followed the women up the stairs.

Keisha, Eve, and Lisa spent most of the following day preparing a welcome feast, now that everyone had arrived and all were moderately adjusted to the same time zone. When Tia first saw the two huge rib roasts and all the side dishes waiting on the buffet, she'd thought they'd have leftovers for a month. Now, as the twenty-three adults and two children cleaned their plates, she realized how badly she'd underestimated the appetites of a houseful of Chanku.

She'd also underestimated the depth of her own emotions, how it would actually feel to sit in a room filled with family and friends, packmates all, who had come from all across the country just to be with her when she gave birth to her babies.

She flashed a grin at Luc. The look he gave her in return took her breath. Goddess how she loved him!

Tia pushed her plate away, stood up and clapped her hands to get everyone's attention.

"Is it time?"

Tinker's big laugh had everyone going. He'd been asking that same question for at least a month now.

Tia glared at him. "No, Tinker. For the gazillionth time . . . *not yet.*" Grinning broadly, she glanced at everyone along the long table, but when she finally paused, she focused on her father and her heart pounded in her chest. "Dad, Millie . . . I am so glad you're here. All of you. I'm not exactly sure when this big event is going to happen, but I want to thank everyone for coming, and Anton, Keisha, Stefan, and Xandi for once again graciously opening their home to all of us."

She glanced at Anton. He sat with his fingers steepled in front and his chin resting at their peak, but he quietly nodded his response. Still looking at him, she added, "Anton always says we're strongest when we're together. Having all of you here when I'm delivering just . . ." Her voice cracked and she took a minute to regain control. "Well, you have given me a wonderful gift, and I wanted to thank every one of you."

She touched Luc's shoulder. His big hand covered hers. "And," she said, feeling a little foolish, "I imagine a lot of you have already guessed it since I look like a beached whale, but yesterday Logan confirmed what Luc and I have suspected all along—Mom got her way on this one. I was almost sure I popped out one egg, but it looks like we're having twin girls."

She laughed at all the raised eyebrows and the applause. "Okay, so I guess not everyone figured it out. I'm surprised, as humongous as I am. I feel as if I'm carrying an entire soccer team, but thanks to Anton's brand-new, state-of-the-art clinic, I got to see both our little girls yesterday when Logan did a sonogram. And yes, there are only two in there." She cupped her hands over her huge belly. "Thank goodness!"

Luc rolled his eyes. "I'm actually relieved. I was thinking litter . . . I figured she had at least four in the oven."

Tia thumped him on the head with her fingers before she sat down. Her dad smiled at her and she caught his thoughts.

*Your mom must be so proud of you, sweetie. I just know she had a hand in this.*

*Thanks, Dad. I think she did. I was afraid it was me, but there's no way I'd do this to myself!*

Tia helped Mei and Jazzy clear the table and then wandered out to the great room where everyone had gathered. There were a couple of chess games going, and Anton and Stefan were chasing the babies around on the floor, much to Lily and Alex's delight.

Oliver was trying to do a magic trick Stefan had taught him, and the laughter from his corner of the room told Tia he wasn't having much success. Millie, Manda, and Adam had gathered in another corner to talk. The three of them held hands, as if they needed even more of a connection than most. Watching Millie and the two children she'd not known until they were adults, had Tia fighting tears.

To have babies taken away . . . she covered her belly in a protective gesture. The pain for Millie must have been indescribable. Now that she carried her own babies under her heart, Tia felt as if she understood her stepmother better than ever. Thank goodness Ulrich and Millie had found each other.

Tinker glanced up from his chess game with Logan, caught her eye and grinned. "Is it time yet?"

Before Tia could answer, half a dozen voices shouted, "No!" and Jake threw a pillow that Tinker deftly caught.

Then he ducked his head and went back to the game. Laughter ebbed and flowed around her. There was a subtle, subliminal buzz that let Tia know a few in the room were mindtalking to carry on private conversations. Oliver gave a triumphant shout and Mei clapped her hands. Luc turned from his spot on the couch beside Baylor and Shannon and smiled at her.

*I love you,* he said. His thoughts drifted over her mind with the strength of a caress.

*I love you, too.* Then she felt it, a painful tightening that radiated from her back and across the lower part of her belly. The sense of pressure more than pain took her breath. It lasted close to half a minute, and when it was over, everyone in the room was staring at her.

"Is it time?" Tinker's question didn't make anyone laugh this time.

"I don't know. But that was definitely different. Not quite like a Braxton-Hicks contraction." She shook her head. They were still almost a week early. "Logan? How do I know when I'm really in labor?"

Logan stood up. "Let's go take a look. I can tell if your cervix is beginning to thin out. You were dilated at two centimeters last time I checked." He crooked his arm, held out an elbow. Tia slipped her hand around his arm and exited the room like a queen with her escort.

Luc was right there with them.

Jazzy Blue glanced up as her mate walked back into the great room with Tia and Luc. They'd all been anxiously waiting for news. Logan smiled at her and shook his head.

"It's going to be a long night, folks. Tia's only had one very light contraction, so her labor's hardly even started."

Shannon stood up and hugged Tia. "Poor baby. Aren't there drugs you can take to get things going?"

Logan sat next to Jazzy and draped his arm around her shoulders. "There are, but it's always better to let things happen naturally. Luc and Tia are going to do a few slow laps around the house, see if that gets things going, but she definitely appears to be in the early stages of labor. This is the easy part."

Tia stuck out her tongue at Logan. "Easy for you to say, Doc."

Luc helped Tia on with her coat and grabbed a jacket for himself. "We'll be outside walking in circles if anyone needs us."

Jake leaned around Shannon and gave Tia a kiss on the cheek. Then he grinned at Luc and said, "Maybe you should just get her a hot walker . . . you know, those machines they use to exercise horses? Put a bridle on her and turn it on . . ."

"Not funny." Tia glared at him.

Luc laughed. "As usual, your timing sucks, Jake. I knew I should have left you on that mountain." With that cryptic comment, Luc gently led Tia from the room.

Jake stared after them with a pensive look on his face.

Jazzy watched Jake and sensed something more than just a light quip. The guy could be such a contradiction—quiet one minute, then acting like a smart-ass and tossing in a crazy insult the next. She'd seen him get the entire room to laughing, but now he just looked sad. "What'd he mean by that, Jake?," she asked. "Leave you on what mountain?"

Jake turned around and shrugged. "It's a long story."

Adam walked in from the kitchen and handed a cold beer to Jake. "It's gonna be a long night."

Jake gazed around the room as if judging everyone's mood, or maybe he was just trying to build up the nerve to tell his tale. Jazzy wasn't sure which, but she settled back against Logan and waited.

After a brief hesitation, Jake sat down on a footstool in front of Shannon. She rested her hand on his shoulder and he glanced back at her for a long, quiet moment. Then he looked around the silent room again, at everyone who watched him so intently, and sighed.

"Well, if you really want to know . . ."

# Chapter 3

# Jake

"There's no doubt in my mind, if Luc had left me on the hill in question, I'd be dead." Jake took a long swallow of his beer. Then he held the bottle in his right hand and stared at it for a few seconds as the memories washed over him. So much had happened since that chance meeting high in the Sierra Nevada mountains. His life hadn't merely been saved.

It had been forever changed.

"Fourteen, maybe fifteen years ago, I was a paramedic, working in the North Bay, in Santa Rosa. My life sucked, to put it bluntly."

He laughed, but he knew there was no humor in it. There hadn't been much to laugh about in those days. "I'd reached a point where I was searching really hard for a solution to life's many mysteries. Unfortunately, I conducted most of my search at the bottom of a bottle."

He took a swallow of his beer. Shannon squeezed his shoulder and he glanced at her and smiled. She was the only reason he'd even consider telling his story, the only reason he'd ever choose to revisit that disturbing period of his life.

"I'd taken a few days off to go to the mountains. It seemed the only place I had a clear head anymore was deep in the forest, somewhere far away from people and accidents and crap in general. From death. The past week had been absolutely shitty. A little boy without a car seat in a bad accident. We couldn't save him, but his drunk mother wasn't even scratched. A toddler who wandered away from her nanny and drowned in a neighbor's pool. Kids' deaths were . . . well, my head was really fucked and I was desperate to get away."

He raised his head and looked at Jazzy to get the nightmare images out of his mind. She was the one who'd asked, after all. "I'd planned to camp," he said, "but I took enough whisky to open my own bar. The more I drank, the worse my future looked. I had some rope in my backpack and that stupid saying kept going through my head—give him just enough rope to hang himself. Well, I had enough rope."

He reached up and touched Shannon's fingers on his shoulder, desperate for a more powerful connection. She was the one who grounded him. The one who made him whole. She was also the only one who knew the whole story, even though he'd never actually told her. She'd been there, in those dark memories in his mind when they bonded. He had no secrets from Shannon, but he'd never actually told anyone. Never said the words. Not even to Luc. Especially not to Baylor. He'd kept his pathetic past hidden all this time.

As if it mattered. "It was late in the afternoon and I had one bottle of cheap whiskey left. I had it all worked out. I was going to walk as far as I could before it got dark, finish the bottle, climb a tree, and tie one end of the rope to a branch and the other around my neck. I was too big a chicken to jump, but I figured if I was drunk enough, I'd eventually fall off. Problem solved.

"I saw a big oak up ahead and it looked perfect. Branches were all arranged like a ladder. Had a great view of a pretty little valley. I figured it had Jacob Trent written all over it. I took a swallow of the whisky. I remember looking at the bottle and realizing I was running out of booze and I wasn't drunk enough yet, and that bothered me." He paused, remembering. "When I looked up, that's when I saw it."

Just thinking about that moment, that pivotal turning point in his life, caught him. He didn't see Anton's beautiful home or the people sitting around, watching him. He saw the wolf. The most beautiful creature he'd ever seen in his life, the way it stood there, staring at him.

"It was huge. A big, black wolf, but it stopped in the trail, blocking my way, not threatening me at all. I remember staring at it. I didn't feel at all drunk, or crazy, or even depressed. And the strangest thing happened. It was like it was in my head, like I could hear the wolf's thoughts, but they weren't the thoughts of a wolf. They were a man's thoughts. A kind and sympathetic man.

"I stared at it so long I lost track of time. Suddenly I realized it was dark and the wolf was gone, and I was still standing there in the trail. Still had the rope in my pack and an empty whisky bottle in my hand.

"I figured I'd had an alcoholic blackout. I tossed the bottle, sort of shook myself, and stared at the tree. I knew there was a reason I had to climb it, but for the life of me, I couldn't remember why. Then I heard someone coming up the trail behind me. I turned around, and saw a man I'd never met before. For some odd reason, though, he felt familiar."

"I asked you if you had a flashlight."

Jake's head snapped up. He hadn't heard Luc and Tia come back inside. Luc stood in front of him, watching him with a sort of half smile on his face, and the memories flooded Jake with a bittersweet sense of the inevitable. His entire life had changed at that moment. "Yeah," he nodded. "You said you'd gotten too far from your camp and the sun went down before you expected. I had a flashlight. I went with you, back to your camp."

Luc helped Tia get as comfortable as she could in a chair next to Shannon. Then he sat down on the floor beside Jake and leaned against Tia's legs.

Jake smiled at Tia. "Any luck?"

She shook her head. "One measly little contraction. Not dilated any more than the last time Logan checked. At this rate I'm still going to be pregnant at Christmas."

"I highly doubt that." Jake reached over and patted her knee.

Jazzy interrupted. "What happened when you went back to Luc's camp?"

"Ah . . . the rest of the story." Jake smiled at her. It was so much easier to talk about it than he'd ever imagined, but these were his friends. His pack. "Luc gave me this honkin' big pill and said it would take away all my cravings for alcohol." He laughed. "As much as I loved the booze, I had to think long and hard before I took it, but I've never wanted to get drunk since."

He'd lost his cravings for alcohol, but something else took its place. Even now, so many years later, when Jake thought of those first few days after Luc started him on the nutrients, he got hard. He'd always had a healthy libido, but everything changed that night.

What had been a powerful sex drive quickly became a living, breathing entity, a constant state of arousal that the handsome young man he now shared a campsite with seemed to handle with ease.

Luc told Jake that a craving for sex was one of the side effects. That, and an increased sensitivity to light and sound, to scents on the wind. A world that had been unrelentingly gray and depressing was suddenly filled with the songs of birds in flight, of small creatures squeaking and rustling in the grass . . . and more.

The beat of his own heart and the rush of blood through his veins. Sounds that somehow connected him more to himself, to the man he was, the man he should be.

They sat by the fire one evening. He'd been taking the pills for a week and he hadn't had a drink the entire time. In fact, he hadn't even thought of drinking.

All he could think of was Luc. His name, Lucien Stone, repeated like a mantra in Jake's mind. Luc lived in San Francisco. He worked for some kind of investigative agency. He was single . . . and he was, without any doubt, the most beautiful man Jake had ever seen.

He glanced up and looked through the flickering light of the campfire. Luc was watching him with what had to be the same hunger Jake felt. His stomach seemed to roll into a knot and his cock got hard. It didn't make any sense. None at all.

Jake shook his head. "I'm not gay. I've never been all that particular about my sex partners, even had a couple of guys give me blow jobs before, but I'm not into guys."

Luc smiled at him as if he understood all the crap going through Jake's head, and he nodded. "I know. I'm not either."

Jake rubbed at his arms. "I think I'm allergic to those pills you're giving me. My skin's itching like crazy."

"Could be. Beats drinking yourself to death, don't you think?"

Jake laughed and tossed a twig into the fire. "Yeah. It does. Luc, I . . ." He swallowed and stared. Luc had gotten up to grab another piece of wood. He had an absolutely perfect body and moved with the grace of a jungle cat. When he knelt down to add wood to the coals, Jake had to clasp his hands in his lap to keep from reaching out to touch him.

Luc didn't seem to notice, but when he finished stirring the fire, he sat on the same log as Jake. Sat close enough that their shoulders touched. Sat close enough that the heat from Luc's thigh seemed to brand Jake.

Yet, in spite of the heat, the contact made Jake shiver. He felt his balls draw up close to his body and his cock ached, trapped there between his tight denim jeans and his thigh. He bit back a groan and realized he was gnawing on his bottom lip.

"It's okay, Jake. I'm feeling it, too." Luc didn't look at him, but his voice roughened with the same arousal slicing through Jake, the same unbearable need. "Whatever you want, Jake. However you want it. I'm okay with anything. What we do stays here, on the mountain. No one ever has to know."

Jake looked up at the smoke spiraling into the star-studded sky and he thought of where his life was going, how the rope he'd planned to hang himself with was still coiled neatly in his backpack. He knew then, without any doubt, that he'd been given another chance by this quietly amazing man.

He understood he was being offered an even greater gift than his own life. Friendship. Love. A sense of connection, if only for the time they spent together on the mountain. It was still more than Jake had known his entire life.

He turned slowly and looked into Luc's eyes. He hadn't noticed their color before. Amber. The same unusual shade as his own, but he took it as a sign, as one more connection he could share with another human being.

Jake had never kissed another man. Never even imagined himself doing anything like it, but he leaned close to Luc and met him halfway. Their mouths touched and the sensation was unlike anything he'd experienced in his life. He didn't remember moving, but suddenly they were standing, holding on to each other, mouths locked in a deep kiss of lips and tongue and teeth and breathing in each other's breath.

He heard the clink of their belt buckles knocking together, felt the thick length of Luc's cock behind heavy denim and knew Luc was as trapped as he was. As desperate. Laughing, too horny to feel embarrassed, Jake broke away from Luc's mouth, and with shaking hands reached for Luc's belt buckle.

There was no hesitation in Luc, no awkwardness or lack of control. When he reached for Jake's pants, he simply unhooked his belt and flipped the snap open. Jake froze as Luc's fingers lifted the tab on his zipper and slowly, one metal tooth at a time, tugged it down.

Jake's hands stilled and he held his breath, fingers locked tightly on the upper edge of Luc's waistband. Jake's zipper parted and then Luc was going to his knees, tugging Jake's pants down low on his hips, reaching in through the open fly and cupping his balls through his cotton shorts.

Jake had never experienced anything like this in his life. Every sensation magnified. Every touch exquisite torture . . . the heat of Luc's big hands holding him, the hot promise of each breath as he leaned forward and stretched his mouth over the ridge of Jake's cock, suckling his shaft through the warm cotton knit.

Jake's knees buckled and he grabbed Luc's shoulders for support. Luc sat back on his heels and laughed. There was so much joy in the sound. So much freedom. Jake didn't ever remember sex being joyful, desire anything but a basic need to deal with. His hand or a convenient lay . . . it had never mattered before.

Luc mattered. What he thought, how he felt, what he wanted. All of it mattered and the fear built in Jake, that he couldn't be enough. He'd never been enough and he didn't want to fail. Not this time. Not with this man. Not now.

"You won't." Luc slowly stood and rested his palms on Jake's shoulders. "You can't fail at anything, Jake. This is not a test." He leaned his head close, rested his forehead against Jake's. "And if it were, I can promise you, you've already passed."

"I don't understand." Jake rolled his head back and forth against Luc's and he felt his throat thicken, as if he might break down and cry. "I don't understand any of this."

Luc tilted his chin and kissed him again. Softly, gently. If he'd wanted to, Jake could have closed his eyes and imagined a woman's lips on his.

But he desired Luc. Wanted it to be Luc's mouth, Luc's cock. His strong male body pressed close to Jake's, showing him things he'd only imagined.

Neither of them said a word, but they pulled apart and slowly removed their clothing. When they were both naked, Jake expected to feel nervous or at the least, silly, standing here in the firelight, stark naked with the biggest boner he'd ever had in his life. Instead he felt a sense of communion, a feeling of connection, once again, to a man he'd known barely a week.

They stared, unabashedly studying one another. Luc was almost as tall, maybe six four to Jake's six five, but broader in the chest, heavily muscled with a thick mat of dark hair that arrowed down to a flat belly.

His cock was huge—long and thick with heavy veins running the length of the shaft. Unlike Jake, he'd been cut, and the broad glans was shaped like a ripe plum and every bit as big.

Jake had never taken a man in his mouth before. At this moment, he had no other choice. He had to taste the thick bead of cream resting at the narrow slit, needed to feel the silky skin against his lips, the smooth crown filling his mouth, stretching his lips. He dropped to his knees and wrapped his hands around Luc's buttocks, pressed his face against his groin and inhaled the rich, musky scent of another man.

He knew what he liked when he got his own cock

sucked. It was a simple enough thing to turn the process around, to run his tongue the full length of that thick shaft, to dip into the damp slit in the tip of the glans and sample the salty, almost bitter taste of Luc's seed.

Jake lifted Luc's sac in his hand, palming the hard orbs inside and rolling each nut between his fingers. Then he wrapped his lips around the slick crown and sucked. Luc groaned, thrust his hips forward, and tangled his fingers in Jake's long hair.

Jake sucked him deeper, ran his tongue along the full length and tasted more of Luc's seed. He wondered if he'd be able to swallow another man's ejaculate, wondered if he even wanted to suck him until he came, but before he could decide, Luc pulled himself free of Jake's mouth. Blowing as if he'd run a mile, Luc leaned over and rested his hands on Jake's shoulders. His cock bobbed in front of Jake's mouth, shiny with saliva. Slick and wet and unbelievably tempting.

"You're trying to kill me," Luc said. "Right? I thought you said you'd never done this before."

Jake laughed and wiped the back of his hand across his lips. "Never. Why'd you want me to stop?" He should have felt awkward, kneeling in front of a naked man. Instead, he felt like laughing. He wanted to lean close and lick the white bubble off Luc's cock. Wanted to, and so he did.

"Enough. Hold on. Shit . . ." Luc raised his head and stared into the darkness. "I knew it. He is trying to kill me." Muttering, laughing, Luc leaned over and grabbed his pants, reached in the pocket and found a couple of foil packets. "You want top or bottom, because it doesn't matter to me. Man, I am so ready to fuck."

He grabbed his cock and stroked himself a couple times, totally at ease with his body. And huge. Really huge.

Jake blinked. He hadn't thought that far ahead. Hadn't

thought of this at all, but he raised his head and realized he felt uncomfortable now on his knees, eye level with another man's package. It was too real, too graphic. He stood up. Taller than Luc. That was a good thing. "I don't know. I've never . . ."

"I have. Either's fine with me. Sometimes for a first time, top's easier, but whichever you decide, you can trust me."

*Trust me.*

Jake hadn't thought about drinking for a week. Hadn't thought about killing himself, about the job, or death, or the fact he'd been on a downward spiral, ready to hit bottom.

All he'd thought about was sex. Sex and Luc, always in the same sentence, the same breath. "Bottom," he said. "Show me what to do. What you like."

They spread one of the sleeping bags on the ground and left the second one rolled up. Jake lay on his back with his knees bent and Luc shoved the rolled bag under his butt so it lifted him up. He felt awkward like this, but Luc said it was better. Not as vulnerable as he might feel on his hands and knees.

As exposed as he felt, Jake found that hard to believe. He lay there with his ass in the air, his knees bent and his feet flat to the ground. His cock and balls hung in the breeze, unprotected. He felt helpless and utterly defenseless.

Luc knelt between his legs. Jake expected him just to shove his cock inside. He waited for the pain because damn, he knew it would hurt, but Luc didn't do anything of the sort. He stroked Jake's thighs and ran his hands over his belly. He leaned forward until their bellies touched with their hard cocks trapped between them, hot and heavy and wet with pre-cum. Their nipples touched and their balls brushed together. Luc reached between their bodies and stroked Jake's sac, slipped his hand lower to stroke his perineum. Then he gently ran his fingertip over Jake's pucker, pressing, releasing, pressing until Jake was lifting his hips, anxious to meet Luc's touch.

His legs quivered. Lightning stuck wherever Luc stroked him. Every nerve ending was charged but the most sensitive place wasn't his cock, it was that tight little puckered hole in his ass. Luc was using some kind of lube because Jake was slick and soft down there and the muscle fluttered and clenched against Luc's fingertip. When Luc shoved a finger inside, Jake was more than ready.

There was no pain. None at all.

Luc pressed deep. In and out, in again. Jake's perception of sensation seemed to ramp higher than anything he'd ever experienced. He could have sworn he felt the ridges of Luc's fingerprints, a tiny snag on his fingernail, a callus. Luc added another finger and Jake planted his feet, lifted his hips and pushed back against it, forcing Luc deep inside, until both of them were panting. Their chests billowed in and out and their hearts pounded, and they weren't even fucking yet.

Luc backed away. Jake groaned with a sense of loss, of total abandonment, but Luc was back, his cock sheathed in latex. He bent Jake's knees and pushed his legs close against his chest. Then he pressed his cock against Jake's ass. Jake felt the thick head bump his buttocks. The tip of the condom felt slick, as if Luc had covered it with lube. It left a damp spot against the back of his thigh.

Luc grabbed himself and found his target. He shoved hard against Jake's anus, pushing that big, broad cock of his against that tiny little hole.

Jake froze. His muscles clamped tight. There was no way in hell Luc was going to shove that monster up his ass, no way . . .

But Luc was stroking Jake again with his fingertips, easing the way in and relaxing the taut muscle. The soft brush of callused fingertips against nerve endings all ready to spark sent jolts of sensation racing through Jake. Before he could react, before he had time to consider the next step, Luc had replaced his fingers with the tip of his cock and pressed forward.

Needy, so damned aroused he couldn't have stopped his body from reacting if he'd tried, Jake met him. He lifted his hips to Luc's invasion, felt the tight muscle guarding his anus relax. He groaned with the long, dark slide of Luc's cock deep inside his body, the sharp burn that was equal parts pain and pleasure when his sphincter stretched to accommodate Luc's girth.

Luc slowly pressed forward. When the soft curl of his pubic hair tickled Jake's butt, Luc held perfectly still. Slowly, Jake felt his muscles begin to relax, felt the burn subside and a new warmth take hold. Both of them panted. Jake thought they sounded like a couple of big dogs after a long run.

Stuffed full, his body slowly adjusted to what was an entirely unparalleled invasion. The lingering pain of entry slowly, subtly, gave way to pleasure. Jake opened his eyes, unaware he'd closed them when Luc first entered his body. Once again he found himself staring into eyes the image of his own. There was something important about that, something he should understand, but now all he wanted was for Luc to move, to make the pleasure grow, to take him even higher.

He'd never been penetrated—not with fingers or sex toys, and most definitely not with a man's cock. He'd never experienced a connection with another man that was even remotely similar, but for some unfathomable reason, as Luc slowly withdrew and then pressed forward once again, Jake thought of the women he'd fucked. So many women . . . the countless, nameless, faceless women who, over the years, had been receptacles for his hard cock, and if not for the condoms he always used, for his seed.

Jake realized he felt more for the man fucking him now than he ever had for any of those women. Felt a greater connection, a stronger emotional link with Lucien Stone than he'd experienced with anyone before now.

Had the women felt this with him? Had he ever given any of them the same feelings Luc now shared with him, the sense he was a vessel, a treasured receptacle for the man's cock? He couldn't imagine any woman feeling this complete during sex with him.

Not as complete as Jake felt with Luc.

*Impossible.* Jake knew he was an adequate lover, but he'd never shared his soul. Never given anything of himself. Luc gave everything. Jake's mind and body soared, caught in the gentle rhythm of Luc's slow and deliberate penetration, in the sense of the man who made love to him as if he truly cared.

Jake wrapped his hands around his shins and held his legs bent tightly against his chest. His cock bobbed against his belly, hard and dripping, the little eye pointing directly at his chin. He almost laughed. Was he going to shoot all over his face when he came . . . ?

Shit. When he climaxed while another guy fucked his ass.

Luc seemed to read his mind. Their connection grew more powerful as Jake's arousal, tempered by confusion, grew. When Jake wondered about his cock shooting jizz all over his face, Luc wrapped a hand over the thick shaft and slowly, almost reverently, stroked him.

As if he understood Jake's fears.

Almost as if he offered answers to his questions.

Jake watched those long fingers sliding up and down his cock, watched the cowl of foreskin as it partially covered the glans and then retreated once more, mesmerized by the vision of another man beating him off, another man's hand lovingly stroking his dick.

The sensation was so intense, so entirely visceral, he jerked his gaze away from the sight and looked up, directly into those clear amber eyes, sparkling now in the dying light of the campfire.

And it happened. Something so unreal, so intense that Jake forgot to breathe. A link, unlike anything he'd ever imagined. A clear telepathic link with another person. Without any warning he was there, inside Luc's head, his cock trapped in the damp warmth of Jake's rectum, sliding in and out against the hot clench of strong muscles and wet heat.

He felt the sleek stretch of soft skin over an erection as hard as steel, the wet flow of pre-cum as his hand rolled over the broad glans on each upward stroke, and the fascinating slip and slide of a foreskin, a small structure alien to Luc.

Jake heard the silent litany, repeated over and over in Luc's head, the words *don't come, hold on, don't come, hold on . . .*, so clear they became Jake's words, his own mantra until the two of them seemed caught in sexual stasis, balanced precariously between need and desire, caught on the precipice between unbearable lust and ultimate perfection.

Luc smiled and Jake knew he'd been caught, knew that Luc realized his thoughts had been stolen. In that one instant, the act that had been a sharing, a joining of two souls, exploded into something more—a challenge. A battle of wills, of two strong men, each trying to outlast the other.

Now when Luc grinned at Jake, Jake winked. What had been deadly serious took on another sense altogether—of challenge, but of play, too. Exhilarating, thrilling beyond the extreme, yet it was something totally unexpected, and for Jake, an entirely new level of arousal.

Luc's thrusts sped up and he slammed into Jake faster,

harder. His hand slipped up and down Jake's cock at the same speed, sliding in the thick streams of pre-cum now pouring from the tip.

Sensation poured over Jake—the penetration that seemed to fill his entire body, the exquisite pleasure and perfect pressure of another man's hand wrapped around his cock. He felt himself sliding over that edge, slipping precariously toward climax, taking the ride alone while Luc plundered his body with perfect control.

Desperate, unwilling to give in to an orgasm fighting for release, Jake slipped his hands between his legs, brushed the thick root of Luc's cock and cupped his balls in both hands.

Jake almost laughed at Luc's sharp look of surprise when he squeezed lightly and pressed a fingertip against Luc's ass. Luc's hips jerked—in and out a half dozen times in rapid succession, and Jake knew he'd won, knew he'd held on, knew . . .

His victory was short-lived. Bombarded with shared sensations and visuals—from Jake's point of view, from Luc's, so many, so intensely visceral, it was all Jake needed, more than he could take without shooting like a burning star off that precipice and tumbling into orgasm, shouting loudly with Luc's cry echoing in his ears.

But it wasn't a cry. Not at all.

It was a howl. The victorious call of a wolf, claiming the night.

They lay together for what seemed like hours. Jake's hips were still raised on the sleeping bag, though it had flattened out under the combined weight of two men. Luc sprawled across his chest, but his cock was still inside Jake and his fingers still wrapped around Jake's cock.

The oddest thing, though, happened in his head. Luc was still there, his thoughts an open book to Jake, just as Jake knew his thoughts were to Luc.

*I don't understand,* he said. *It doesn't make any sense.*

*It does,* Luc answered. *You will.*

Jake felt Luc's chest bouncing against his, and recognized his silent laughter for what it was . . . an excuse for words, because there were no words.

Jake had no desire to move. None. He'd never felt this complete, this connected, to anyone in his life. Nor this confused. So many images, so many more questions, but they were questions that made him revisit a past he'd tried to forget.

He'd grown up with a succession of relatives raising him until the time came when no one knew how to handle the kid who couldn't or wouldn't follow the rules.

He'd lived on the streets, tried some drugs, drifted in and out of empty relationships and dead-end jobs, but without a high school diploma he'd been headed nowhere fast. At least he'd recognized a need for more education, and finally, with a small scholarship, he'd gotten his diploma, gone on to junior college, and then completed paramedic training.

Somehow, he'd thought that helping people in trouble would give him the connection he'd always needed, but it hadn't helped. Nothing helped. He'd floundered, lost and frustrated.

Until now. Luc had known. Somehow he'd tapped into that part of Jacob Trent that had been searching in vain all his life . . . only it was hard to find something when you didn't know what you were looking for.

Luc had shown him exactly what that was. During the height of climax, as orgasm had swept over both of them, Jake had seen his own holy grail, and he'd grabbed hold of it with both hands.

*Chanku.*

He had no idea what it was, what it meant, but he knew one important fact. Somehow, Luc and the black wolf were connected. And so was Jake. Their paths were meant to cross.

This night was meant to happen.

They made love again, and then again. Jake took the top, then Luc again. Each time more intense. Each time giving Jake a greater sense of who and what Lucien Stone really was.

What he, Jacob Trent, was. And in the morning, after he and Luc had bathed together in an icy stream, washing bodies sticky with semen and sweat and saliva, Luc had finally demonstrated everything Jake had tried to understand throughout the most important night of his life.

Luc shifted. There, in the morning glow of a rising sun, with the towering Sierra Nevada as their backdrop, Luc Stone turned into the same black wolf that had saved Jake's life just one week ago. Then he'd shifted again, and he was once more just Luc . . . and Jake broke down and cried.

He sat there by the cold embers of the night's fire, beside the sleeping bags that were twisted in knots and covered in dirt and pine needles and wept like a baby. All those years, those lost and wasted years of searching and wanting, of strange dreams and even stranger desires, finally made sense.

One week later, after more sex, more love, a greater connection with any other man or woman than he'd ever known in his life, Jake made his first shift.

Before the week was out, he quit his job and joined Ulrich Mason's special investigative company, Pack Dynamics. He became a part of the team that already included Lucien Stone, Miguel Fuentes, and Andrew Jackson Temple. Since that day, he'd never looked back, and he'd never once regretted meeting Lucien Stone, the man who not only saved his soul, but forever changed his life.

# Chapter 4

Jake raised his head, more than a little surprised by the utter silence, even more by the fact everyone had remained in the room while he told his convoluted story. He was even more surprised that his face was wet, covered in tears. Embarrassed, he scrubbed his cheeks with his palms. Then he turned to Luc.

His friend wept openly, as did Tia.

"Hey man, I . . ."

Luc shook his head, wiped his face with a handkerchief and grinned. "I'm just thinking how bad I'd feel, knowing all this now, if I'd actually killed you that night at the cabin at Lassen. It's a good thing my aim was off."

"That night in Lassen, I probably deserved it." He looked at Tia when he spoke, but she merely shook her head in denial. He damned well had deserved it, but Luc and Tia appeared to be well past that sordid affair. "I will always owe you, both of you, for your forgiveness. A lot of people wouldn't have gotten past my stupid stunt."

Jazzy sniffed and wiped her eyes with the tissue Logan handed to her. She smiled at her mate, frowned at Luc, and then turned to Jake. "What happened at the cabin?"

Jake dipped his head. His skin flushed hot and then

cold as shame washed over him. It hurt to admit it, here in front of everyone, but as long as he was spilling his guts . . .

"I made a complete ass of myself. It was ugly and it never should have happened. We all knew Tia and Luc were in love, but they hadn't mated yet. We were up at the place in Lassen, the whole Pack Dynamics crew except for Ulrich. We were all screwing around, quite literally . . . except for Luc."

Jake glanced at Luc and was surprised to see him smiling. Encouraging him to continue. Amazing. If Luc had tried anything remotely similar with Shannon, he'd be dead now.

He shifted his glance back to Jazzy. Luc was obviously a better man than he'd ever be. "Luc had gone downstairs. He left the room while Tia was with all of us. I imagine he wasn't real comfortable watching the woman he loved with his packmates."

Jake shook his head and took a deep breath. It physically hurt to remember something he'd just as soon forget. Without realizing, his hand had gone to his neck, and his fingers covered the pale scar where Luc had torn his throat open.

"It was just Tia with Mik, AJ, Tinker, and me. The sex was really intense . . . and really good." He shot a quick glance at Tia and then looked away. "Tia was amazing and everything was going great. At least, until I lost control. I still don't know exactly what I was thinking, but I shifted and tried to mate with Tia as a wolf—I wanted to get to her before she bonded with Luc, even though I knew she loved him. Some weird part of my brain told me if I got to her first, she'd love me instead."

Luc actually laughed. "It wasn't your brain doing the thinking at that point, bro."

Jake nodded his head, still blown away by his own stupidity. "I imagine you're right. Anyway, Luc heard the commotion and shifted. He came after me as a wolf. A really pissed off wolf. He almost ripped out my throat. I'm damned lucky he didn't hit anything vital, because no one would have held it against him if he'd killed me. I was dead wrong. It was attempted rape, no matter how you look at it."

Tia's fingers brushed his shoulder. "I forgave you, Jake. So did Luc. That's all water under the bridge."

He turned to her and sighed. There was so much love in her eyes. So much understanding. "You're more generous than I deserve," he said quietly. "It'll be a long time before I can forgive myself."

He tilted his head and gazed up at his mate. Shannon's cheeks were damp and her green eyes sparkled. "I'm still in shock that Shannon actually loves me, in spite of all she learned when we bonded. I don't deserve her, either."

"You're right." Shannon flashed her cocky grin, but her eyes were filled with love. "You really don't deserve Shannon. She's much too good for you."

Jake's tension completely melted away. He looked out across the room and sighed. "Shit. I'm in for it now."

"Oh!"

Luc spun around and stared up at his wife. "Tia? Sweetie, are you okay?"

She took deep breaths in and out, then once again before all the air escaped from her lungs in a loud *whoosh*. "That was a good one." She rubbed her hands over her rounded belly and took a couple more deep breaths. "I'm fine, now." She waved her hand at the bunch of them. "You may all go back to what you were doing."

"What were we doing?" Jake grinned at Tia.

"Telling your sordid tale," Mik said. Then he softly added, "Thanks, bud. That took guts." He glanced across the room and grinned at Anton. "Now, the one I really want to hear is Anton's. How'd you and Oliver link up? You two have been together longer than any of us."

"Sort of like an old married couple," AJ added. He nudged Mik. "I think they're even starting to look alike."

Anton laughed. Then he slowly nodded his head and smiled at Mik and AJ. "You're right. We have been together a long time. We met when Oliver was a teenager and I was a young man doing sideshow magic in a circus. It's been . . ." He glanced toward Oliver. "How long has it been?"

"Twenty-five, twenty-six years. I was about seventeen. I remember it was winter because the circus was over-wintering in Florida. February, maybe?"

Oliver's clipped British accent seemed more pronounced than usual, his voice deeper. Jake wondered what memories Anton's simple question might have raised. Oliver took a deep breath, blew it out, and the moment passed. He turned toward Mei and grinned. "It was definitely a long time ago . . . probably about the time you were learning to walk."

Mei punched his shoulder.

The teasing went on for a few more minutes. Jake tossed a few barbs at Mik and AJ, teased Oliver and Mei. He'd always felt just a little bit apart when they all gathered, as if he never quite fit, but since spilling his guts he was actually beginning to relax. He'd never been comfortable talking about himself, yet now he realized he felt lighter. As if a burden had been lifted.

A sound caught his attention and Jake turned around. Tia was panting again. Luc sat beside her now with one hand supporting her back, the other resting lightly on her very pregnant belly.

Tia groaned and leaned against Luc. "How long was that?"

Luc checked his watch. "A little over twenty minutes since the last one."

They both shot disgusted looks at Logan.

"I said it was going to be a long night." He shrugged,

grinning. "Don't shoot the messenger." He got up and knelt in front of Tia. Then he placed both palms on her belly and closed his eyes. Everyone in the room went quiet. After a couple of very long minutes, Logan smiled and sat back on his heels.

"You have two very impatient little girls in there. I can sense them. They're anxious but not frightened, and they are both very healthy." He shook his head and grinned. "Sure beats a sonogram. I'm amazed by what I can learn from them."

Luc frowned. "Are you mindtalking? They can't talk yet, can they?"

Logan shook his head. "No. I'm not trying to link mentally with them, though I can pick up their moods. I'm actually going inside the womb and looking at things on a cellular level. Sort of the way Adam taught me to repair injuries, only I'm just snooping around. Everything's fine. Just moving at a typical snail's pace." He stood up and went back to his spot on the couch. Jazzy crawled into his lap and snuggled against him like a little kid.

Keisha wandered back into the room after changing the baby. She handed Lily to Anton and then sat down beside him on the other couch. He settled the sleeping baby in his arms and gazed around the room.

Everyone switched their focus from Tia to Anton. "I'm assuming Logan knows what he's talking about," he said. "I guess I've got time to tell you how this all began." He smiled fondly and dipped his head in respect to Oliver. "How all of us here, together as a single pack, a single family, would not be as we are, if not for Oliver."

Oliver glanced sharply at Anton. "How can you say that?"

Keisha answered him. "Because he wouldn't have survived his years in Europe and Asia if you hadn't made certain he ate and slept and occasionally bathed. Remember, I've been inside this man's head. We all owe you, Oliver."

Anton raised his eyebrows. "Especially on the bathing part . . ."

"I'll second that." Stefan wandered in with Alex sleeping on his shoulder. The one-year-old was out like a light, but Stefan, just like Anton, seemed unable to put his child down tonight. His gaze met Anton's, and there was a definite twinkle in his amber eyes. "Oliver told me what it was like, following you around during your years researching the arcane arts."

"I was afraid of that. I wasn't very pleasant company during that period, but our story—mine and Oliver's—started many years earlier. It began when I first met Oliver and had what I can only call my first premonition. I've never told Oliver, but I knew from the moment I met him that he would change my life."

# Chapter 5

## Anton and Oliver

Anton settled back on the leather couch and gazed at his infant daughter instead of his packmates. He knew many of them were curious about him, about his past. No one but Keisha knew his personal history. Even Stefan was aware of only a few of the details, but maybe it was time. There should be no secrets among family, and he counted every person in this room as part of his family. His pack.

This was Lily's story as much as his. The bloodlines that had mingled and created him had also helped to create his perfect little girl.

She was so beautiful, so absolutely flawless. Would she ever truly understand the legacy she carried? The burden as well as the gift of her unique bloodline? The blood of an ancient race ran through Lily's veins, just as it did everyone in this room. In this, they were all connected, each to Lily, and Lily to each of them.

Anton's prayer for his daughter was that it would always be more of a gift than a burden—just as it was for him—and he gazed at Lily as he spoke.

"My parents were immigrants to this country." He didn't remember his father, but somehow, he recalled his mother. Flashing eyes, dark, dark hair, her joy in her only child tempered by overwhelming sadness.

"My father was Serbian and French. His parents had met when my Serbian grandmother vacationed in France with friends many, many years ago. My mother was Romanian, of Gypsy blood, and she and my father left Europe shortly after they married. They came to this country to avoid persecution shortly before World War II. My grandmother, a widow by then, came with them. She is the one who raised me."

He brushed a finger gently across his daughter's brow. "Lily is named for her. Lily Milina. My paternal grandmother's name was Milina Cheval. I remember her much better than I do my parents, because both of them died when I was very young. My father found work in a factory near Chicago. He was killed in an explosion in the mid-fifties, when I was still a toddler, not much older than Lily. I remember my mother only as a very sad woman. She never got over her grief. I don't know if my father was Chanku, or if my mother knew of her birthright, but one day my father didn't come home. By the time I was four, my mother had faded away to little more than a shadow, and then she was gone. After that, it was just Grandmama and me for the next ten years. I was fourteen when my grandmother died."

Keisha's hand brushed his shoulder. He turned his head and drank her in. His throat felt tight, but it wasn't from the story he told or the tragedy of an unhappy childhood. It was his love for Keisha. She was so beautiful, so good and powerful that the emotions she stirred made his heart ache. She gave him strength and empowered him. Instead of diminishing her own strength, it seemed to make her even stronger.

Keisha's love blessed him.

He turned away before his feelings for her unmanned him. He didn't want to weep, not when there was so much joy in his life. Sometimes he felt like an emotional fool, but so often the love he felt for his mate overwhelmed him. He looked away from her so that he could better focus on his story.

"I was left entirely on my own when my grandmother died, but I survived. Because we were poor and my parents had been immigrants, no one cared that an old woman had passed on, or a young boy was left on his own. Grandmama loved magic. She'd taught me what she knew until I was a master at sleight of hand. I remember how she called it *léger de main.* She was so proud of her French, but she was even more proud of me. I was adept at misdirection. My skill kept me fed after she died."

He laughed, remembering. "It's a testament to her teaching that I was never arrested for stealing. I worked the streets and improved my skills. I dabbled in magic and became fascinated by what I thought of as real magic."

He'd always wondered if it was a result of his mother's Romanian blood—his Gypsy heritage—that seemed to give him such natural talent. By the time he was in his late teens, he'd begun to build a name for himself.

And then he discovered the circus.

"I loved everything about the circus. The smells and the sounds, the transient life, the people. In hindsight, I imagine this was my first experience of living in a pack . . . and how I loved the women." He laughed then, and glanced at Keisha. She merely rolled her eyes.

"I knew nothing of Chanku, but I certainly had the libido. The circus was a good place to satisfy my needs. Women were freer, men were accommodating. I was happy there, and my fame was beginning to grow." He grinned at Keisha. "On stage, my love, not in the bedroom."

She stuck her tongue out at him.

He laughed and looked across the room. Oliver raised his head as if Anton had called to him. They had always had a powerful link, one that existed long before they understood why.

"Then I met Oliver. He showed up one day looking for work, while we were in winter quarters down in Florida. I can still remember the first time I saw him, this skinny little black kid with skin like dark coffee and a world of intelligence in his eyes. His feet were bare. He wore his torn jeans and ragged T-shirt as if it were Armani. I liked his style and I was immediately drawn to him—he was quick and funny and very, very smart. I also found him extremely attractive but he wasn't the least bit interested in me sexually." Drily, Anton added, "Once I got past the fact that my amazing charm had absolutely no effect on him, we became friends."

Oliver laughed. "You were always, and still are, charming, Anton. You were also a bossy, overbearing pain in the ass, but I loved you anyway."

"Shows you what amazing taste you had, even then. Of course, at the time I didn't realize what it was that made me want you so badly, nor did I understand your lack of interest."

He silently asked Oliver if he wished to explain. Oliver merely smiled and nodded, but he stared at his clasped hands as he spoke.

"What Anton didn't know, what neither of us knew, is that we were both Chanku. Subconsciously we must have recognized our common lineage, but at the time we didn't understand what it was. As most of you are aware, my lack of sexual interest was physical. I had been castrated as a child. I had no sexual desire for anyone. That didn't mean I couldn't love."

Oliver raised his head. The look he gave Anton told more than words ever could. "I loved you then, Anton, with all my heart. As I do now."

Oliver's words swept through Anton, a sensation so powerful it was physically painful, as if he couldn't contain the depth of emotion. He bowed his head, acknowledging Oliver. It took him a moment to find his voice, which sounded uncharacteristically ragged even to him. "Thank you. You know my love for you is as strong as my love for my mate and my daughter. You will always be my son, my brother, my friend." Anton held Oliver's gaze for a long moment, remembering.

They had been through so much together.

Then he turned and looked directly at Adam Wolf and shook his head. "I still think what you did for Oliver was absolutely impossible, you know, but thanks to you and your amazing ability to fix what is broken, he can now experience what each of us demand as our birthright—sexual love and the ability to shift. Of course, Oliver managed to take it one step further."

Mei snuggled close against Oliver. "Personally, I think it's great that Oliver can shift into either a wolf or a snow leopard. He deserves it after what he went through for so many years, though I could do without that barbed cock of his."

Everyone laughed, but Tia grunted and started to pant. Luc stared at his watch until her contraction ended. "Wow. That was a good one, but we're still fifteen minutes apart."

Tia grumbled. "Didn't feel so good to me."

Logan sat up. "Actually, I sense they're getting a little stronger. Maybe it won't be such a long night after all. We've got the birthing room all set up in the clinic. We'll move you there when the contractions get down to a few minutes apart."

Tia shifted her position and caught Anton's eye. "Talk faster. I want to hear the rest of your story before Logan runs me out."

"Yes, ma'am." Anton saluted, but he looked at Ulrich, not Tia. Worry was etched on the man's face. It couldn't be easy, watching his daughter, knowing what lay ahead of her tonight. Anton glanced at Lily's perfect little face and felt a welling up of sympathy, an almost visceral fear for her.

The females were definitely the stronger sex. Thank goodness he'd had Oliver watching over him for all those years, or he might never have made it. Did it take two men to equal one woman? He slanted a quick glance at his mate. Keisha grinned at him, and he knew she'd caught his errant thought . . . and agreed.

He chose to ignore her. "Oliver and I grew very close. I became his sponsor and helped him get his citizenship. Eventually, I hired him as my personal assistant. My act was beginning to draw huge crowds and I needed someone to help me with the business side of things."

Oliver laughed. "You needed someone, period. If any man needs a keeper, Anton, it's you."

"There is that. You can finally relax, though. Now Keisha manages my life."

"No," Keisha said. "Oliver can't relax. You, my dear, are a full-time job for both of us."

"As I was saying . . ." He flashed a grin at Keisha. "Oliver became my assistant. Eventually we outgrew the circus. When I took my act to Las Vegas, Oliver went with me, but even as my career and fame were growing, I felt as if the most important part of my world was missing. I just didn't know what it was."

Oliver interrupted. The pride in his voice almost brought Anton to tears. "What Anton's not telling you is that, at the time, even Hollywood came calling. He performed in a couple of specials for television that drew huge audiences and went on to win awards, including an Emmy. They wanted him to act. More than one studio approached him about making movies. A few of the scripts were really good. He turned it all down."

Anton nodded. "That's true. I was at the peak of my career when I walked away, but I was absolutely miserable. I knew there was something missing. I thought it was my quest to become a wizard, and the fact I'd not mastered the arcane arts I'd wanted to understand, but it was more. Much more."

"He cancelled contracts in the middle of the season," Oliver said. "As his assistant, I was the one who had to get him out of everything. I told people he'd had a breakdown, that he was going into a facility for treatment. I made it sound so bad, they wanted out of the contracts, but I figured it was worth the rumors about drugs and all the bad publicity that followed in order to get him out of his commitments as quickly as I could. I was worried about his mental and emotional health and I feared the rumored breakdown might become fact. Since Anton was adamant his public career was over, I decided not to worry about the repercussions. He willingly burned all his bridges. Not many men could walk away from that kind of success, but Anton did."

And he hadn't missed any of it. Not one bit. "Thanks to Oliver, I was able to get out of my obligations without too much fuss, quietly get my finances in order and slip out of the country. Over the next three years, we traveled through Europe, the Middle East, and Asia. I focused entirely on my quest to learn everything I could about necromancy. I was determined to become the most powerful wizard alive." He shrugged. "You all know me—how single-minded I can be."

He should have expected the laughter. He just hadn't thought it would last for so long.

A few minutes later, Tia doubled over and began panting again. Luc checked his watch and the room went quiet while Tia worked through her contraction. "Sorry, babe. Still fifteen minutes apart."

Finally Tia caught her breath. "Keep talking, Anton. You're helping to take my mind off this."

"At your command, m'dear." Anton focused once

again on Oliver. "Thank goodness I had Oliver to see to my care. He made sure I ate, that I occasionally slept, that my luggage wasn't stolen and my body odor didn't become too offensive."

"I think you just liked it when I forced you into the shower and scrubbed your back."

Anton smiled and nodded. "That's true. It was the closest I got to sex in the three years of our travels. I don't recall ever being celibate that long in my life, but I was learning the arts I had longed to understand. My skills were growing. I was beginning to understand some of what I must have inherited from my mother, the inherent Gypsy traits that are so much a part of who and what I am."

Oliver nodded. "Then Anton found some scrolls in an old abbey in England that changed the course of his search. A single word on one of the pages that he couldn't ignore. The word was *Chanku*. We packed up and went to Tibet."

"That we did." Anton looked around the room, at the beautiful women, the handsome men, all of them like him in so many ways. Connected by their common heritage.

All of them *Chanku*.

"It was a lead that wouldn't let me go. Something about the word resonated with me, and from what I read, I knew we had to go to Tibet. That's where it all came together. Everything I ever knew, ever believed in, was upended. I was drawn to a monastery, a beautiful old place on the Himalayan steppe, that high plateau country at the foot of those majestic mountains. It is a world so ancient, so amazingly wild, and it called to me with a powerful voice. I remember standing in front of the huge gates with a sense of homecoming. I'll never forget how the monk looked at me when Oliver and I first entered the compound. He nodded and smiled, as if greeting an old friend. Then, without even asking why I was there, he took us into a dark cavern beneath the temple where hundreds of scrolls were stored. When I read them, everything suddenly made sense."

"But Anton . . ." Shannon's interruption brought him back to his home, out of that musty cave where his mind had taken him.

"How could you read them? What language were they in?"

He nodded, slowly. "That was the most amazing thing."

The monk was clothed in a roughly woven robe the color of the red dirt they'd hiked through to reach the isolated temple. Oliver was exhausted from the long journey they'd traveled on foot. Anton felt exhilarated, as if he'd taken some sort of drug that made his heart race and his mind spin.

Colors seemed brighter, sound more intense. His muscles twitched and his skin seemed to shiver, not from the intense cold, but from something both internal and external. He had no explanation, but he'd almost been overcome by the sense of destination, the feeling his search had finally taken him to the source of his questions, the one place in the world he might find answers.

He and Oliver wore heavy boots, thick pants, and warm coats against the cold wind that seemed to blow without ceasing, but the monk who met them at the gate was dressed in nothing more than his robe. His feet were bare and one shoulder exposed by the cut of the garment, yet he seemed perfectly comfortable in the frigid air.

Anton shivered as he and Oliver followed the man deep into the bowels of the caverns located beneath the temple. They hadn't asked for anything. Had not explained the reason for their visit. Not a single word had been exchanged. In fact, if anyone had asked him, Anton couldn't have said what had drawn the two of them to this isolated sanctuary in such a desolate place.

The scrolls he'd read in England had only hinted at the

place they needed to find. Once they'd arrived in Tibet, he'd somehow known this monastery was his destination. He remembered thinking that this was truly magic, arriving at precisely the place he needed to be without any directions.

They followed the silent monk into a long, narrow room, where the man pointed to a wall with shelves carved into the stone. Without direction, without questioning the need that drove him forward, Anton went unerringly to a carved chest set in the midst of many other similar boxes and containers.

He held his hand over the chest, unable, at first, to touch it. His palm tingled. The sensation spread until his hand shook, and his body trembled, but he waited, one hand hovering over the thick dust on the intricately carved lid.

He felt a sense of age, of something larger than himself. Something wondrous. Oliver waited silently beside him, but Anton knew Oliver felt it, too. In fact, there was a sense of communication, as if Oliver knew what was in his mind, in his heart.

He'd never been a religious man, never questioned the spirituality that had been part of his core since his earliest memories, but it clearly came to him, standing in that dark and dusty cavern, that it was not a god he served, but a goddess. A powerful feminine figure with unimpeachable dominion over his life. He understood that hers was a benign power, an ancient, yet omnipotent strength directly linked through the females of the people she both ruled and protected.

They'd strayed from her in times long forgotten, though she'd not forgotten them.

In Anton, she saw their return.

She did not ask for worship. Wanted no sacrifice. Did not require a tithe of any kind. She merely wanted to be remembered.

Acknowledged and remembered.

The concept unraveled in his mind in a heartbeat. Too much to comprehend, too powerful to ignore. He filed the sense of obligation away, stored it where he might study it later, at a time when his hands weren't trembling in anticipation, when his heart didn't feel as if it might beat out of his chest.

He took a deep breath and blew a puff of air across the top of the chest. Dust swirled away is if he'd used a powerful blower, not the strength of his lungs. The carvings, almost hidden beneath an ages-old layer of dust, were now perfectly clean, shining in the pale glow of the monk's lantern.

Impossible, but he didn't question the phenomenon until much later.

Carefully, Anton undid the gold latch and lifted the lid. Inside, scrolls were stacked three deep. Their age was impossible to determine, but the scent of centuries drifted from the chest. Anton seemed to know exactly which one to reach for, knew to lift it carefully from beneath the others, to carry it to a large table made of stone and lay it on the clean surface.

The monk had not spoken a single word. He followed silently with his lantern and set it on the table. Anton slowly removed the silk wrappings protecting the first scroll. It was fine vellum parchment of the rarest kind, made from the skin of unborn calves, though he had no idea how he knew such a thing.

Again he thought of the Goddess. Again, he accepted her presence in this place, in his life.

And he thanked her.

Then he unrolled the parchment and carefully spread it out. Script covered the surface and the scroll appeared almost new. He knew how to read Latin and German, and he could read and was conversant in French as well as Romany, the tongue of his mother's people, but the beautifully drawn characters on the scroll made no sense to him at all. Confused, expecting more, he glanced at Oliver.

Oliver shook his head. He had no idea. Discouraged, Anton turned once more to the scroll. This time, the script seemed to rearrange into words he understood, letters that made perfect sense so that the meaning was clear to him. Again, the sense of the Goddess was strong within the cave. Without questioning how or why, Anton once again whispered a word of thanks, something that even now had become automatic for him.

To thank the Goddess for her gifts. To thank her for knowledge—for this life he was still trying to understand.

Oliver couldn't read the scroll—the script made no sense to him—but Anton could, and he did. Scroll after scroll, throughout the long night and into the next day, reading and learning what he could of the people he now knew were called Chanku. Though there was nothing of their evolution, nothing to tell him how they began, he learned of their lives here, at the place of their birth. He read of their matriarchal society and the control the females had over their bodies. He learned of their powerful sexuality, the fact that their bodies needed sexual release the way most species required food.

The more he read, the more he came to believe he'd discovered his own heritage, the secrets that had eluded him all his life. When he finally read of their exodus, the need, as their numbers grew, to find new hunting grounds rather than prey on their human neighbors, he knew he'd almost found the answers.

Their exodus took them in all directions of the compass, away from the grasses that fed a need specific to their bodies. Grasses that provided the select nutrients which gave them their amazing ability to shift form.

To become creatures other than human.

During the long hours, Oliver left and then returned with food and water. Anton couldn't recall if he actually ate or drank, but when he'd finished the last scroll and carefully wrapped it in its silken sheath, he finally understood what had been missing in his life.

He knew, for the first time, exactly who and what he was. He finally understood what an amazing legacy his mother, through her blood, had given him. In the most powerful epiphany of all, he knew his spiritual deity, the Goddess who had always been with him, even when her presence had eluded his understanding. She had no name, no physical stature, but she was as real as Oliver, the man who stood beside him.

And, like Oliver, she would always be there, always a part of him.

A gift of equal importance was the knowledge that Oliver might share the same legacy, the same heritage as Anton.

When he finally put the chest back on the shelf, Anton realized he was physically and emotionally stronger than he'd ever been in his life. He thanked the Goddess with a sense that, in the course of the long night, he had become intimately acquainted with the deity who had been with him for so long. He thanked the monk and left a sizeable donation for the small community living within the monastery's walls.

A community charged with protecting the written history of an amazing people. A people thought to be forever lost.

Anton told Oliver he was ready to return to America. Confused by Anton's sudden decision, Oliver went ahead and made the arrangements. He never questioned his friend. This had, after all, been Anton's journey. His own private pilgrimage.

Before they left the area, Anton had huge quantities of the native grasses baled and shipped to the property he'd purchased in Montana during his years on stage. Though he'd never actually lived here, it was a beautiful home. Isolated and wild, it was the one place he'd always known he could come to when his fame overwhelmed him.

Now it became his sanctuary. The retreat where he would finally discover whether or not the scrolls told the truth.

Here he would learn if he had the ability to become a wolf.

He would finally prove whether or not the story of the Chanku was more than mere legend.

"I began eating the grasses. From what I read in the scrolls, I learned there were nutrients in them that could be found nowhere else, and I was amazed at how delicious they were. It was as if I'd discovered a taste my body didn't know it craved. I didn't tell Oliver what I was doing, what I had discovered. I had to be sure it was real, that the dreams I'd had for so many years, vivid dreams of running as a wolf, of hunting and howling at the nighttime sky, were more than just dreams. When it happened, when I shifted for the first time, and I stood there in the forest on four legs, my senses on fire, my hearing unbelievably acute, I knew I had been reborn."

He raised his head and stared at Oliver. "That's when I made the first of many mistakes to come. Once I had shifted, I knew I was right—I truly had seen the same qualities in Oliver. I recognized my dearest, my only friend, as Chanku. I began giving Oliver the grasses. I ground them up and added them to his food without telling him, fully expecting him to join me as a wolf.

"Within days, his telepathic abilities surfaced. I was ecstatic. This was proof that my theory was right. He was Chanku! I told him what I'd been doing, explained everything I had learned in that cavern in Tibet. I shifted for him and told him he would join me in a matter of days, that we would run together as wolves. His anticipation—and mine—built, but weeks went by and he couldn't shift.

That's when I realized the fact he'd been castrated had robbed him of the chance to embrace his heritage. That cruel mutilation had taken more than his sexuality, more than his manhood. It had taken his Chanku birthright."

Anton had to look away. There was no anger in Oliver, no sense of condemnation. There never had been, no matter how badly Anton deserved it. The regret he felt would always be part of him. A reminder of his own sin of hubris. It was difficult to say the words, to actually speak aloud of his arrogant presumption that he could do as he pleased with another's life.

He tried, but he couldn't keep his voice from breaking. "I had done something even worse than the bastard who ordered Oliver's mutilation so many years ago. Because of the castration, Oliver already had been cheated out of the normal life of an intact, sexual male. Then I came along and offered him something he'd never known to want, something he'd never missed. I, in all my arrogant wisdom, gave him the nutrients. I showed him the wolf when I shifted. I promised him he would have this amazing gift. Because of my presumptuous act, he glimpsed what could never be his. And then he missed it. Terribly. It was my fault, but Oliver was the one who suffered for my mistake."

Keisha shook her head. "You say the words, but one of these days, my love, you will truly understand that taking away someone's choice is wrong."

Oliver immediately disagreed. "No, Keisha. I've never regretted it, even during all those years when I couldn't shift and it set me apart. The telepathic link gave me a sense of connection I wouldn't otherwise have known. A connection more important than anyone here will ever understand."

Then he grinned and winked at Adam Wolf. "Besides, thanks to Adam, everything worked out just fine. It's too bad we didn't have you around when Anton pulled a similar trick on Stefan."

Oliver turned to Anton and grinned—turning the tables, so to speak. Anton had to look away. He turned his head, and found himself gazing directly into Stefan's dark eyes.

Another of his horrible mistakes. He rarely allowed himself to wallow in all the errors he'd made during his long and convoluted life, but tonight seemed to be the time for telling tales and clearing away the mysteries.

He wasn't sure if he was strong enough to tell this story, though. His fault with Stefan had been inexcusable, yet Stefan had forgiven him almost from the beginning.

He'd even forgiven rape.

As if Stefan's five years in hell, courtesy of Anton Cheval, had never even occurred. As if Anton's violent and uncontrolled attack against a man he loved hadn't happened. Maybe it was a story that needed to be told. And, just maybe, tonight was penance for at least some of the wrong Anton had committed against the ones he loved the most.

Keisha's thoughts interrupted his. *Come with me, my love. I need to put Lily to bed in case Tia needs me. I sense her time growing closer.*

Anton nodded, but he guarded his thoughts. Did she really need him, or was his beloved mate merely saving his sorry ass? No matter. He'd take whatever rescue came his way.

Thank goodness one had been offered.

It was Baylor Quinn who asked the question—who forced the issue. "What trick was that, Anton? What happened between you and Stef?"

# Chapter 6

# Anton and Stefan

*What happened?*

He'd asked himself that question for far too long. Damn, but he loved the man. *Stefan Aragat, magician extraordinaire.* Who wouldn't? Kind and generous, a loyal friend, a wonderful lover. An absolutely beautiful man, inside and out.

It was hard to believe how terribly they'd begun, but this should be Stefan's tale to tell. Still, Anton thought how he'd love to stay and hear what Stefan had to say about those horrible years.

Years when Anton had thoughtlessly exiled the famous Stefan Aragat to his own personal hell.

But Keisha needed him, at least for now, so Anton stood up and tugged his mate to her feet. "I'm going to help Keisha get Lily to bed so she'll be ready when Tia needs her. Besides, I'm absolutely certain Stefan would prefer telling our tale with me out of hearing."

"Preferably out of the country," Stefan mumbled, but he flashed a wink at Anton as he and Keisha left the room.

"That's assuming you're interested," Stefan said as he handed Alex to Xandi. From the laughter and rude comments, he figured they must be.

Xandi took the baby and kissed Stefan. "You're on your own, big boy. This little guy needs to be in his own bed." *And I want to be ready, too, when Tia needs me.*

He nodded and watched her leave the room behind Anton and Keisha. Damn, but he got hard just looking at that perfect bottom poured into tight jeans. It had been that way since the first time he saw her, half frozen and near death in the snow. He'd known then that if she died, he was lost, as well.

But hadn't he already been lost? Condemned to a living hell, a victim of his own unrestrained ego and Anton's unbearable pride. Two strong men, deeply flawed yet irrevocably connected, their lives forever entwined.

So much had changed in just a few short years. He couldn't suppress a shudder as he remembered that night so long ago. A time before Xandi, before he had any idea of what his future would bring.

Reluctantly, Stefan turned away as Xandi left the room. He realized at once he was the focus of everyone's attention, so he settled back in his chair and took a sip of his cognac. Staring into the amber liquid, Stefan quietly took all of them back to that time, over eight years ago.

"Like a lot of us who came from dysfunctional families, I had a pretty shitty childhood, so I won't go into that." Growing up in foster care seemed to be something many of them had in common. It made him sad now, knowing what he did about the Chanku, to think of all those mothers who'd never learned of their birthright. They couldn't cope with unfulfilled lives and disillusionment, much less with their children.

They'd all lost so much—mothers and children alike.

*What a waste . . . what a terrible, useless waste.*

Stefan blinked and realized he'd been broadcasting. Every single person in the room was nodding in agreement. They understood. All of them knew exactly what he meant. He cleared his throat and went on. "Needless to say, like Anton, I was on my own at a fairly young age. Another thing we shared in common was actually the link that brought us together—and I'm not talking about genetics. I had discovered magic as a kid, only mine was purely of the tricks category. I had the ability to fool the eye, to make my audience see things that weren't there, to miss things that were. I was very good at it, but I wanted more. I wanted real magic. The kind of real magic I witnessed when I saw the amazing Anton Cheval perform in Las Vegas one night."

He glanced at Oliver and caught him smiling. "Go ahead, Oliver. Laugh if you will, but what Anton did was already magic, long before he went on his quest to study wizardry. We're talking major *woo woo* factor. I remember watching him perform and being in awe. He had showmanship like I'd never seen, a fluid, rhythmic manner of moving his body about the stage that was a dance, like watching ballet. He did things that should have been impossible. He was talented. He was beautiful. Anton Cheval *was* magic."

Stefan paused as memories swept through him. "I wish you guys could have seen him. He had command of the stage, his audience, even the crew working on the sidelines. No one could figure out how he did what he did with such marvelous ease."

Pausing, he looked at the faces around the room, knowing the men, at least, would understand. "I didn't realize it at the time, but I fell in love with Anton that night." He took a deep breath and glanced down at his folded hands, remembering.

"I wasn't gay, you see." He raised his head to the knowing nods of a few of the guys. They understood exactly what he meant. A lot of them had gone through the same period of sexual confusion, the questions of gender identity that never seemed to fit any preconceived label. Not really gay, not bi, not hetero. Not all the time or all at once or even once in a while. They just couldn't find anything that fit the confusing desires that ruled their lives.

"All I could think of was how much I loved women. How could I possibly lust after a man I'd never met? I excused it as nothing more than misplaced hero worship and tried to put my desire for him out of my mind. I didn't contact him then. I think I was afraid of my feelings more than anything, but I went back to learning my craft, doing my shows and trying to put my feelings for Anton into a tight little box where they couldn't affect me. I kept track of him, though. I followed him through every form of available media, until Anton suddenly disappeared.

"When he left the stage, he left a huge void in the industry. In some perverse way, I took his disappearance personally, as if he'd left me, not the industry as a whole. I was terribly disappointed that someone I so admired had reportedly had a complete meltdown. How could he do this to me?"

He laughed. As if Anton were the only one with ego issues! "The stories were all over the place, none of them good, though I have to admit, his departure helped my career tremendously. My show slipped into a lot of the nightclub slots Anton cancelled, and my star began to rise. I even did a television special, but within a year or so, I knew I'd reached my peak. I wanted to be the best, but I was floundering and there was no way I could improve without help. I still performed in Anton's shadow. I needed a mentor, and I wanted the best. There was only one I would even consider—I chose Anton Cheval."

He laughed. "That, my friends, took real balls. I didn't contact him, or ask him for his help. Hell, I was at the top of my game and I was damned good. My ego knew no bounds. I had heard of Anton's home in Montana, so I found out where it was and I went to him. I merely assumed he'd been in rehab like the gossip rags were saying. I had no idea he'd only recently returned from his studies abroad. I think he was so shocked I would just show up on his doorstep, he didn't think to turn me away."

"I wasn't there," Oliver said. "Anton met him at the door. I'd gone to Barbados, to the city where I'd been raised, determined to find the man who had had me castrated. The man who not only had taken away my chance to be a fully functional male, but had also taken something even more important—my ability to embrace my newly discovered Chanku birthright. When Stefan arrived here at Anton's home, he found Anton alone. Stefan didn't realize Anton even had a personal assistant, something that became important later on."

"That's right." Stefan gazed fondly at Oliver for a moment. A complicated individual if ever he'd known one, but someone Stefan could never fully repay. He winked at Oliver and returned to his tale. "I went up the stairs and knocked on that imposing front door you've all been through. To my surprise, I discovered that the only one here was the great magician himself, Anton Cheval, star of stage and screen, rattling around in this big old house all by himself. I introduced myself and told him I had come to learn his secrets."

In reality, the day Stefan came to Anton's door hadn't been exactly the way he'd described. It seemed like another life, now, when he thought about it. He still remembered walking up the curved staircase, knocking on the door. Expecting a butler, at the very least. His shock at the man himself opening the door had left Stefan speechless.

Speechless, in shock, and instantly aroused. The attraction to a man who looked enough like him to be his brother was disconcerting, to say the least. Tall and lean, his hair long and curling against his shoulders, Anton Cheval even had eyes the same unusual color as Stefan's.

It was like looking into a mirror of himself just a few years older, but even more unsettling was the almost visceral sexual reaction Stefan experienced. He still remembered his cock growing hard, his breath hitching in his chest.

When he finally brought himself under control, it was as if he'd walked into a vision of sorts. An alternative universe where nothing was as it seemed.

Cheval had taken him in. Humbly, he'd apologized for the mess as his assistant was away for a few weeks, but he'd welcomed Stefan into his home, into his life . . . into his world of magic and spells and a spiritualism older than time.

They ate simple meals, played chess in the evenings, and studied from dawn until dusk, but it wasn't enough. Unrest, a sense of anxiety, grew between the two men. At the time, Stefan hadn't recognized it for what it was—a powerful sexual tension that practically vibrated in the air between them.

One night they argued. He couldn't remember what started it, but in retrospect, the topic wasn't important, and the argument had escalated over nothing. He'd been young and cocky, frustrated by his inability to perform some of the illusions Anton seemed to create so easily.

Of course, at the time he hadn't realized that what Anton Cheval did was so far beyond mere magic tricks, so much more than illusion, that he was on another level altogether. Stefan had fought the need to learn the deeper, mystical laws of true magic. He wanted the quick fix, the illusory tricks he thought were behind Anton's act.

Anton had been beyond insulted. Later, he admitted to Stefan he'd begun to resent him for his unwillingness to apply himself to the lessons Anton wanted to teach. Yet without even working at it, Stefan's natural talent and his growing abilities were beginning to outshine even Anton's.

Neither man had recognized, at the time, that the level of arousal each of them experienced was fueling their Chanku abilities. They were trying to manipulate sex magic without realizing the source of their power or its potential.

What forced them to the tipping point, though, hadn't been about magic at all. Long after Stefan was gone, Anton realized and later admitted the truth. Like oil and water, they were two highly sexed Chanku males, alphas both, attracted to one another on levels neither one recognized, yet unable to take the small step that would have given them both the sexual satisfaction their bodies craved.

Complicating the situation even further—Anton had been with men before and accepted his open sexuality. Stefan hadn't.

Anton was used to being sought out by sexual partners. The idea of having to pursue another man for sex was beyond his experience. He hadn't known how to take the first step.

Neither had Stefan. He hadn't figured out there was even a step to take. Anton was a man and so was he, ergo, there could be no sexual desire. With that mindset and lack of action, their need simmered and the tension built, until it finally reached a point where reason snapped.

Stefan would never forget the night he lost control and shouted at Anton. Called him a fake. Insulted the man he had begged to mentor him. And Anton Cheval, the man who never seemed to rattle, who held such unimaginable control over himself and his emotions, cursed him.

Stefan remembered the anger, the horrifying, uncontrollable anger he'd felt, that this man wouldn't share his knowledge. His reaction had been totally out of character, entirely over the top. Now, of course, so many years later, he could look back and see it purely for what it was—his libido driving him to a man he loved, and his prejudice holding him back, denying the feelings that were so powerful they'd taken over all sense or reason.

"On top of an awful lot of sexual confusion, Stefan didn't know I'd been giving him the nutrients for almost a week." Anton stepped into the room. He stood behind Stefan's chair and rested his hands on Stefan's shoulders. "This comes under the label of another of Anton's big mistakes." He rubbed Stef's shoulders as he spoke. Stefan raised his arms and covered both of Anton's hands with his.

Anton sighed. "I'd forced a man with a greater than normal sex drive into an untenable situation. Suddenly his libido was no longer under his control. His drives were controlling him and his adrenal glands dumped an overload of the hormone into his system, which pushed his Chanku genes into an action they weren't fully formed to produce. When I cursed him, he shifted, but without enough of the nutrients, his shift was incomplete. He was almost entirely a wolf, huddled on the ground on four legs, his ears flat to his skull, but there was still some of the human in him. He was terrified."

Anton touched Stefan's hair and cupped his palm along the side of his face. "So was I. I had no idea what to do. How to help you. You spoke telepathically because your voice wouldn't work. You begged me to turn you back, to make you human again, but I didn't know how to do it. And so I made another terrible mistake. I let you think that the curse was no more than you deserved. I told you that when you could apologize to me for your hubris, I would turn you back into a man."

Anton bowed his head. "As if your arrogance was a greater sin than my own."

Stefan turned and looked at his mentor, his lover, his closest friend—a man he had hated enough at that time to kill if he hadn't been so afraid of condemning himself forever to life on four legs. He smiled at Anton. "You knew me well enough already to realize my pride wouldn't let me apologize to you, didn't you? I figured out years later that you hoped like hell I wouldn't ask for your forgiveness, at least until you figured out how to turn me back. Wouldn't have looked good at all if I'd said I was sorry right away, and you'd have had to admit you were clueless."

Anton grinned at him. "Have you ever heard me admit a failure?"

Stefan nodded slowly. "Yes, my friend. On occasion I have. We all make mistakes, but yours tend to be doozies."

Anton threw his head back and laughed. "So true. But I didn't abandon you, if you'll recall. Even though I was totally pissed off at you and your unbearable ego."

"You were just mad because you didn't get laid while I was here trying to learn your tricks and spells, you faker."

Anton's eyes were actually twinkling. "There is that. But I sent Oliver to you and he saved your sorry ass . . . at least, until Alexandria came along and helped you see the light."

Thank the Goddess for Xandi. He might not have survived if not for her. But that night, his first night as a wolf, had been an unbelievable, but all-too-real nightmare.

Stefan turned away from Anton, unwilling to hurt him with the terrible memories that still gave him chills. "Anton saw to it that I got home safely, but I have very little memory of the ride back to Oregon."

Trauma had blanked much of it. He recalled weeks at home as a nightmare when he'd hunted as a wolf to survive and wondered what would become of him. He learned later that Anton had left him with a hypnotic command that interfered with his recollection of actual events—so much of what he recalled of those first days, stories and events he'd told Xandi when they first met—had never really happened.

What Anton had planted in Stefan's mind about Oliver still amazed him. It proved once again how powerful a man the wizard was. "I know now that Oliver showed up at my door the day after the driver left me at my home. At the time, I thought I had been on my own for weeks, but I realize now it was the day after I got home. I'd never met Oliver before, but I greeted him as an old friend. I thought I'd known him for years, that he'd been with me since I was a young magician, just starting out. It wasn't until later I learned the truth."

Oliver laughed at Stefan's dry comment. "Anton had planted a powerful hypnotic suggestion so that Stefan would accept me. I immediately flew home from Barbados and moved in with Stefan as if I'd lived with him all along. He believed I had family nearby, so when I occasionally needed time to connect with Anton, I would use a visit home as an excuse."

"Thank the Goddess I had Oliver, old friend or not." Stefan sent Oliver a smile of thanks. "I walked on four legs, had no opposing thumbs and couldn't even open a door without help. I wasn't prepared to live in the wild, yet I couldn't live alone in my home. I could not have survived without Oliver. He very literally saved my life."

Chuckling, Oliver said, "There were days I thought about ending it for you and putting you out of your misery."

"I probably deserved it." Stefan gazed about the room. "What Oliver's not saying, and what I didn't know, is that he was dealing with his own issues at the time. The trip to Barbados had been less than satisfactory."

Oliver nodded. "True. When I got there, I discovered my owner had died. Unfortunately he died peacefully of natural causes." He laughed, but there was no humor in it. "It seemed unfair. I wanted him to suffer, at least a little. As I had. As I still suffered. I did find his daughter, my old playmate. She's very wealthy with a successful husband and a couple of spoiled-rotten kids. She barely remembered me. There was no point in telling her what her father had done to insure she had an acceptable playmate.

What happened to me wasn't her fault, but I couldn't help but think how little my life had meant to her. I'd been mutilated, had served her for many years, and yet I'd been forgotten as if I was nothing more than a castoff toy. My life meant nothing to those people. They had changed it in such a horrible way, yet to them I was entirely expendable."

"Not to us, Oliver. Never to any of us." Stefan stared into his friend's eyes, remembering those first traumatic days. "Like I said, I'm glad you decided against putting me out of my misery, though I wouldn't have blamed you. I was an angry, bitter, frustrated man." He laughed, breaking the tension. "And horny. Damn was I horny! Five years without sex, and Oliver wasn't the least bit interested."

Oliver laughed. "Even if I'd been a functioning male, I don't think I would have been interested. You were ugly, Stefan. Real ugly."

Manda's soft voice broke into their teasing. She'd been so quiet, sitting over in the corner in a big, overstuffed couch all snuggled up against Baylor, that Stefan had forgotten she was even in the room. Her time as a partial wolf had been a nightmare . . . a long, unrelenting horror story many times worse than his.

"Did you have a tail?," she asked. "Did it hurt? My joints were all wrong and the pain was constant."

Stefan shook his head. "No. Mine was nothing like what you had to deal with. Nothing even close."

Manda had suffered terribly for a quarter century, trapped in her painfully misshapen body, mistreated and tortured by a man who had promised to save her.

Stefan's five years had been a cakewalk compared to hers.

"Fortunately, my physical combination of human and wolf was more an issue of what I could and couldn't do. I don't really remember pain, and I was lucky enough to eventually get rid of the tail. Over time I was able to reverse some of the shift. Obviously, if I'd been getting the nutrients, I might have been able to complete the shift one way or the other."

Anton glanced Stefan's way. "I wish I'd known then what I eventually learned. I didn't realize that Stefan merely needed more of the grasses." His shoulders slumped and he stared at his hands once more. "Another one of those mistakes of mine."

"Like I said, when you make 'em, they're doozies." Stefan leaned close and touched Anton's shoulder. He sensed Anton's need for connection, for absolution from at least a few of his own sins of hubris. "It all worked out eventually, my friend."

Anton smiled, but he didn't raise his head. After a moment, Stefan leaned back in his chair. He steepled his fingers, unintentionally reminiscent of Anton's typical pose.

"I finally reached a point where I could walk upright and my hands became more functional. I attributed it to spells I was casting, but now I know it was merely my desire to be human, combined with the physical changes from the grasses I'd had while at Anton's. Still, it was a relief, being able to zip my own pants, brush my teeth. Eat at a real table with a knife and fork. For some reason, though, I couldn't get rid of the fur or the bestial face."

"Or the cock, thank goodness." Xandi walked into the room and stood beside her mate. "I met Stefan five years after he'd partially shifted. He'd been living in his self-imposed exile all that time. I had a car accident and got lost during a blizzard. He found me, unconscious and half frozen in the snow, and took me to his bed to warm me. When I finally thawed out, we made love all night long. I didn't see him at all that first night because he kept the room in total darkness, but I'd never had such amazing sex. Never felt a man's cock swell inside me and tie me to him. It was unreal."

She leaned over and kissed him on top of his head. "Even more than that, I'd never linked telepathically with anyone. When we linked during sex, and I had orgasms that were so amazing they seemed impossible, I knew I'd found my soul mate."

Stefan grinned and reached for Xandi. He wrapped an arm around her waist and drew her close. "And, true hero that I was, after I'd fucked her silly all night long, I left her in a snowdrift on the side of the road the next morning."

Xandi leaned over and kissed him. "I said you were sexy, sweetie. Not that you were smart. You did come back for me."

"That was my doing." Oliver wrapped his arm around Mei. "I told him if he left you out there he was a damned fool. Then I threatened to leave if he didn't go back for you."

"Well, Stefan can't help being clueless. He is who he is, but I love him anyway." Xandi leaned over and kissed Stefan's cheek. "See? You have Oliver to thank for the fact you're still alive, my love. If you hadn't come back for me, I might have hunted you down and murdered you in your sleep."

"There is that . . ." Stefan glanced toward Luc and Tia. Luc was checking his watch once again. "How far apart?"

"That one was just ten minutes, and they seem to be getting stronger."

Tia huffed out a big breath. "There's no 'seem' about it. These suckers are definitely stronger."

Logan raised his head. "Like I said . . ."

Everyone in the room chimed in with, "It's gonna be a long night."

"Funny, guys. You're all just a barrel of laughs." Grumbling, Tia settled back against Luc and glared at Stefan. "Well? Aren't you going to tell us how you and Anton ended up not killing each other?"

"Which time?" Xandi kissed Anton on the cheek. Then

she turned her attention to Stefan and planted a big one on his mouth.

Before he could even kiss her back, she'd broken the kiss, laughing. "Take your choice. For all their smarts, these are two of the most clueless guys I've ever met."

Stefan turned and quirked one eyebrow at Anton. "She's going to pay for this, you know."

Anton nodded slowly, but it was obvious he was fighting a smile. "Oh yes. Most definitely. She'll pay."

Stefan reached for Xandi and tugged, pulling her off balance. Giggling and flailing her arms, she tumbled into his lap, but it was more than obvious she wasn't fighting him very hard.

He held her there with her perfect bottom resting on his suddenly wide-awake cock and enjoyed every moment while she squirmed and wriggled to make herself comfortable.

Finally she sighed and settled down, but he was solidly planted at the juncture of her thighs, well aware of her heat and weight and feminine shape.

Stefan wrapped his arms tightly around his mate and held her close, but his gaze was directed at Anton. "When I realized that Xandi actually loved me, half man and half beast that I was, I knew I had to end the curse. I needed my life back, and the only way I knew to make that happen was to apologize to the wizard. I contacted him telepathically, I in Oregon, he in Montana, but such was the power of my need that I was able to touch Anton's mind. I thought my abilities came from a spell I cast. I had no idea our mindtalking was part of being Chanku, that it was powered by my frustration and anger."

Anton broke their visual connection and gazed about the room. "I had given up on ever hearing from Stefan. I knew of his progress from the regular reports Oliver gave to me. I'd thought of giving Oliver more of the nutrients for him, but I was afraid of what would happen. Afraid he wouldn't know how to control the abilities more of the grasses would give him."

Oliver shook his head. "Even now, you can't admit the truth, can you, Anton?"

Anton's head shot up. He frowned at Oliver. "I don't know what you mean?"

"Be honest. With yourself, at least. You didn't want to give him the nutrients because you were afraid if Stefan had the power to shift back to his human form, he wouldn't need you."

Anton stared at Oliver for an uncomfortably long time. Then he turned and gazed steadily at Stefan. "I never . . ." He shook his head. "Dear Goddess. He's right, you know. I was afraid you wouldn't come back to me. Stef, I . . . I don't know what to say."

"It all worked out, my friend. Everything worked for the best."

Xandi kissed Stefan's jaw. "It sure didn't look that way at first. When the driver let us out in front of Anton's home, Stefan had gone from quiet and introspective to rude and obnoxious. It took me a long time to figure out what he was thinking, but when we were met at the door by an old servant who was, we discovered, actually Anton in disguise, Stefan was all bullshit and bluster. I was ready to punch him in his muzzle."

Stefan rolled his eyes. "You probably should have."

Xandi laughed. "I didn't have time. Next thing I knew, I was bare-ass naked and magically stuck to the wall, the old man had turned into a wolf, and then he attacked you."

"I raped him." Anton spoke so softly, Stefan was surprised anyone even heard, but from the shocked gasps from around the room, it was obvious everyone caught what he said.

"It got my attention."

Anton's head came up at Stefan's droll comment. "What?"

Laughing, Stefan tightened his arms around Xandi. "Why do you think I acted like such a horse's ass when we arrived? I wanted you to take the first step. I knew I didn't have the guts. If you hadn't done what you did, the two of us would have gone on forever, waltzing around the real issue."

"Which was?"

Smiling broadly, Stefan slowly shook his head. "The fact we were hopelessly attracted to one another. I was still fighting that whole guy on guy issue, and you were still hung up on my arrogance versus yours. Face it, Anton, we're two stubborn men, alpha males, for want of a better description, who were unwilling to admit the real issue was the fact we wanted nothing more than to get naked and fuck."

"And if you'll recall," Xandi said, turning to smile at Anton, "once I suggested you two do just that without all the strutting and posturing and alpha male bullshit, everything worked just fine."

Anton sighed, but his shoulders were shaking and it was obvious he was doing his best not to laugh. "She's right, you know."

Stefan held both hands over Xandi's ears and leaned close. "Don't let her hear you say that. She's impossible enough as it is."

"Deservedly so, gentlemen." Xandi crossed her legs and leaned back against Stefan's chest. "Get used to it."

# Chapter 7

## Tia and Shannon

"Xandi, I do like your attitude." Shannon gave Jake's shoulder a solid bump with her knees. Then she patted him on the head. He growled.

"Thank you, m'dear." Xandi dipped her head in a regal attempt at a bow. She glanced at Luc. "How long?"

"Eight minutes. That's a little closer, but . . ."

This time, as if they'd planned it, everyone sang the familiar line. "It's gonna be a long night."

Oliver ended with a high-pitched warble and the group broke into laughter.

"Funny. You're all just hysterical." Tia grumbled and tried to look miffed, but she was obviously enjoying the attention, if not the contractions.

"I think we sounded great." Xandi glanced toward Shannon. "Didn't you and Tia know each other from the time you were little?"

Shannon nodded. "That we did. Our mothers were friends before I was even born. When my parents were still married, we lived really close to Tia's family in the Marina District in San Francisco. I was still little when my mom and dad split up and my mother ended up moving to an apartment in the Tenderloin. She died when I was five, and I went back to live with my father."

"That's the thing I never understood," Tia said. "My mom was Chanku. Your mom must have been, too, or you wouldn't be, yet your mom died of cancer. I didn't think we were supposed to get cancer."

"Shannon's mom never knew she was Chanku." Ulrich's deep voice sounded unbearably sad. "Camille, Tia's mother, recognized I was Chanku, but she only knew to go by eye color. I remember Shannon's mom, and she had beautiful green eyes, just like Shannon. In hindsight, I imagine their shared heritage was part of the reason they were such good friends, but we never suspected Shannon's mom was like us. Since she didn't get the nutrients, her body never developed the immunities that protect the rest of us."

"I wondered, too." Shannon barely remembered her mother. She recalled their little apartment on Saturday mornings, curled up on the old couch, wrapped in a colorful afghan with her mom and watching cartoons on television. She remembered eating cereal at the rickety table in the kitchen while her mom drank coffee and smoked one cigarette after another.

Even today, the smell of cigarette smoke reminded her of her mom, but in a good way. She hadn't known it was bad for you when she was only five. She just knew that it was fun to watch the gray smoke curl into the air. She could still see her mom blowing perfect Os of smoke across the table for Shannon to poke with her finger.

"I never liked your dad." Tia slanted a glance at Shannon.

Shannon burst out laughing. "I never did, either. I haven't seen him since we graduated from Briarwood." She glanced at Ulrich. "Does he still live down the street from the Marina house?"

Ulrich shook his head. "Not any more. I heard he remarried and moved out of the country. Mexico, as I recall."

"Nice of him to let me know, don't you think?"

Jake squeezed Shannon's hand. She dipped her head to smile at him. "Don't worry. I haven't thought of him in years. He was so awful to my mom and he hated having me underfoot." She turned back to Ulrich. "I always suspected you paid my way at Briarwood. Did you?"

Ulrich sighed. "Yes, I did. He had the money but he . . ."

"Thank you." Shannon shook her head. "Please, don't make excuses for him. I don't know what I would have done if Tia had gone to boarding school without me. I will always appreciate your generosity. Tia was my lifeline when I was growing up."

Ulrich glanced fondly at his daughter. "I doubt Tia would have gone without you. You two were practically joined at the hip."

"We were the M&M girls. Murphy and Mason." Tia barely got the words out before another contraction took her voice. Luc checked his watch. Logan, who'd been dozing on the couch next to Jazzy, opened one eye.

Luc shook his head. "Still eight minutes."

Logan closed his eyes. Jazzy started laughing. "It's got to be a doctor thing. He can sleep anywhere, and then when someone needs him, he's wide awake."

"Hopefully it won't be too long before we need him, hon." Shannon sent Tia a sympathetic glance. "I'd almost forgotten the M&M girls thing, but Ulrich's right. We were like sisters from the time my mom died until you left Boston to come back here to teach."

Tia laughed. "Well, not exactly sisters. Friends with benefits?"

"Really great benefits." Shannon shot a guilty look in Ulrich's direction.

He waved her off. "Why do you think I sent you to Briarwood with Tia? The white hair doesn't mean I'm stupid."

Tia sat up and stared at her father. "You knew?"

He chuckled. "That you and Shannon were doing more at your sleepovers than sleeping? Yes, I knew. I also remembered what it was like being a teenager with a sex drive that made absolutely no sense when I compared myself to my friends. I figured whatever was going on between you and Shannon would keep you from spending all that energy on boys."

"Dad! I can't believe you . . ."

Ulrich shook his head. "Just wait until those little girls of yours are teenagers. You'll have a lot more sympathy for your old man's decisions then."

Shannon noticed everyone in the room was grinning as they watched Tia and Ulrich's back and forth. Every one of them remembered those years when they suddenly realized all they could think about was sex, but they were too young to follow through with their overwhelming desires.

"Ulrich, for what it's worth," she said, "Tia and I were eighteen before we acted on our desires."

Tia glared, wide-eyed at Shannon. "You're not going to talk about that, are you?"

"Why not?" Tinker grinned at Tia. "I, for one, want to know what two gorgeous young women finally did when they, well, did what they did."

Luc stood up and tugged on Tia's hands. "C'mon, sweetie. Shannon's going to talk whether you're here or not. Let's go move around a little and see if we can't get things going." He helped Tia into her coat and tugged her toward the door.

She stopped in front of Shannon. "My *father* is in this room, Shannon!"

"I know. Isn't it great?" Laughing, she patted Tia's hand. "Enjoy your walk."

"Argh!"

Obviously doing his best not to laugh and failing miserably, Luc dragged Tia out the door that led to the deck.

Shannon shoved her hair back from her eyes and grinned at Tinker. "So, you want details, eh?"

She noticed Tinker wasn't the only one who nodded, and it wasn't just the men. "I hate to disappoint you all, but until Tia's eighteenth birthday, we had an entirely G-rated relationship. We were both homesick at boarding school, but it was the only solution for two young women without mothers. My father and I were entirely estranged by then, and Ulrich was so busy with Pack Dynamics he didn't have the time to keep a close eye on a beautiful daughter . . . especially with Luc and Jake around."

She smiled at Ulrich. "That's the main reason you sent us off to Briarwood, isn't it? To get Tia away from the guys?"

He nodded. "You're right. I wasn't worried about Mik and AJ because they had each other, but I worried about Luc and Jake. They hadn't noticed Tia yet, but I didn't want her around when they finally did. An all-girls school far from home made a lot more sense. If the two of you were together, so much the better."

He looked down at his folded hands and sighed. Millie rested her hand on his shoulder, and Ulrich raised his head once again. "I knew Tia was Chanku, but I didn't know how to tell her. It was so hard after her mother died. It was bad enough dealing with things like menstrual cycles and crap like that. There was no way I could tell my beautiful teenaged daughter she was not only going to be able to turn into a wolf, she'd want to screw every guy she met once it happened. For some reason, I didn't worry about Jake so much, but I kept seeing Luc and Tia together, and when she was just a kid it didn't compute."

Shannon sent him a sympathetic smile. "I don't know how you should have handled telling her she was Chanku, but you did the right thing, sending us to school. We both excelled there and did well with the structure. When we took our relationship to the next step, finally, it was exactly right for both of us."

Lisa Quinn was the one to ask, "How'd it happen?"

Lisa had become Tia's lover since mating with Tinker. The four of them—Tinker, Lisa, Luc, and Tia—lived together in the Marina house in San Francisco. Shannon had expected to feel some jealousy over Tia's attachment to the tall, quiet, dark-haired beauty, but it was impossible not to love Lisa.

Just as impossible as it had been not to love Tia.

As usual, Tia was at her desk in their dorm room at Briarwood, wearing nothing but an old T-shirt of her dad's and a pair of bikini panties. Her nose was buried in her physics book. On her eighteenth birthday, no less.

"Look what I got for your birthday, sweetie!" Shannon swung the bottle of dark rum under Tia's nose. "I got cola, too. And a bag of ice. We are gonna party tonight!"

Tia raised her head and brushed her frizzy blond hair out of her eyes. "You are nuts. I have that physics test tomorrow and if I don't study . . ."

"You might get an A minus instead of an A plus? Horrors!" Shannon set the rum down and closed the thick physics book Tia had been glued to since classes ended hours ago.

She grabbed a couple of glasses, filled them with ice and poured rum halfway to the top. Then she added the cola and passed one to Tia.

Tia stared into the fizzy drink. "What's it taste like?"

Shannon laughed. "Hell, I don't know. But there's one way to find out." She took a sip. Then she took another. It was delicious!

"This is good!" Tia drank almost half of hers before she set her glass on the desk. "Where'd you get it?"

"It's Mr. Hinkley's stash."

"The janitor?"

Shannon nodded. "Yep. I saw him hide it in the coat closet and I snagged it during lunch break."

"What if someone had caught you?" Eyes wide, Tia looked at her drink and then back at Shannon.

Shannon shrugged. What did it matter? No one had caught her, and she'd surprised Tia with something special. It was the least she could have done.

A couple hours later, she'd discovered exactly how much more the two of them could do together.

It had begun so innocently. Sitting there together, drinking rum and cola, they'd talked about everything under the sun. Then they got to sex. Shannon had lost her virginity when she was barely thirteen, but Tia kept her head buried in her books and avoided boys and sex with almost as much energy as Shannon used to obtain both.

"Haven't you ever had an orgasm?" Shannon sipped her drink and stared at Tia over the top of the glass.

"I think so. I don't know." Tia shrugged and finished her drink. She immediately made another one and sat on the floor across from Shannon. She leaned against the side of the bed and studied the drink in her hand. "How can you tell?"

Shannon shook her head. The room spun a bit and finally settled down, but she couldn't have possibly heard Tia right. "What d'ya mean, how do you know? You just know, silly. When you play with yourself, you know, when you masturbate. Don't you come then?"

Tia blinked like a wide-eyed, caramel skinned, blond-headed owl. A virginal owl. "I don't do that."

She really had to stop drinking. Shannon focused on Tia. "You don't do what?"

"You know . . . masturbate. It just sounds yucky."

Shannon realized she'd been staring at Tia for so long she was making her nervous. Finally she burst out laughing. How could her very best friend not even . . . sheesh!

"Sweetie, you don't know what you're missing." Shannon carefully set her drink down on the floor. She stood up, checked the locks to their room, closed the curtains and turned off all the lights except the one in the bathroom.

It sent a soft glow across both beds . . . enough light to see, but not enough to make things too bright.

Tia stared at her, obviously plowed on the rum and cola, but she was still sober enough to follow every move Shannon made as she set the stage in their cramped little dorm room.

Shannon had never given another girl an orgasm before, but plenty of guys had done it to her. There was no way in hell she was going to let Tia Mason get another day older without at least finding out what she'd been missing.

What were friends for, anyway?

Shannon held out her hand. Tia grabbed it, and Shannon tugged her to her feet. Both of them wobbled a bit before they caught their balance. Shannon said, "I think that's enough rum and coke," and she took Tia's drink out of her hand and set it on the desk.

"Sit here." She shoved lightly and Tia sat on the edge of her bed. Shannon grabbed her panties and tugged them down over her hips.

"What are you doing?" Tia reached for the waistband.

"I'm going to show you what an orgasm feels like. I can't believe you don't know. Every girl's had them by now."

Tia bowed her head as Shannon pulled the panties over her bare feet. "Except me. I am such a nerd."

"Not after I get through with you. Shannon's super sex education class is about to begin."

She knelt between Tia's knees and looked up at her best friend in the whole world. "Do you know where your clit is?"

Tia nodded. "Somewhere down there."

"I don't believe this." Shannon had never touched another woman there, but she'd spent plenty of time touching herself. She carefully parted Tia's folds and pointed to the glistening little nub barely poking out of its protective hood.

"That, my love, is where it all happens. Touch it."

"Eeeuw. Really?" Tia stared at Shannon. Then she put her finger on her clit. "Wow. It's sensitive."

"Exactly. Look, I don't want to gross you out, but this is what Teddy did to me last week, and it's amazing. Lie back and close your eyes."

Confused and definitely drunk, Tia did as she was told.

Shannon spread her friend's thighs apart and touched Tia's delicate lips.

"What are you doing?"

"Shut up and keep your eyes closed. Think of what this feels like, not what I'm doing. Imagine a really good looking guy down here."

"I don't know any good looking guys. I go to an all-girls school, remember?"

"What about Lucien, that guy who works for your dad?"

"He's old."

Shannon laughed. "Yeah, but I know you think he's hot."

Tia sighed. "He is hot. Have you ever seen his shoulders?"

"That is so not what I'm looking at when I look at Lucien Stone."

Tia's head popped up. "You look at him, too?"

"Well of course I do. He's gorgeous. He and that other guy, Jake."

Tia lay back down. "Well, you can have Jake, not Luc. He's mine, so keep your eyes to yourself."

"You just said he was too old."

"Fifteen years isn't that much older when you're grown."

"You're eighteen, Tia. You're an adult."

"I don't feel like one. I've never had an orgasm, remember?"

"Now that's something I can deal with. Pretend I'm Luc and we're all alone and he's going to make you come."

"I can do that. He's gorgeous."

"I know. We've already been over that. Now shut up."

This was a first, but Shannon knew what took her over the top. She loved sucking a guy's cock and even liked it when they came in her mouth. Sucking on a girl couldn't be all that much different. At least with another girl, she knew what she liked. With a guy it was all guesswork, though they were usually pretty easy to figure out.

She ran her finger between Tia's labia, separating the tender folds. Then she leaned close and blew a soft puff of air against her clit. She could have sworn it looked bigger, almost like it had swollen a bit beyond the tiny little hood of skin surrounding it.

Very gently, Shannon pushed the skin back, exposing Tia's clit. Then she touched it with the tip of her tongue. Tia jumped, but she kept her mouth shut.

There was the slightest glistening of moisture at the mouth of her vagina. Shannon ran her finger back and forth, touching the small dark slit, occasionally brushing lightly over Tia's clit with her damp fingertip.

Tia moaned a soft, tortured sound of need.

Shannon grinned. Obviously she was doing something right. She slowly pushed her finger inside Tia's pussy. Immediately, strong muscles clenched tightly around her knuckle.

Shocked, Shannon felt the pulse between her own legs. She hadn't considered the effect touching Tia might have on her own healthy libido.

Encouraged, she slowly slipped her finger in and out of Tia, sliding in her slick fluids. At the same time, she leaned close and ran her tongue between Tia's swelling labia. At the top, she softly licked Tia's clit.

Tia's hips jerked and she pressed close against Shannon's mouth. Shannon carefully pressed her finger deeper, well aware of the fragile barrier of Tia's hymen. Then she placed her lips gently around her clit and sucked.

Tia arched her back and screamed. Her hips thrust forward and Shannon's finger went deep, all the way inside.

*Shit. All that issue over a little bit of tissue . . . but Tia's virginity is obviously down the tubes.* Shannon kept sucking and licking, shocked by the amount of cream suddenly lubricating the soft folds between Tia's legs.

Shocked and very pleasantly surprised. She held her finger deep inside Tia where it was trapped by the powerful muscles clasping and releasing. Slowly she licked and sucked as she brought her best friend down from her first orgasm.

Long moments later, Shannon sat back on her heels and grinned as Tia raised up on her elbows and stared, wide-eyed, right back at her.

Tia opened her mouth, closed it. Opened it again. "Okay. Now I see what you mean when you say you just know." She flopped back down on the bed. "I almost expected to see Luc's face."

"Sorry. Maybe you can ask him to do it next time."

Tia giggled. "Yeah. Sure. Like I could just go up to that gorgeous man and say, hey, Luc, will you suck my clit?"

Shannon snorted. Doubled over giggling and finally fell back on the floor, rolling with laughter. "Bet he wouldn't turn you down!"

"That really is amazing. I think I've done that in my sleep. I have these weird dreams, and . . ."

"Wet dreams. Guys get them all the time. Girls too, but they don't talk about them as much." She rolled around and sat up, but for a brief moment she really couldn't look Tia in the eye.

There was a lot they didn't talk about. Shannon didn't want to discuss dreams. Hers were weird enough. Running through dark forests on four legs. Killing things, for crying out loud. And sex. Sex with a wolf beneath a silvery moon. She'd feel that long, slick penis slide deep inside, then the swollen length of animal cock locking their bodies tightly together . . .

No. It was safer to show Tia what a climax felt like than to talk about dreams.

"I want to do what you did."

Shannon's head shot up. "What?"

"I want to make you come, too. I want to come again. Gosh, I feel like I've got a lot of time to make up for!"

"I thought you were drunk." Shannon felt like she was grinning at a total stranger, but her pussy had suddenly come to life.

"So did I, but what you just did seems to have cleared my head." Tia flipped around until she was face-to-face with Shannon. Resting on her belly, she propped her chin in her hands. "I thought we were friends, but now I'm beginning to wonder. I bet there are all kinds of things you've been holding out on me."

"Maybe." It was hard to get the words out through the grin she was trying to control. "But we'd both have to get naked. And you'd have to put your mouth on me where I put mine on you."

"Okay."

"Okay? Just like that? Okay?"

Tia shrugged. "Why not."

*Why not? Why not, indeed!* Shannon was naked before Tia had a chance to change her mind. The twin bed was small, but with Tia on her back on the bottom, and Shannon kneeling over her, propped up on knees and elbows with her mouth over Tia's pussy, they managed.

Good Goddess, how they managed. She'd never forget that first gentle exploration of Tia's tongue, the way it felt to have another woman suckle her clit and her nipples.

They'd opened up an entirely new level of their friendship that day. One that endured, stronger than ever.

"We'd actually reached a point, by the time Tia moved back to California, where we knew that we weren't truly lesbian, we weren't really bisexual, we were just ourselves, but we didn't know who those selves were. When Tia found Luc, and shortly afterward Jake rescued me, well . . ."

Shannon tilted her head and smiled at Jake. He still sat on the floor, his back against her chair and one arm looped over her thighs. "Jake did more than rescue me. More than change my life. He saved my life."

Jake kissed her denim-covered knee. "Works both ways, sweetie. You saved mine, too. I love you."

Shannon brushed away an unexpected rush of tears. "I love you, too." Then she glanced up. Someone was missing. "Where's Ulrich?"

Millie giggled. "He made it through your story as far as the rum and cola, but when you started talking Tia and orgasm in the same breath, he excused himself and left the room."

Anton's eyes twinkled, but he solemnly shook his head. "I imagine there are some things fathers just do not want to know about their daughters."

Shannon shook her head, laughing. "And here I thought I was telling the censored version."

"Censored?" Tinker's shocked expression cracked everyone up. "That was censored?"

"Of course it was. You don't think I'd tell you guys anything really personal, do you?"

"Oh, no . . ." Tinker shook his head in exaggerated fashion. "Never. There's nothing personal when you're talking about licking another girl's clit for the first time."

Ulrich stepped into the room just in time for Tinker's comment. He made an abrupt about-face.

"Stop! It's okay. You can come back." Giggling, Shannon waved Ulrich back into the room. "I'm all through talking. It's safe, Dad."

Ulrich walked across the room and sat next to Millie. She patted his hand. "I won't let them tease you, dear. It's okay."

"I needed to check on my daughter." Ulrich's lips twitched.

"And, how is your daughter?" Millie smiled sweetly at him.

"Miserable. They're doing laps around the house, but her contractions are still eight minutes apart. I think they'll be out there for a while. Luckily, it's a mild night."

He turned and glared at Tinker. "And you, my friend, have no room talking about my baby girl."

Tinker dipped his head. "Yes, sir."

"I could tell stories about you that would shock everyone in this room."

"I'm sure you could, but you won't get the chance." Tinker hugged Lisa close against his side.

"Oh? And why is that?" Ulrich arched one amazingly eloquent eyebrow.

"Because I'm going to tell my own story." Tinker winked at Ulrich. "And if it gets too personal, you have my permission to leave the room."

# Chapter 8

# Tinker

"I was always an outsider," Tinker said. He kept his gaze firmly fixed on Ulrich Mason. "Until Ulrich dragged my ass out to San Francisco and force-fed me those honkin' big pills of his."

Ulrich laughed. "C'mon, Tink. It wasn't quite like that."

"Close." Tinker laughed. Then he felt Lisa's eyes on him and realized he was doing exactly what he always did—he was making a joke out of something because he was afraid of the truth . . . afraid to be serious.

Tonight, everyone else had been honest and upfront, warts and all. He glanced at Jake and caught the other man staring directly at him.

*You can do it, Tink. It only hurts when you laugh.*

*Guess that means I should stop laughing, eh?*

Jake flashed him a big grin. Tinker searched for control of the sudden bout of nerves that hit him. He found Lisa, her love a constant, glowing strength in his heart. A strength she shared without hesitation.

He could do this. With Lisa beside him, he could do anything. "I guess I should start at the beginning," he said, "which for me was being abandoned when I was a toddler. It was a little Midwestern town outside of Cincinnati. For all I know, my mom is still alive. I might even have siblings out there, Chanku like me, but not knowing anything about their birthright."

He rubbed the back of his neck and felt the tension in his taut muscles. "I worry about that. Worry I might have blood brothers and sisters who haven't got a clue what their lives could be like. In a lot of ways, though, I was lucky my mom didn't want me, because the family that raised me, did."

He grabbed Lisa's hand and held on. His lifeline. She was always there, loving him. Like Ulrich and the pack, a constant in his life.

"The problem is, they were well-educated, white, middle class . . . right down to the nice neighborhood, the minivan, and the white picket fence. The neighbors were great, I had a lot of friends and the only thing I didn't have was any clue how to be a black kid. I never saw racism, never got singled out for my color."

He laughed softly, remembering. "Boy, was I naïve! They kept talking adoption, but for some reason, it never happened. When I was fifteen, the couple I had always known as my parents were killed in a car accident. I went from the perfect American middle-class life to getting tossed back into the system. Only now I wasn't a cute little two-year-old, I was a big, gangly teenager who'd been raised like a white kid. Funny thing, though, no one else got it. I was supposed to fit the stereotype. I played chess, not basketball. I liked to work on computers—that's how I got the name Tinker, always tinkerin' with stuff. I'd been in the school band . . . I was great with a trombone but didn't have a clue how to be black. In a heartbeat, my peer group changed. I was still grieving the deaths of the only parents I'd ever known, and some big black kid was calling me out to fight."

He realized he was squeezing Lisa's fingers so hard he'd cut off her circulation. He loosened his grip. She squeezed him back. "I was big for my age and scared enough to fight dirty. After a while, the other kids left me alone. I graduated from high school and joined the Army. When I was twenty-two, I ended up in Afghanistan right after nine eleven. A couple years later, when my tour ended, I came home and decided not to re-enlist. There was no point. I was just as much an outsider in my *band of brothers* as I'd ever been as a kid."

"Have you felt that way since you joined Pack Dynamics?" Ulrich's soft voice broke into Tinker's moment of silence.

He looked directly into Ulrich's amber eyes and nodded. "Yes and no. Overall, I knew I was part of the pack. I was respected and loved . . . I never doubted that and I don't, now. But Mik had AJ, Luc eventually had Tia and even though I was included in their relationship, I still felt like the odd man out . . . again. Until I met Lisa." He turned just in time for the kiss she planted on his mouth. "Something that never would have happened if Ulrich hadn't brought me to San Francisco."

Jazzy yawned. Logan was sound asleep, stretched out now on the couch with his head in her lap. "How'd that happen? How'd Ulrich know you were Chanku?"

Ulrich answered. "I saw his eyes."

Tinker smiled at Jazzy. "That was purely coincidence. Ulrich happened to be watching the news when I was interviewed coming back from Afghanistan. He called me the next day and offered me a job. Sent me tickets to fly out to San Francisco and take a look at his operation."

"Tink had no idea what we did or who we were, but as soon as I met him at the airport, I knew my first guess had been right. He was definitely Chanku."

Tinker nodded. "I'll never forget that first night. He took me to the house on Marina, introduced me to the guys. I remember feeling as if they were all sizing me up, and I didn't like it a bit, but it brought out my stubborn streak. I'd succeeded at everything I'd ever done without ever feeling as if I belonged. I didn't need to belong here, either, but I was sure I could do the job Ulrich offered." He chuckled. "The pay was real good."

Ulrich laughed. "The chip on his shoulder was a foot wide and a mile long, at least, but after Luc, Jake, Mik, and AJ went back to their place in the Sunset, I poured Tinker a drink and told him about us."

Tinker grinned at Ulrich. "Yep, and after I'd had a few swallows, the dude stripped his clothes off. I thought he was nuts."

Again, that imperious eyebrow rose. "I'd been trying to explain what the Chanku were. I had no doubt Tink was one of us, but I could tell he wasn't swallowing my story. So I did the only thing I knew worked—I took off my clothes and shifted."

"That definitely worked. I just about shit my pants."

Lisa jabbed him in the side. "Probably why Tinker pulled the same stunt on me. What is it with these guys?"

"I think they just like to get naked and show off their boy toys." Eve's soft, southern drawl cracked everyone up. "It's a guy thing."

"Guy thing or not, it got my attention. I took the pills for a week, but as the days went by, I started thinking maybe he'd tricked me, that I hadn't really seen what I thought I saw. I mean, a guy turns into a wolf? No way." Tinker shook his head. "And then, one night we were all eating dinner and I cut into my steak and realized it was just about raw. I like my meat cooked well done . . . or I had. This was just the way I wanted it. I think that bloody piece of meat convinced me where actually seeing the wolf couldn't."

"I remember that night." AJ bumped Mik's shoulder with his. "Remember the look on Tink's face? Sitting there at the dinner table with that chunk of bloody steak on his fork, staring at it like it was going to attack?"

"That was about a week before you actually shifted, wasn't it, Tink?"

Mik's smile reminded Tinker of a lot more about that week.

A week where everything he'd ever known about himself, his sense of who and what he was, and most of all, his awareness of his own sexuality, took a massive one-eighty.

They took him to the cabin up at Lassen for his first shift, just Luc, AJ, Mik, and Tinker. Jake stayed behind, working on some project with Ulrich, so it was only the four of them. He'd already figured out that Mik and AJ were gay, but he wasn't sure where Luc fit in, and he had no idea there'd be sex with four guys involved.

He was only thinking of his first shift. The chance to find out if what Ulrich promised him was true—that he truly shared a most remarkable heritage with these men.

His overactive libido had always been an issue, but he'd dealt with it as quietly as he could. Over the years, he'd grown really well acquainted with his right hand. No way in hell did he want to risk fathering a child without marriage. He'd never condemn a baby to grow up like he had, without a family. Those fears of abandonment were all too real for Martin "Tinker" McClintock, no matter how tough a guy he'd turned out to be.

As far as sex with other guys . . . it wasn't going to happen. He had no problem with other gay men, but that was not his way.

That first night in Lassen upended a lifetime of preconceptions. He'd never forget that first shift, that sense of vertigo when his point of view went from somewhere over six feet off the ground to almost ground level.

He'd suddenly been staring at his feet—two big paws with curved black nails, and when he raised his head, he was surrounded by wolves.

Three big males, all watching him out of the same amber eyes. He'd suffered a moment of blind terror, the fear they would rip him to shreds before he got his bearings, but then Luc nipped his shoulder and took off running.

Sights, scents, sounds . . . an entirely new world met him when they raced into the deep forest. They'd hunted, each of them managing to catch at least one rabbit that night. They'd bathed in a hot spring after shifting back to human and he'd been utterly shocked when AJ and Mik climbed out of the pool and shifted—and Mik mounted his partner as a wolf.

He'd had no idea they were bonded mates.

And that was only the beginning.

His arousal had been growing all evening, but it peaked at that point. The combination of his first shift, the sensual nature of his acute awareness of the world around him, the mere fact he was naked with a really good looking guy, sitting together in a bubbling hot spring watching two wolves who were also men, fuck their brains out.

Whatever the reason, when Luc moved close to Tinker and reached for his cock, it seemed like the most natural thing in the world to mirror every move Luc made. They sat there, two big, powerfully built naked guys, slowly, carefully beating each other off.

His big hands barely circled Luc's girth, but Tinker wrapped his fingers around Luc's heavy shaft and cupped his balls with his other hand. It was absolutely amazing. Even more so when Luc's thoughts entered his mind, when he shared how Tinker's hands felt on his body, the strength of his grip, the warm, callused support of his palm.

Tinker had never experienced such an exquisite climax in his life . . . and the night was just beginning.

Tinker's breath was still slamming in and out of his lungs and his balls hadn't quit tingling when Luc rose up out of the water and stood beside the small pool.

Luc held out a hand to Tinker and tugged him out of the water. AJ and Mik were still together, lying on the ground, tied like a couple of dogs. Moonlight glinted off their sharp teeth and their eyes glowed green as they panted, tongues lolling, ears pricked forward.

The whole thing was surreal.

Tinker was utterly fascinated by the entire scene—Luc, himself, Mik, and AJ. None of it seemed real, especially the fact he was already hard again. After a climax like he'd just had, it should have taken a lot longer before he was erect, but here he was, hard as a post and raring to go.

Luc shifted and he followed. The two of them headed back to the cabin. He wondered about AJ and Mik, when they'd come back, but he also wondered about what he'd just done with Luc. No guy had ever touched him before, at least not with permission.

There'd been a few times in high school when, in spite of his size, he'd been outnumbered in a fight. Part of the pecking order always seemed to revolve around some sort of sexual domination, but there'd been no posturing with Luc.

No, it had just been sex. Two guys beating each other off. No big deal . . . or at least, that's what he tried to tell himself.

Luc shifted as soon as he reached the deck in front of the cabin. "I'm going to take a shower. There's room for both of us if you want to join me."

Tinker's head snapped around. "Join you? In the shower?" Instead of feeling awkward, he realized his cock had twitched in expectation. This was just too weird.

Luc reached out and touched Tinker's arm. "You're Chanku, bud. There's no gay or bi or any other label. Once you shift, your libido sort of takes over. Sex is sex, unless it's your bonded mate. Then it's unreal, from what I've heard." He shrugged. "I wouldn't know, since I'm not mated, but Mik and AJ were gay before they were Chanku and they took it a step further with a mating bond. They said it's a whole different level of intimacy. For the rest of us, though, sex is just to keep us sane."

"I've never been with a guy. What we did tonight, at the hot spring . . . that was a first."

"I thought so. Did you like it?"

Tinker nodded. "I did. I thought it would feel awkward. It just felt really good."

Luc tugged his arm. "C'mon. A shower will relax you." He glanced down at Tinker's cock and laughed. "Well, not all of you."

It was amazingly easy to step into the big shower behind Luc. The tile was a deep cobalt blue and he hadn't been kidding about the room. There were shower heads at each end and benches where you could sit while you bathed.

At first they washed themselves quietly, scrubbing pits and crotches, washing hair, rinsing. Aware, though. So unbelievably aware that he shared a shower with another man who was interested in him as a sexual partner.

Tinker's curiosity built and his arousal grew. Luc was an absolutely gorgeous man, all muscle and sinew with dark hair and a killer smile. He was a couple inches shorter than Tinker, though Tinker doubted he could take Luc in a fight.

Of course, fighting was the last thing on his mind. He realized he didn't know the first thing about sex with another man. Did they suck each other off? Jerk off like they'd done earlier? He'd heard about anal sex between guys, but he'd never even done it with a woman, much less a man. Why, though, did he feel that little muscle in his ass sort of tighten and release when he thought about it?

They dried off. Tinker folded his towel very neatly and hung it on the rack, so aware of Luc standing beside him, doing the same thing, he wanted to scream to relieve the tension. He knew his body looked calm and collected but his brain was spinning like a top. His cock was hard as a rock and that damned little muscle guarding his asshole was twitching and puckering like nobody's business.

Luc acted like nothing out of the ordinary was going on, like he showered with another horny guy all the time. Maybe he did. Maybe he and AJ and Mik and Jake all fucked together on those mattresses Tinker had seen in the loft.

Big old king-size mattresses pulled together to make one big bed on the floor. Plenty of room for big guys like all of them.

Room for all four of them. He hadn't really thought of that. Was that Luc's plan? For all four of them to fuck? AJ and Mik were gay . . . did he want to fuck with a couple of gay guys?

He knew Chanku couldn't get diseases so AIDS wasn't a concern, but the whole idea was something he'd never really thought of, the idea of another man sucking his dick, a guy shoving his cock inside another man's ass . . . inside *his* ass.

Shit. He almost moaned. The visuals were hitting him hard and fast as he followed Luc out of the bathroom, but all Luc did was grab a pair of clean shorts out of his bag and slip them on.

Tinker did the same. Then he followed Luc into the kitchen and grabbed the cold beer Luc tossed to him. AJ and Mik came in, all windblown and laughing. They headed into the bathroom together.

They'd be in there washing and scrubbing each other. Would they fuck in the shower, too? Damn, he had to get his head under control. Had to quit thinking about guys together screwing each other because he didn't do that. He'd never been that way, but for some reason he hadn't even thought of a woman since his shift.

All he'd thought of was sex and Luc. Sex and AJ and Mik. Sex. Hell, even his hand looked good, and if there'd been a woman here, she'd look damned good, too. Luc hadn't been kidding about that supercharged sex drive.

"No, Tink. I wasn't kidding at all."

Tinker snapped around and stared at Luc? "How'd you . . . ?"

"You haven't learned to put up good barriers yet. You're broadcasting your thoughts."

*Oh, shit.* "All my thoughts?"

Luc nodded. "Every damned one." He grinned, leaned against the kitchen counter, and sipped his beer. "I don't have a plan, you don't have to fuck anyone you don't want to, and we won't make you feel like you're doing anything wrong if you choose not to have sex with any of us. That's not how we are."

He glanced down at the boner tenting Tinker's shorts and then brushed his hand over the massive erection tenting his own pair. "We are, however, highly sexed creatures. No longer entirely human, not restrained by the rules of human society. We fuck when we're horny, eat when we're hungry, and run through the forest as wolves when the time is right. We're Chanku, Tinker. As you become more familiar with your new reality, you'll discover things that mattered before don't mean a damned thing now—that includes sexual preference and color, even age. Did you know Ulrich was in his sixties? I bet if it wasn't for the white hair, you'd never guess."

Tinker thought of the head of Pack Dynamics, a charismatic, intelligent gentleman of indeterminate age. His bearing alone set him apart, his white hair made him look older, but in retrospect, his body and features were that of a much younger man. A very handsome man. "You guys have sex with Ulrich, too?"

Luc shook his head. "No. Not that we haven't invited him. He chooses not to screw the employees—figuratively and literally."

The bathroom door opened. AJ and Mik walked out

wearing jogging shorts and nothing else. Mik was still toweling his waist-length hair. On some men, hair so long and thick might have looked effeminate, but on the massive Hispanic, it merely added to his look of pure, barely restrained power.

Tink had never asked, but Mik looked like he might be at least part Native American. Whatever his racial mix, it had all come together perfectly. He wasn't as physically beautiful as AJ, but when the two walked into the room, Mik was the one you saw first.

AJ walked up to Tinker and threw an arm over his shoulders. "So, what do you think? Did you ever imagine what it would be like, running as a wolf?"

Tinker nodded. "Actually, I did. In my dreams. It's a million times better in real life. Amazing. I can't believe it's something I can just do . . . you know, when I want. In the movies . . . well, I thought you had to wait for a full moon."

Luc laughed. "That's werewolves. They're not real, just legends. We're shapeshifters, and we're definitely real."

Mik grabbed a beer out of the refrigerator and handed one to AJ. "I understand what you're saying, Tink. I was raised by my grandfather, a Lakota Sioux. He believed in spirit guides and the ability of some people to walk as animals, so for me, it was all about the mythology, my people's core beliefs. That was part of my life, growing up. When I found out I was one of the same creatures I'd heard of, it wasn't easy to separate it from the spiritual upbringing I'd had."

They moved out into the front room, the four of them appearing relaxed and at ease. Tinker talked about his time in Afghanistan and his sense of always feeling apart.

He was shocked to learn that AJ and Mik were lovers in prison, as surprised by their criminal history as he was to learn Ulrich had somehow gotten them out before their sentences had been served.

Luc had been a rookie cop. He didn't explain why he'd left the force, but whatever it was still filled him with guilt and a sense of unfinished business.

They talked of cases they'd been on, how their workload had increased since nine eleven, and how much they looked forward to working with Tinker. He wasn't sure how it happened, but somehow they'd moved the conversation from the living room to the loft. The lights were low, the room comfortably warm.

Tinker's leg cramped up and Mik offered to rub it out. Before he knew it, AJ was working one leg, Mik the other and Luc had straddled his butt to rub his back. Tinker dozed in a state of unbelievable sexual bliss. The sensual pleasure of three powerful men rubbing his sore muscles went beyond anything he'd ever known.

There was no choice to make, no thought of stopping events that Tinker realized he fully wanted to proceed. When one of the guys tugged his shorts off, he helped. When Luc helped him to his knees, Tinker went without hesitation, and when AJ crawled beneath his belly and suckled Tinker's swollen cock between his lips, it seemed perfectly natural for Tink to take AJ's thick erection in his mouth.

He'd never tasted a man. Hadn't realized how much the scent of male musk would turn him on, how he'd love the feel of smooth, sleek skin over a rock hard shaft. Hadn't considered what it would feel like to dip his tongue into the small slit in the end and taste a man's flavors . . . especially when that same man was doing the same thing to him.

AJ's fingers traced his balls and his lips swept up and down the length of Tinker's shaft, consuming his attention to the point where Tinker was barely aware of Mik behind him, of Mik's fingers rubbing the slick and sweaty crease of his ass.

When he finally noticed, it was only because it felt so

good when Mik pressed against the puckered little muscle with lube-slick fingers, pressed and released and pressed again until he'd breached the opening with one thick fingertip. Tinker groaned around the mouthful of AJ's cock and if he'd really thought about what was going on he might have freaked. Mik added another finger, driving deeper. Again, Tinker might have resisted if it hadn't felt so damned good.

AJ's mouth was doing amazing things to his cock and balls, suckling him deep, rolling his nuts around with his tongue, Mik was making a lot more headway into his ass than Tinker imagined possible, and he'd lost track of Luc altogether.

No matter. This was all a dream. A most amazing dream, and he hoped he wouldn't wake up for a long, long time. He'd never felt so connected, so wanted or loved. His mind was awash with images—AJ's thoughts and Mik's, and they were loving thoughts, inclusive thoughts, and Tinker was right in the middle.

Not the new kid on the block, not the one who was different. His color didn't matter, the fact he still had so much to learn about his new reality—none of it mattered. He was one of the group, a member of Pack Dynamics.

He was Chanku.

AJ's mouth worked magic on his cock and his climax was growing close. Mik's fingers stretched him wider, deeper, and before Tinker had a chance to protest, he felt the broad head of Mik's cock sliding deep inside as Mik swiftly pulled his fingers free.

One for the other, only the other was huge. Mik eased past his sphincter, slowly stretching the taut muscle beyond what his fingers had done, stretching and pressing, sliding oh, so slowly inside.

There was no way in hell he could explain the sensation, a burning pain that was more pleasure than anything he could have imagined. Simply put, he was getting fucked in the ass, something he'd been taught to abhor. It was wrong, it was sick . . . it was the most erotic experience he'd ever had in his life.

AJ's lips slid up and down his cock and he tried to mimic every move with his mouth on AJ, but damn, he wanted to concentrate on what Mik was doing, on the heat and the amazing pressure, the fullness that sent shivers of sensation through his balls and cock, fusing him with AJ, connecting the three of them through mouths and dicks and the blood thundering in their veins, in the pounding cadence of hearts and lungs.

Luc was there, slipping into Tinker's mind as easily as Mik had slipped into his ass, and he almost laughed with the joy he felt, the connection to three strong men loving him, loving each other.

Mik opened his mind to the dual sense of Luc fucking his ass while Mik fucked Tinker, of AJ sucking Tinker's cock with his hand wrapped around Mik's balls. Their disparate experiences became one single event in Tinker's head—four men moving in a rhythm that defied anything and everything Tinker thought he knew about sex and men and, most importantly, himself.

Mik's hands gripped his flanks with bruising strength and he plowed hard and deep into Tinker. AJ's cock twitched between Tinker's lips and he knew what was coming, knew it was his choice to suck and swallow or pull away.

There was no choice at all. He was part of the whole, a minor segment of one mass of sensitized male flesh moving in a most amazing rhythm, a rhythm that took them to the peak, held them there for a brief moment in time that stretched on forever.

When they hit the top and flew over the edge, they flew as one pulsing orgasm, the four of them together, bodies thrashing and lungs bursting. It seemed to go on and on, the flow of seed from cock to mouth. Tinker swallowed it all, licking AJ's thick shaft and trapping each drop of his cum between his lips.

Just as AJ did for him.

Finally there was no more, yet still he licked and suckled AJ's cock, unwilling for this to end, for this amazing climax to be over. Tinker rolled to one side so their massed weight wouldn't hurt AJ, but he kept his cock in his mouth. Still connected, their bodies shuddering in the final throes of orgasm, blowing like bulls, they slowly came down from a most amazing high.

Tinker lay there stunned with the experience. This was so far beyond anything he'd ever imagined, he had no framework to explain the way he felt, the way his body reacted.

Then AJ got the giggles.

Tinker felt AJ's body shudder beneath his leg. He thought at first he was crying, but Mik, still planted firmly inside Tink's ass started to laugh, and in seconds they were all rolling on the mattresses, laughing until they cried.

Long moments later, Tinker finally caught his breath. "What's so fucking funny?" he asked.

And they started all over again. Finally Luc pulled out of Mik and Mik pulled free of Tinker's ass. The two of them headed down the stairs to the bathroom to dispose of condoms Tinker hadn't seen them put on.

AJ spun around and lay next to Tinker. "That was a first, you know."

"Sure as hell was for me."

AJ laughed. "For us, too. We've never done a four-way before. Even when Jake's been here, it just hasn't happened. Three of us at a time, but four? We weren't sure how to make it work."

"Trust me," Tinker said drily. "It worked."

"That it did." AJ raised up on one elbow and stared steadily into Tinker's eyes. "Did anything we do bother you? Did you feel at all awkward?"

Frowning, Tinker shook his head. "No. I kept waiting to be embarrassed, or to think I was doing something really bad, but it was all good. You guys made it work." He shrugged. "I was only thinking of pleasure. Yours. Mine. Mik and Luc's. Pleasure and sensation and how good it all felt."

He looked away for a moment, and then turned back to AJ. "I was thinking how I felt as if I belonged here. With you guys. I didn't feel as if I was barging in where I didn't belong, where I wasn't wanted. That's a new feeling for me."

"Good. I'm glad you feel that way. You do belong. You're one of us. You're Chanku. We don't play by the old rules. In a lot of ways, we make our own as we go, though none of us really know that much about our history. Someday I hope we find out. I want to know more. For now, though, I'm just glad that Ulrich found you. You belong with us."

Tinker raised his head and looked across the room at AJ. "You will never know how much your words that night meant to me, AJ. I felt as if I'd found a home after drifting for way too long. You, Mik, and Luc accepted me as if I'd been with you all along. You never made me feel as if I didn't belong. I still had my own hang-ups, but I can't blame them on any of you."

Lisa leaned close and gazed up at him. "We all had hang-ups, sweetie." She laughed softly. "We probably still have them, but now we know better than to worry. We take pride in them."

"Excellent point." He kissed her cheek. "I'm going to take my hang-ups and go outside and check on Tia and Luc."

"I have something I'd like to ask Ulrich." Adam had been so quiet, Tinker'd almost forgotten he was in the room. "I've heard a lot about Tia's mom, Camille, but how'd you meet? How come you didn't know about Keisha? You lived in the same town."

Millie smiled at Ulrich. "Looks like it's your turn on the hot seat, m'love."

"Millie? You're supposed to get me out of trouble, not push me into it." Ulrich shook his head. "How could you?"

"Very easily." She laughed. "Read my lips. It's your turn."

Laughing, Tinker stood up. "Time for me to take my hang-ups and go." He kissed Lisa again, tipped an imaginary hat in Ulrich's direction, and stepped outside to look for Luc and Tia.

He found them sitting on a bench by the back door. "Why don't you two come inside where we can pick on you?"

Luc hugged Tia close to his side. "We were going to, but we heard Adam ask Tia's dad about her mom."

Tia patted the bench next to her. "Sit down and join us. I really want to hear what Dad says about my mother. He would never talk about her very much, so I don't know a thing about their early years."

Tinker sat next to Tia, stretched his arm across her shoulders and rested his fingers on Luc. Connected like this, it reminded him of the days before Lisa. These two had always included him. They'd never made him feel like a third wheel.

Just the opposite, actually. All the issues he'd had, had been his own. Like Lisa said, they were his hang-ups . . . he might as well appreciate them. He nuzzled Tia's neck and planted a kiss on her ear. "Can't you listen if you're in where it's warm?"

She chuckled. "Of course I can, but I doubt he'd talk about personal things if I'm in the room."

"Excellent point." Tinker settled close against Tia and focused on the soft voices coming from inside the house.

# Chapter 9

## Ulrich & Camille

Ulrich slanted a glance at Millie and got her sweet smile in return. There was no guile in this woman. No jealousy, no anger, and never a sense of regret. She'd learned to let go of the past, and for her, there'd been more than enough to let go of.

What would his life have been like if he'd found Millie instead of Camille first?

For one, he wouldn't have had Tia. Nor would he have known of his amazing Chanku legacy. No, Camille was the one who gave him the life he had now. Camille Anne Jones. Damn . . . she was an incredible woman, and an alpha bitch like no other.

"When I was a young cop in San Francisco," he said, "I was assigned an area of the city that included Golden Gate Park. I couldn't believe I'd finally gotten it as my beat. I'd always been drawn to wild places, and after the jungles in Nam, the park was like having my own forest . . . only there weren't as many people shooting at me."

He shook his head, reliving that amazing night and the very first time he saw her. "It was 1975. I was a thirty-two year old cop, fairly new to the San Francisco Police Department. I'd gotten home from Vietnam and out of the service four years earlier. I went straight into the SFPD, and while I liked the job, I didn't love it. I didn't love much of anything, to be honest, but Golden Gate Park came close, and now it was my beat. It was late, almost time to head back to the station and clock out, but I'd gotten out of my patrol car to check for drug dealers in an overgrown area of the park near Stanyan Street when I heard something rustling in the bushes. I drew my service revolver and flipped on my flashlight.

"Green eyes reflected back at me. My first thought was I'd scared up a coyote, but a moment later a woman's voice said not to shoot, that she was coming out. She stepped out of the shrubbery looking like some sort of exotic Nubian goddess. I still remember what she wore, a gauzy, multi-colored peasant dress. Her feet were bare and her black hair rippled over her shoulders and down her back in thick curls. Her skin was dark as bittersweet chocolate. It looked smooth as silk, and damn, but it was obvious she wasn't wearing a bra under her dress." He laughed. "It took me all of two seconds to fall in lust."

She looked him up and down with those gorgeous amber eyes and then she had the audacity to wink at him! "You planning to shoot me, Officer?"

Her sassy comment caught him off guard. He drew himself up to his full height and put on his best cop face. "What are you doing out here, miss? It's almost midnight. Kind of late to be wandering around the park by yourself, don't you think?"

She'd somehow moved closer without him realizing she'd taken a step, and he holstered his weapon before she ran into the damned barrel. He caught a whiff of her scent and the hair on the back of his neck stood on end. Whatever she was wearing hit him like a drug. His cock was suddenly straining against his zipper and a trickle of sweat ran down the middle of his back.

He tried to take a breath but his lungs wouldn't expand. She stared at him with the oddest expression on her face, like she was looking right through him, as if she saw into his soul.

Then she tilted her head and slowly ran her tongue over her lush lower lip, leaving a shining trail across its full surface. He wanted to lean close and taste her, but that could get him fired in a heartbeat. Instead, he watched her as if she were a wild thing, a feral creature that might fade away into the night.

"I like to run at night," she said. Her voice was soft and low, and it sent shivers of arousal down his spine. "I'd rather be in the woods, way away from the city, but I live here. The park's better than sidewalks and streets."

He glanced down at her bare feet, at the long gauzy skirt floating around her ankles, and laughed. He sounded like he was choking, so he cleared his throat and tried again. "You don't look as if you're dressed to run."

She raised her eyes, and then her chin and smiled at him. Her teeth glistened like ivory against her dark, dark skin and her eyes glinted green from reflected light. Her scent enveloped him with a sense of need unlike anything he'd ever experienced.

"You might be surprised." She tilted her head and studied him out of the corner of her eye. Flirting. She was flirting with him!

"When do you get off duty, Officer . . ." She paused, leaned forward and read his name on the tag above his badge. "Mason?"

He had a strong personal code, one that included staying far away from the people he encountered in the line of duty. When this woman spoke, his code evaporated. It no longer existed. He realized he was looking at his watch.

She was looking at him.

"I clock out at midnight," he said. He never did this sort of thing. But he had no choice. He couldn't lose her.

Not when he'd just met her. "There's an all-night coffee shop, over on Haight . . ."

"The one with the really great glazed donuts?" She planted both hands on the flare of her perfectly rounded hips and cocked her head. Smiled wider.

"Yeah. That's the one." He nodded his head and relaxed a little bit. She knew the place. That made her somehow familiar, not a complete stranger. They'd been to the same coffee shop. Maybe sat in the same booth . . . never together. Not yet. "I have to turn in my reports and change clothes, but I can be there by twelve-thirty."

"I'll see you there." Her amber eyes were twinkling when she turned away and headed across the damp lawn. Her bare feet didn't make a sound as she disappeared into the darkness.

He was in his squad car heading back to the station before he realized he didn't even know her name.

It seemed to take forever to get out of his uniform, grab a quick shower, dress in his civvies, and turn in his reports. A couple of guys stopped him to ask questions, the captain wanted to set up a meeting for later in the week. He was practically shaking with impatience when he finally got into his little red '68 Mustang and headed out to the coffee shop on Haight.

He was about five minutes late by the time he parked and almost ran the half block to the restaurant. He saw her through the window, sitting alone at the same booth he usually chose. Her back was to him and the thick fall of her dark hair and the sleek curve of her spine made him hard all over again.

He greeted the waitress as he walked through the door and slipped into the seat across from the woman. Her hair glistened like midnight in the harsh glare of the overhead lights. She was still wearing the gauzy dress that seemed to cling in all the right places.

She'd slipped into sandals, but she wore no makeup or jewelry. She didn't need it. He'd never seen a more alluring female in his life.

"I'm sorry I'm late. There are always a million things to do before I can get away." He glanced up as the waitress approached and said he'd just have coffee. The woman already had a cup in front of her. The waitress poured a cup for Ulrich, topped off his companion's, and sashayed away.

"I would have waited for you, no matter how late you were." She sipped her coffee and smiled at him through the steam.

That stopped him. A spiral of pure, male satisfaction circled his groin and settled in his balls. He paused with his cup halfway to his mouth. "What's your name? You never did tell me . . . but then, I think I forgot to ask."

She smiled. "I know. I realized that as soon as I left." She held out her hand. "Camille Jones, Officer Mason."

He wrapped his big paw around her long, slim fingers and felt a jolt that seemed to charge up his arm and straight to his already interested cock. Her eyes flickered and the corners of her lush lips turned up in a wide smile. Had she felt it, too?

"That's a beautiful name. Camille. As I recall, they named a really deadly hurricane after you a few years ago."

She laughed, and once again it felt as if the sound touched him. "People who know me would consider the name perfect for a big storm. Preferably an unpredictable one."

"That's probably good information to have. My name, by the way, is Ulrich." As he said it, he wondered why anyone would stick such a name on an innocent baby. He always felt as if he had to grunt to say it.

"I can't imagine naming a baby Ulrich," she said.

He felt that shiver up his spine again. Was she reading his thoughts?

"May I call you Ric?"

*Damn,* he thought, *call me whatever you want, so long*

*as you call me.* "Of course." He felt flustered for some strange reason. He wasn't sure what it was about her that affected him so powerfully, though her subtle scent seemed to weave in and out of his brain, as if tying him into knots of pure desire. It had been a long time since he'd been with a woman, but he'd never reacted to another female the way he was reacting to this one. Carrying on a simple conversation wasn't easy, not when he wanted to sling her over his shoulder and take her home with him. "Do you live near here?"

She nodded. "Yes. With my sister and her husband and their little girl, over on Lincoln. What about you?"

"I just bought a place in the Marina District. It needs a lot of work, but I've got the time to fix it up."

She shook her head. "I love that area. You're remodeling it by yourself? You're not married?"

"I wouldn't be sitting here with you if I was involved with anyone else, married or not."

She nodded in agreement. "That's good to know. I'm not, either. Involved, married . . . whatever. I'd like to see your place sometime."

He shrugged as if it were no big deal, that it wasn't almost one in the morning, that he hadn't just come off a ten-hour shift. "Anytime. Whenever you like."

She sipped her coffee and smiled at him over the rim of her cup. "I'd like that very much. Tonight?"

He swallowed. There was no doubt in his mind what she was offering. "Tonight would be perfect," he said. Praying.

"Good."

No doubt, either, what they'd both just agreed to. "Are you parked nearby?"

"No. I'm on foot." She set her cup down and gazed directly at him. He realized her eyes were the same odd color as his own, an unusual shade of dark amber. Not really brown, not really green.

"You shouldn't be walking around here at night. It's not safe." He stood up and tossed a couple dollars and change on the table to cover the cost of two coffees and the tip.

"I've never had a problem." She gave him a saucy wink, and for some odd reason, he believed her.

He held out his hand. Camille took it without hesitation. It was hard to draw a deep breath and there was an odd buzzing in his ears. He was taking her to his home. She was coming home with him. Either way he looked at it, this beautiful, sensual woman was going to be in his bed tonight.

He helped her into the Mustang, fastened her seat belt for her and got a cheeky grin as thanks when he inadvertently brushed her left breast with his arm. There was no traffic this late at night and the street was empty when he pulled into the driveway of his house. He got out, opened the garage door and parked the Mustang inside.

He helped Camille out of the car and unlocked the door to his house. He flipped the light on and they walked directly into the kitchen from the garage. This was the one room he'd finished. The new appliances glistened in the overhead light and the light birch cupboards and white tile made the fairly small room appear much larger.

"I like it." Camille ran her fingers over the smooth wooden cabinets and even opened the refrigerator to look inside. "This is most definitely a bachelor's refrigerator."

She was bent at the waist to peer inside, but she glanced over her shoulder and laughed at him. "Leftover pizza and two six-packs of beer." She straightened up and closed the door. "Is that your dinner tonight?"

Bemused, he shook his head. "No. I ate on duty. I was just planning to come home and get some sleep. It was a long shift."

She sort of sashayed across the room, hips swaying, eyes twinkling, and rested her hands on his shoulders. "And here I am, keeping you awake."

"Here you are." He rested his palms on her hips and

wondered if there was anything under that gauzy skirt beyond warm, naked woman. "But I don't mind that you're keeping me awake." He leaned close and kissed her, a light, teaser of a kiss that tested her willingness.

Her lips were full and soft and slightly damp, and they parted beneath the gentle thrust of his tongue. She tasted of rich coffee and warm woman. Her body swayed toward him, and her breasts connected with his chest. He felt her nipples through his shirt, hard little points of heat. His pecs tightened in response.

She moaned. The soft sound removed his last breath of reason. He swept her into his arms and carried her out of the brightly lit kitchen, down the dark hallway, and into the master bedroom.

He hadn't bought any furniture for this room, but the king-size mattress and box springs on the floor had clean sheets, and the soft glow of a streetlight filtering through the window threw just enough light to see by.

He knelt on the floor beside the mattress with Camille still in his arms, and he held her like that, devouring her with open-mouthed kisses that she met with an almost feral intensity.

She scrambled out of his arms onto the mattress and lifted the hem of her dress. She knelt there, staring at him for what felt like forever with the fabric bunched in her hands and the soft curve of her knees showing beneath the edge of her dress. Then she slowly tugged the hem up, up over her thighs and hips, over her waist until she bared her full breasts.

*Holy shit.* She wasn't wearing panties, either.

She tugged the dress over her head and tossed it to one side. Kneeling there, naked and glistening in the moonlight, reminding him once again of an exotic queen staring down at her subject.

Ulrich reached for the ribbed bottom of his sweatshirt and ripped it off over his head. Before he could unfasten the snap on his jeans, Camille was there, opening the snap and lifting the tab of his zipper. She lowered it slowly, baring the upper curve of his shaft. Once she got the zipper open, she spread the placket wide and shoved his jeans down past his hips.

His shorts went with the denim, but she only lowered his pants to the point where the crown of his cock was still trapped beneath the elastic of his boxers. For some reason it made him feel more naked, his shorts riding low on his thighs, his butt bare to the cool night air. Camille slipped her hand beneath the elastic band and filled her palm with his sac.

Groaning, Ulrich thrust his hips forward, silently begging for more. She stretched the elastic and freed his cock and balls. He knelt there, trembling with lust while the most beautiful women he'd ever been with in his life played with his genitals as if she'd discovered a set of new and amusing toys.

She stroked his cock with her left hand, cupped his balls with her right, and the sensations were beyond amazing. If she didn't stop right now, her gentle touch was going to take him right over the top.

Laughing, he pulled out of her grasp and sat on the floor so he could untie his shoes. It took him mere seconds to finish undressing while she watched him with undisguised interest.

He knew he was big, but then he was big all over. Still, a lot of women had a change of heart when they saw just how much of him there really was.

Not Camille. As soon as he was naked, she sprawled on her back and spread her legs. When he knelt between her thighs and lowered his mouth to her belly, she seemed shocked. "What are you . . . ?"

He raised his head and grinned. "I'm having my evil way with you." Then he sat back on his heels and lifted her legs over his arms, pulling her close until he could taste every bit of her.

She didn't relax until his tongue swept the length of her soft folds and valleys, and when he circled her clit, the sound she made was more of a garbled scream than a moan. She was already wet and swollen and obviously ready, but he wanted to make sure he could enter her without any pain or discomfort.

Her scent was an aphrodisiac. He couldn't get enough of her, couldn't breathe in enough of her unique perfume. She tasted like ambrosia, her cream a mix of sweet and salt unlike any woman he'd ever tasted before. Her dark, sleek skin felt like silk beneath his hands . . . silk over steel. Unlike most women he'd known, she was lean and muscular with the powerful body of an athlete.

He used his fingers to dip deep inside her pussy, and when she didn't show any aversion to anything he did, he pressed a fingertip against her anus and slowly pushed inside. The moment he breached her tight sphincter, she stiffened in his arms, arched her hips and pressed her mons against his mouth, climaxing hard and fast as he licked and suckled her clit.

He brought her to climax one more time before he reached for a condom. Panting, eyes twinkling, she stopped him. "No. It's okay. I want to feel you inside me. I won't get pregnant."

She didn't need to ask him twice, and his only thought was, thank God for birth control pills. He grabbed his cock at the base and rubbed the thick head between her thighs, trailing the crown through Camille's lubricating cream. She opened for him and he slipped between her folds, stretching and pressing, slowly moving deeper into her welcoming heat.

She was hot and tight and her muscles rippled along his length, stretching for him, making way for him. She moaned, but it was a sound of pure pleasure and it was all he could do to keep from coming.

Her long, muscular legs wrapped around his hips and

her heels dug into his butt. Her fingers tightened against his shoulders and he rode her, slamming in and out, harder, faster than his size and most women ever allowed. It was good—it was beyond good, it was freaking fantastic.

And then it got better.

He almost cried out at the shock, the unbelievable sensation of Camille's thoughts melding with his. He sensed her first as a tendril of sensation sort of tickling the edge of his consciousness.

Then she filled his mind, full-blown and as clear and lucid as verbal speech. Except she was pure sensation and unbelievable arousal. Then he was in her head, sharing her feelings, her sense of his size and heat, of his hips slamming into hers with bruising strength, the slap of his balls against her ass, the pure bulk and weight of him.

She reveled in his mastery, wanted more of him, wanted his strength and his length and the pure element of possession she felt in his taking.

He *was* Camille. He felt her climax sizzling along nerve endings unfamiliar to him, and it sparked his own. He shared the first ripples of her vaginal muscles, the ache in her womb, the speed of her heart thundering away in time with his.

In perfect time. They beat as one, breathed as one, climaxed as one—an orgasm that went on and on, forever.

It was a long time before he regained any semblance of coherent thought. A long time before his body quit pulsing and spasming in what had to be the most powerful, most fulfilling climax he'd ever experienced in his life.

And jerk that he was, he'd collapsed full upon her, his entire weight pressing Camille into the mattress. He planted his palms on either side of her shoulders to raise himself off, but Camille clasped him with her arms, held him with her legs.

"Don't go." Her voice cracked. "I don't want this to end."

Was she crying? He turned his head and nuzzled the soft skin beneath her ear, raised enough to kiss her cheek and felt the wash of tears across her face.

"Are you okay?" He kissed those full, soft lips of hers and wondered if he'd ever get enough of them. "I didn't hurt you, did I?"

She shook her head. He heard her sniff. "I'm amazingly okay."

He smiled against her throat. "No, you're mainly just amazing." He was getting hard again, his cock already pressing against her vaginal walls, reacting to the steady pulse and throb of her ebbing orgasm.

His hips were already moving. He hadn't intended to love her again so soon—hadn't dreamed he'd be ready so fast—but she was moving with him, her body pressed tightly to his, her breasts flattened beneath his chest. He wrapped his arms around her and lifted, sitting back on his heels and bringing Camille with him. Her legs tightened around his waist and she buried her face in the crook of his neck. Her cheeks were still damp with tears.

He'd never brought a woman to tears with sex before. That was definitely a first. Everything about tonight was a first. He'd never taken a woman to bed so quickly after meeting her, never been intimate with a woman of color, never had a mental connection such as the one he'd shared with Camille.

"What was that?" he asked. He rubbed his chin over the top of her head. "How did you get in my head?"

She laughed, but there was definitely a choked quality to the sound. Was she laughing at him? He couldn't tell.

"I'll tell you later. First I want you to finish what you started."

He chuckled and thrust harder. Faster. "You want to finish? I was thinking of just doing this all night long."

"Ah, a man after my own heart. But don't you have to get some sleep before work tomorrow?"

He shook his head. "I'm off tomorrow. Got all day and all night to keep you in my bed. Unless, of course, there's somewhere else you need to be?"

She pulled back and smiled at him. Her long hair was tousled and falling over her shoulders, across her breasts. Her lips were swollen from his kisses, and glistening tracks across her cheeks marked where her tears had fallen. He'd never seen anything sexier in his life.

"There's no place I need to be," she said, punctuating her words with a quick kiss beside his mouth. "No place but here. Make me fly again, Ric. That was amazing. I need to do it again."

So did he. And he did, so many times that night he lost count. Each time they connected, and each time the connection grew stronger, clearer, until he realized he could communicate with her mentally even when they weren't having sex.

They'd done it so naturally the next morning, over coffee. She'd asked him for a refill when he got up to get his. He'd turned and taken her cup without hearing a word, other than what she'd asked in his head.

When he placed her freshly filled cup in front of her and sat down at the table, he'd asked her again. "What's going on, Camille? I can hear your thoughts. You can hear mine. Who are you?"

She lowered her gaze and stared into her steaming cup for a moment. When she raised her head, there was a look of pure determination on her face. "It's not who I am, but what I am." She reached across the small table and covered his hand with hers. "It's what you are, too. Why you can hear me. Why you and I can make fireworks happen when we make love. What I have to show you, tell you, can't leave this room. Will you promise me?"

He frowned and stared into those amazing amber eyes of hers and realized he'd promise her anything. Say anything, if it was the only way to keep her. After this past night, there was no way in hell he was letting her go. He nodded.

She smiled. Then she stood up, slipped out of her gauzy peasant dress and turned his entire world upside down.

With a saucy wink, Camille Jones disappeared, and a beautiful wolf sat in the middle of his kitchen floor.

Ulrich chuckled as he gazed around the great room at all the familiar faces. Each one of them had their own story, their own unique memory of the first time they'd shifted, but they shared a common theme. One of disbelief, expectation, maybe of fear, yet they'd all embraced their new reality.

Not one of them would ever regret it.

"Camille told me her ability had been handed down through her mother's line, that both she and her sister, CJ, had been able to shift since they were teens. Their mother had taught them to eat a certain kind of grass."

It too, had been handed down through their mother's line, and the seeds were carefully maintained and the grasses grown through generation after generation.

In fact, that was how CJ had met the man who was Keisha's father. José Rialto was a gardener and she'd gone to him for help in growing the grasses. CJ had given up on ever finding a mate like she was, another Chanku. Only Camille had held out. She'd known there was a mate out there for her, somewhere.

"As far as Camille knew, she and CJ, and hopefully CJ's daughter, Keisha, were the only shapeshifters around. Their mother was the last of her line. She had died in a car accident shortly after CJ's first shift, or Camille wouldn't have known of her own heritage. They hadn't found any others, but Camille said she never gave up hope there was a mate out there for her."

Ulrich glanced about the room again. Tinker, Luc, and Tia hadn't come back in yet, though he sensed they were close and that all was well. He was glad they'd stayed away. He doubted he could have told the intimate details of his relationship with Camille, knowing their daughter was in the same room. Some things were just too personal to discuss with your kids.

His amazing sex life with Camille was one of them.

"I won't say that Camille and I had a perfect relationship. She was too headstrong and I was too stubborn, and neither of us had learned to compromise, but we loved each other. We married about a year after we actually mated. We had an open marriage. She took lovers as did I, though as I gained rank in the police department and after we had Tianna, I settled down quite a bit. Not Camille. She still had her lovers, and she refused to give up her daytime runs in Golden Gate Park. We fought over that, but she was stubborn. She did as she pleased. Unfortunately, it led to her death. Luc was a rookie cop with SFPD when he shot her. It was a horrible tragedy, but not a surprise."

He shook his head and reached for Millie. She had tears in her eyes when she took his hand and squeezed hard. "She will always hold a place in my heart, but it's not the lonely place it was for so long. I'm a very lucky man."

Ric gazed into Millie's shimmering eyes, studied the soft smile on her beautiful face, and could find no words. Instead, he just shook his head and muttered, "The luckiest damned bastard around."

Tia wiped the tears off her cheeks and shivered. Luc hugged her close. "I've never heard how your mom and dad met. It was right near the place where I . . ." Luc shook his head. "I'll never forgive myself for what happened that day."

Tia smiled and touched his cheek with her fingertips. "You're the only one who hasn't forgiven you. Even my mother forgave you. She said it was her own fault, and look at my dad. I think he's happier with Millie than he ever was with my mom. They were together because they're both Chanku and they understood each other on a level they couldn't have found with anyone who wasn't, not because of any abiding love. Her death changed a lot of things, but it wasn't your fault."

Tinker grabbed Tia's hand. "You're chilled, sweetie. I think your dad's all through telling things unfit for your tender ears. Let's go in."

Tia laughed, but then she doubled over and gasped. Tinker closed his eyes and concentrated. He'd been doing his best to take her pain, the way Lisa had taught him. Hurt like hell, but it seemed to be making Tia's labor easier.

He took a deep breath and let it out as the contraction eased. Tia sent him an appreciative glance. "You're amazing, Tinker. Not too many men I know of would take a woman's labor pains."

He laughed and kissed her cheek. "Wouldn't be so bad if I didn't feel it in my damned balls. This birthing babies is not for the weak."

"That's why women get the job." Luc glanced at his watch. "Seven minutes. We're getting a little closer. Are they harder?"

Tia shook her head. "They hurt, even with Tinker's help, but I don't think they're any stronger than the ones I was having a couple hours ago."

Tinker stood up and held out a hand for each of them. "C'mon. Let's get in the house where it's warm." He hauled Luc to his feet, but gently helped Tia when she struggled to stand. With Tinker on one side and Luc on the other, they walked her back inside.

Tinker glanced over Tia's head at Luc. He looked worried, exhausted and frustrated by everything Tia was enduring—typical male stuff, as far as Tinker could tell.

Logan hadn't been kidding when he said it would be a long night. No wonder Lisa hadn't been pushing him to start their own family. After watching what Tia had gone through this past nine months, Tinker wasn't all that sure about the whole parenthood thing anymore.

As far as he was concerned, it appeared to be a lot more fun making babies than birthing them.

# Chapter 10

She couldn't believe everyone was still waiting up. It was almost midnight, yet the main room was full. A few of the guys were dozing, but the women were all alert. She'd felt them touching her thoughts, checking to make sure she didn't need more help with the pain.

*Not yet.* Tinker had been amazingly effective. Luc had tried, but the way to ease a woman's labor pains wasn't something that came naturally to a man. Somehow, Tinker had figured it out. Lisa was a lucky woman to have him as her mate . . . just as Tia was a lucky woman to have him as lover and friend.

Tia glanced toward her father. Ulrich sat with his arm draped comfortably around Millie's shoulders, smiling at Tia.

"How're you doing, sweetie?" He stood up and wrapped her in a big hug.

She caught his familiar scent and fought a powerful desire to curl up in his lap and ask him to make it all better. Instead, she leaned back in his arms and asked, "How'd you do it, Dad? How'd you manage for all those years after Mom died?"

Tia knew he understood exactly what she asked. How could any Chanku survive alone? Without a lover, without the support of the pack. He'd had the guys at Pack Dynamics, but her father had always held himself apart from the younger men. Truly a lone wolf, if ever there'd been one.

She glanced over his shoulder and smiled at Millie. "You too, Millie. You were alone for over thirty years. How?" The enormity of it hit her. Millie had been alone since before Tia was even born. Literally a lifetime, and on top of that, her babies had been taken from her. Tia's imagination couldn't take her deep enough to comprehend such misery.

She choked back her tears. "All of you are here for me. I've never had to go through anything alone. When I was young I had my dad and then Shannon. Now I have Luc, but I have an entire pack, too, and I can't imagine doing any of the things you've done, alone."

She stepped out of her father's embrace. "This is not a rhetorical question." She folded her arms over her very large belly. "How?"

Ulrich let out a big sigh. "Okay." He led Tia across the room and helped her get comfortable in the overstuffed chair beside Luc. Then he went back to sit beside Millie. He leaned forward, rested his elbows on his knees and his chin on his clasped hands as he appeared to contemplate the question. When Ulrich finally raised his head and glanced in Tia's direction, there was very little humor in his smile.

She was reminded, once again, what a handsome man her father was, beautiful in both appearance and actions.

Ulrich sighed again, and slowly shook his head. "I spent a lot of nights, after you were in bed asleep, little girl, curled up in the middle of my big, empty bed as a wolf."

He leaned back, wrapped his arm around Millie and held her close. "I wasn't celibate all those years, far from it, but I realized very quickly that it wasn't sex that I needed or even wanted, it was the mental connection. If you really think about it, it's not sex we crave, it's the connection during sex. The sharing of sensation and emotion, the complete joining we experience. Without another Chanku, that was impossible. After your mother and the amazing connection we shared, sex with anyone else was the equivalent of, to be blunt, masturbation. I might as well have been alone. It didn't take me long to figure out that when I slept as a wolf, I dreamed as a wolf."

He shrugged, and gazed off into the distance. "Maybe it's because we're closer to our feral roots when we take our animal form. I don't really know, but on those nights where my needs were impossible to control, I often found a partner for sex . . ." He cast a sideways glance at Tia, shrugged, and looked away. "Then I would go home and shift. When I slept as a wolf, your mother came to me in my dreams. On those nights it was as if she'd never gone. I'd wake up angry on those mornings, furious with her for dying, for taking the risks that led to her death."

He turned and looked directly at Tia. "She hasn't returned since that night Anton helped me pass over into her world. That was the night she finally moved beyond the veil. I wonder now if those dreams were part of what held her earthbound. If my need and my anger were stronger than Camille's need to move on."

He took Millie's hand in his and turned his attention fully on the beautiful woman he loved. "Once I met Millie, it was as if those dreams never happened." He smiled, and this time his entire face lit up. "I loved Camille, and Goddess knows, I loved the little girl she gave me more than my own life, as I will love her always. But you . . . you are my life now, Millie West. You're everything to me. I love you and I refuse to ever imagine a life without you in it." He leaned close and kissed her.

Tia felt her tears at the same time she felt the next contraction. Luc pressed a hand against her tightening belly and checked his watch as she panted her way through it. Tinker sat close beside her with a look of pure concentration on his face.

When the contraction ended, sweat beaded his forehead and ran down his neck. Tia just shook her head. "Tinker, you're amazing."

"No, sweetie, you're the one who's amazing. I'm just taking the first shift. I'll let the ladies help you out when things really get going."

Laughter flowed around the room. "Tinker's taking the pains for you?" Keisha grinned at both of them. She elbowed Anton in the ribs and he gave an exaggerated grunt. "Now that is a real man."

"My feelings exactly." Xandi stood up and stretched. "C'mon, girls. He's putting us to shame." She reached for Tia's hand. "I bet a shower with friends would feel really good to you about now." She glanced in Logan's direction.

He opened one eye. "Shower. No bath. Make sure she has a place to sit and you use one of the showers with support bars. We don't need her falling."

"Gotcha." Keisha leaned over and kissed Anton. Then she took Tia's other hand and she and Xandi pulled her to her feet. "C'mon. The hardest part's yet to come. A shower will really help you face all the sweaty stuff."

"Beats giving birth soaked in jet fuel, don't you think." Xandi's wry comment brought a long sigh from Anton.

"Since it was Luc's and my wedding you were headed to when the plane went down, it might be a good idea not to bring that up, Xandi." Tia gave an apologetic shrug in Anton and Stefan's direction. Then, with a burst of laughter, she surged ahead and dragged Keisha and Xandi from the room.

When she heard Tinker's sigh of relief, Tia laughed even harder. Logan had been right. It was a very long night. But with her pack around her, she was actually loving every minute.

* * *

Millie watched Tia leave with Keisha and Xandi. She wasn't the least bit surprised to see tears in Ulrich's eyes when she leaned close and kissed his cheek. "She'll be okay, love. She's right when she says she's got the pack to help her through."

Ulrich covered her hand with his. "It's certainly more than you had at that age."

Adam raised his head and smiled at her. "How did you do it, Mom?"

*Mom.* She'd never in her wildest dreams expected to hear her own child call her Mom. Millie wrapped her fingers around Ulrich's arm and hugged him close. One more reason to love this man.

"I've wondered that too." Manda sat in Baylor's lap near Adam, the brother she'd connected with for so many years, but only met the year before. "I had Adam in my head, so I never felt totally alone, but you didn't have anyone."

Millie shook her head. "No, but you have to remember, I had no idea what I was missing. My mother died when I was little and I was turned over to my uncle. He was a cruel and twisted man who thought my mother was a slut and a whore, and I was painted with the same brush. Now I realize she was the product of her genes, but I never heard a nice word about her. Still, the life I had with my uncle was the only life I knew until I met your father, and he was only around for a matter of weeks."

Manda frowned. "I've never even asked if you loved him. Did you?"

Millie thought about Jace and the girl she'd been so many years ago. Had she loved her cowboy? As much as any nineteen-year-old girl can love a tall, handsome man who literally rides into her life on a beautiful sorrel mare. "I thought I did," she said, smiling. "I knew so little about love, and he was the first boy to ever court me. I had to sneak out because my uncle never allowed me to date, but that's probably why I ended up pregnant. I had absolutely no experience with boys."

She still remembered that first time. She'd been so angry at her uncle and disgusted with herself, and all because of the spankings. He'd always spanked her, and when she was a little girl, those big hands slapping her little bare butt had hurt like the blazes.

She got spanked for every infraction, and as far as Millie could tell, there was damned little that wasn't an infraction. It wasn't until she was around twelve or so that she realized there was more going on than arbitrary punishment.

Always a religious zealot, her uncle made her kneel and pray for forgiveness before he disciplined her. Since her spankings were always on her bare bottom, she would have to kneel wearing only her shirt and socks.

It was always that way. She had no idea it was wrong. No idea what kind of normal lives most little girls lived. For Millie, this was her reality.

Until her first menses. She'd never forget the horror of kneeling on the hard linoleum floor in her bedroom and seeing the trickle of blood running down her inner thigh. She'd stared at it, terrified she must be dying. Then she'd started to cry.

Her uncle had been furious. He'd told her she was filthy, that she needed to clean herself and then stay in the bathroom until he got home.

Hours later, he returned. She found a box of thick pads on her bed, but no explanation what to do with them. Ashamed, with no idea what had happened beyond the fact she'd somehow escaped her spanking, she'd worn the things pinned inside her underpants until a friend at school told her about the little elastic belts that would hold them in place.

Still ashamed all these long years later, Millie studied

her toes. "After that, things changed. He never spanked me during my period, but now when he did spank me, it was definitely sexual. I had felt his erection for years when he had me over his lap, but had no idea what it was. The few girls who spoke to me at school would talk about such things. Eventually I realized that the spankings he regularly gave me also gave him sexual gratification. They continued well into my teens."

She raised her head and faced her friends, her family . . . her packmates. Her body felt leaden, as if the weight of all those years with her uncle might actually press her into the ground.

Blinking back tears, she finally admitted something she'd never before said aloud. "What disgusts me is that I actually reached a point where I looked forward to the spankings. I hated him. I hated that he made me take off my pants and lie across his lap."

She shuddered and took a deep breath. This was harder than she'd expected, admitting her weakness in front of her packmates and especially Ulrich, even though he already knew her story. Even more difficult was admitting her terrible behavior to her children. "Most of all," she said, speaking in barely more than a whisper, "I hated the way my body responded. I was disgusted by my sense of anticipation when I knew he would punish me. What was even worse is that he knew how I felt, that by the time I was a teen, I craved the sexual feelings."

Ulrich shook his head, silently denying her words. He tightened his arm around her shoulders and hugged her close. Millie leaned into his warmth and the pure physical strength of the man and felt the pressure ease.

Ulrich kissed her forehead. "You've no reason to feel shame, m'love. He was a sick and disturbed man, an example of someone who was genetically the same as all of us, but who never discovered his heritage. His religious beliefs must have been constantly at war with his sexual nature. I imagine it twisted him up inside. You were reacting as your body intended you to react, yet you were too young and too uninformed to understand any of it."

Millie leaned her cheek against his shoulder. "Uninformed is a pretty mild description of what I was like as a youngster."

"What about your cowboy?" Eve asked. "How'd that happen?"

Her cowboy, in spite of the fact he'd left her alone and pregnant, was a good memory. "His name was Jace, shortened from JC which was short for John Charles." She laughed, remembering. "He was tall and lanky and so handsome. I remember thinking how witty he was when he told me cowboys were long on short names. I met him when he came on to our property before a big storm. He was looking for a couple of heifers that had strayed. I was nineteen and had been punished that afternoon by my uncle. I was so furious with him and myself I'd decided to run away, but then I ran into Jace about a mile from the house. He took my breath, he was so good looking."

She slanted a teasing glance at Ulrich. "However, not nearly as gorgeous as you, sweetheart."

He laughed. "I was waiting for you to explain yourself."

Millie nodded contritely while she bit back a grin. "I figured as much." Then she smiled and glanced at Adam, so tall and strong and handsome. "You take after your father, Adam. You've got his mannerisms, even his way of walking, which is amazing, considering neither you nor Amanda ever knew him."

She felt as if some of the others in the room needed an explanation. "Ulrich did a search on Jace, and discovered he was killed in a farming accident before Adam and Manda were born." She shrugged. "At least it explained why he never came back for me. He never even knew I was pregnant."

Oliver asked the question Millie had often wondered herself. "Do you think he was Chanku?"

"No. I've thought of that, but there was never a real connection between us, at least not any kind of mental link. Until Ulrich, Jace was my only lover."

She grinned at the soft gasp of surprise from the few in the room who didn't know her story. "Anyway, I had nothing to compare him to. I didn't know anything about sex, including the mechanics. I didn't even know what my period meant until one of my friends explained it to me, and then I was more grossed out than interested. My only personal knowledge of arousal was from the strange feelings I got when my uncle stripped my pants off and beat me. At the time, I had no idea what I was feeling was sexually related. Remember, I was young long before there was an Internet. No way to Google what I wanted to learn. Even the romances I loved to read, always in secret, of course, used to shut the bedroom door in my face."

Ulrich cleared his throat. "Might I interrupt and say that Millie is a very quick study. She now knows what happens behind the bedroom door . . . or in the woods, or on the deck, or . . ."

She punched his shoulder and continued as if he hadn't said a word. "Jace and I only had sex a few times out in the old barn near my uncle's house. The first time was a disaster, as far as I was concerned. It hurt. It was messy, and while Jace seemed to have a wonderful time, I wasn't too impressed. I think my main enjoyment was that he was young and handsome and paying attention to me, and I was defying my uncle by seeing him." She laughed, amazed that, even after all these years she could still recall his face and the way she felt when he held her. Nice.

Ulrich, on the other hand, was not a lover she would ever describe as merely nice. Matt, either. No, they went far beyond simple descriptive phrases. Way far . . .

"I never had an orgasm with Jace. I think, if he had

been Chanku, or at least had the right DNA, we would have had a stronger connection. As it was, there was nothing beyond the pleasure of being close to another person who wasn't interested in beating me. Of course, when he didn't come back, I figured he'd grown bored with me and found someone else. It was months later when I realized I was pregnant. Then there was no getting out of the house at all, but I was more elated than upset. I couldn't wait to hold my babies. The thought of those two precious lives growing inside me was all that kept me sane."

She dipped her head and fought the burn of tears. Everyone knew what happened when she gave birth, how her uncle took the babies before she even got to see them. How he gave them up for private adoption so that they were lost to her for all those long years.

Was it the Goddess or fate that brought Ulrich into her life? If not for Ulrich and Pack Dynamics, she might never have found them again. But she had, and life was good, and there was no point in dwelling on things that could not be changed. "The best thing to come of all that happened, besides Adam and Manda," she said, smiling at both of them, "is that my uncle never touched me again. As far as he was concerned, I was dead to him, which is why the ranch wasn't left to me. But, since it became a wolf sanctuary instead, I certainly can't complain. The land is being put to good use, and I obviously don't need it."

She turned and looked into Ulrich's sympathetic gaze. Goddess how she loved the man. "I have no regrets. I lived a celibate life for over thirty years, but I have more now than I ever imagined possible. I have a man I love, who loves me. I have two amazing adult children who make me so proud to be their mother, in spite of the fact I didn't raise them, and like Tia says, I have all of you. My life has never been so rich."

The room was silent, but the sense of support and love

was almost enough to leave Millie in tears. Then Oliver broke the silence—and the mood.

"Celibate?" Oliver shook his head in disbelief. "I mean, c'mon, Millie! I was celibate too, but damn, I lacked the necessary parts. How'd you . . . ?"

She stared solemnly at Oliver, fighting a smile. "Batteries, m'boy. Lots and lots of batteries."

Laughing, Adam slapped his hands over his ears. "I really don't need to hear this."

Manda touched his wrist. Speaking very seriously, she said, "I know. The visual is definitely not something I want to associate with my mother."

In a loud stage whisper, Millie leaned close to Ric. "I guess we shouldn't tell them about Matt."

Adam nodded. "That's probably a very good id—"

Ric raised his head and stared directly at Millie's son. "Possibly, but compared to batteries, Matt's sort of like that bunny that keeps going and going and . . ."

Tala curled up between Mik and AJ and realized she couldn't have wiped the smile off her face if she'd wanted. There was nothing but warmth and love and a comfortable sense of support among all the different personalities gathered together, all of them here for Tia and Luc . . . and for each other.

She raised her head and caught Baylor's eye. Her brother flashed her a warm smile and they both turned to see Lisa looking back at them.

A sense of love flowed through Tala—love totally unlike her feelings for Mik and AJ. Love for her sister and her brother—two people who had essentially been strangers to her when they were all growing up in what had to be one of the most dysfunctional families ever.

Bay had been a teenager when Tala finally came along, the youngest of the three Quinn children. Lisa was just five years older than Tala, back when Tala'd been known as

Mary Ellen, but the years had established enough of a gap that they'd never been close.

Bay was the handsome older brother, the one her girlfriends drooled over and wanted to meet, but of course he'd been totally uninterested in any of his little sister's friends.

For good reason. They were all pretty twerpy at that point in their lives.

Bay must have caught her thoughts. "Definitely a change from our situation when we were kids, eh, girls?"

Lisa merely shook her head and snuggled close to Tinker.

"Thank the Goddess," Tala said. "We sort of defined dysfunctional."

"At least you had a family." Mei hadn't said much all evening, but her soft voice caught everyone's attention. "I was found in a park, umbilical cord and placenta still attached. I figure my mother couldn't get away from me fast enough."

"That's pretty bad." Lisa seemed to shrivel up next to Tinker. "Our mother did hang around, though I don't remember her giving us much attention. She was there, at least until our father shot and killed her."

"Sweetie, you—" Tinker held Lisa close against his side.

"No, it's okay." Lisa sat up a little straighter. "Our mother was ruled by her sex drive, and she was pretty indiscriminate about who she took for lovers. I don't think any of us had the same father. Baylor is the only one the man who raised us even tried to claim as his own, but the most important thing is that we survived. You, too, Mei. She might not have raised you, but she didn't abort you, either. And Eve, you were raised in foster care, too, but you're here now, healthy, alive and mated to a pretty terrific man who loves you."

Lisa paused and glanced at Tala as if asking for strength.

She'd always been the quieter one, but she'd also been the only witness to their father's murder of their mother. Telling her story in court had taken guts, but Tala always felt it had taken a lot out of her, too.

Lisa blushed, as if she suddenly realized everyone was looking at her. "I mean . . . I . . . we . . ."

Jake interrupted, speaking softly over Lisa's stumbling words. She gave him a grateful glance and stayed close beside Tinker.

"I remember when I first met Bay and asked him about his family." Jake smiled and turned away from Lisa. His gaze settled on Tala's brother. The depth of emotion in that simple look almost took Tala's breath. These were men who lived together, who loved each other deeply, passionately. As passionately as they loved their female mates.

"I asked him about his family, and he sort of shrugged, and then he said they could be described in one word: dysfunctional. I'll never forget what he told me. 'My father's in prison for murdering my mother when he caught her screwing the postman. The postman didn't survive Daddy's temper tantrum, either.' I remember thinking how dispassionate he sounded when he described his mother's death, or the fact he had sisters."

Jake glanced toward Lisa. "He said, 'One of them lives under a bridge in Tampa and the other one's divorced and living in New Mexico,' but that he'd lost touch after the trial. I remember trying to control my excitement. I immediately looked at Shannon because both of us realized at the same time exactly what it meant—that there were two more Chanku females out there, women who didn't know who or what they really were. You, Lisa. And Tala. If we hadn't met Bay, there's no way we ever would have found you."

Tala glanced around the room and saw nothing but thoughtful smiles . . . until she made eye contact with Ulrich. The serious gleam in his eyes stopped her cold.

"What . . . ?"

"Look around you," he said, gesturing at each of them. "The fact we are all here together is so serendipitous. Pure chance? Accidents, or . . ." He glanced at Anton and smiled. "Fate. Maybe even the hand of the Goddess. I doubt we'll ever really know, but our stories, the odds of all of us finding one another, are unbelievable. And yet, here we are."

Anton nodded. "So true. There is so much we don't now about ourselves. So many questions of how each of us came to find one another. I'm always trying to learn more. It's not easy. Like why, for instance, there are so many of you from Florida. Are there more Chanku, undiscovered, living in that state? The odds seem good, but there is so little we actually know, so much we need to learn."

Ulrich nodded. "That's another thing. Look at all of us. What do you see? No matter how horrible your beginnings, all of you are healthy and happy with your lives. And you're young. Think about it. Millie and I are the oldest ones here. Only Adam, Manda, and Tia have living parents, but we don't appear to have aged at all like the rest of the population. I haven't changed since my first shift, but even Millie, who didn't shift until she was in her midfifties, looks like a much younger woman."

He glanced at Anton. "Do we age, Anton? Will I someday grow too old to shift? Could Millie still get pregnant if she wanted? Her human body had gone through menopause before her first shift, but will anything change? Will she come into heat like the younger ones? Shannon was infertile, but now that she is Chanku, her reproductive system is sound. When she wants to, she can have babies, all because she shifted. One of the young kids, Deacon, was HIV positive. He's not, at least not anymore. There are so many unanswered questions about who and what we are. Aging . . . I look the same as I did when I first met Camille. That was a long time ago. My blond hair was already almost entirely white, but other than the white hair, I know I can pass for a much younger man."

Millie shot him a sexy grin. "I can vouch for that."

Ulrich growled at her. She laughed and snuggled close. "I guess, now that I am about to become a grandfather, finding answers to so many questions is suddenly more important to me."

Anton nodded. "I understand completely. Stefan and I have had the same discussions, ever since we knew Alex and Lily were coming. Suddenly those questions have become more important than they were before. We have another generation to consider. Unfortunately, the answers are just as elusive."

Tala heard footsteps and glanced up in time to see that Tia, Xandi, and Keisha had returned. Tia was freshly showered with her long hair tied back in a simple ponytail. Wearing a big, fluffy bathrobe and her old beat-up moccasins, she looked like a freshly scrubbed twelve-year-old.

A very pregnant twelve-year-old. Tala felt a yearning deep in her womb. What would it be like, to carry a child? She felt the warmth of both her men, one on either side. Mik leaned close and kissed the top of her head. AJ squeezed her hand. The feeling grew stronger, the sense that it was time, that finally, she might be ready for the next important step. Maybe, just maybe, when her next heat began.

Or not. She couldn't help but think how much easier it would be if the decision were not left entirely to her.

Tia stood in the doorway and listened to her father and Anton talking about the questions none of them could answer. They weren't questions that worried her. No, she was more interested in finally meeting the two little girls she'd carried under her heart for almost nine months.

She glanced up and caught Luc watching her. Her breasts began to ache and she knew her nipples had tightened into taut little peaks, merely from the power of his gaze. Already heavy with the first milk she'd need for her babies, now they ached from arousal as well. She couldn't wait until her body was ready for Luc again. It seemed like years instead of a few short weeks since they'd last made love.

She craved his touch, the shock of sensation to nipples and clit and womb. The warm, liquid reaction of her body pliant and soft, molding to his.

She heard his tender *I love you* in her mind.

She flashed him a big smile. *I love*—a gush of warm fluid ran down the insides of her legs and dripped into the soft moccasins that were the only things that still fit on her feet. She stared at the spreading wet spot on the rug, and raised her head, wide-eyed.

This wasn't quite the liquid reaction she'd been fantasizing.

Luc broke into a big grin. No one else appeared to notice she was currently leaving a huge puddle on Anton and Keisha's expensive Persian carpet. Frantic, Tia spun her head and looked directly at Tinker, but he was talking quietly with Logan and hadn't noticed her.

"Tink?" she said, and when he didn't respond, Tia said it again, louder. "Tinker!"

His head came up. He stared blankly at her.

Tia grinned. Fully aware she had the attention of everyone in the room, she gingerly stepped out of the wet spot. "I think it's time!"

Logan was on his feet in a flash. A big grin spread across Tinker's face. Laughter and silly comments filled the room, but it was all good. Tia stood perfectly still while warm amniotic fluid trickled down her legs and Logan pressed his palms against her belly. When he raised his head, he was smiling.

"It appears only one of the membranes has broken, but the other is still intact. This should get things moving faster, but everything feels exactly the way it should. I imagine your little girls will be here in a couple of hours, max."

Keisha and Xandi showed up with their arms loaded with towels to mop up the mess. Tia hadn't seen them leave the room, but she stepped away from the puddle and grabbed one of the towels from Xandi to shove between her legs.

She should have been embarrassed, but she wasn't, not surrounded by so many who loved her. Luc took a couple of towels from Keisha and folded them into a thick pad so Tia could sit on the couch beside him without staining the leather. No one seemed the least bit upset about the mess she'd made.

The only problem was, now everyone in the room was looking directly at her. Tia didn't mind being the center of attention on occasion, but this was a bit much. She raised her head and caught Tala's intent gaze.

She knew the guys were pushing Tala toward motherhood. And Tala, like Tia had been so many months ago, was still unsure. Of course, with two men to please, Tala's case was a little bit more complicated than Tia's.

It seemed only fair, then, to put the spotlight on Mik and AJ. Tia grinned at Tala, but she spoke to the guys. "Mik, I remember you and AJ from when I was still living at home. You guys were already a pair when you came to live with us. How'd Dad find you? I'd love to hear your story."

Mik glanced at AJ and they both focused on Tala for a moment. Then Mik shrugged his broad shoulders and settled back against the leather couch. "AJ, you were in prison longer than me. Why don't you start."

AJ gave Mik a dirty look, took a deep breath and a sip of his beer. Then he nodded his head. "Folsom was a long time ago," he said. "Another life. One Mik and I try not to dwell on, but it began even earlier, long before either one of us served any time. For me, it started when I was about three, when my mother killed herself."

# Chapter 11

## Mik & AJ

It was something that would always bother him, the fact he couldn't remember anything about his mother before that morning he found her sleeping in the bathtub. That memory was as clear as if it had happened yesterday, a pinpoint of time before his life had changed so dramatically. He saw her now, his beautiful mother with her thick, dark brown hair perfectly arranged and curling over her shoulders, the black silky nightgown she loved, one narrow strap slipping from her shoulder and resting against her arm. The swell of her breasts, her long, slender throat, her skin as white as the porcelain of the tub.

Only she wasn't sleeping, and the thick, red paint staining her brutally slashed wrists and pooling beneath her and around the metal drain of the tub wasn't paint at all.

He shuddered with the memory and drew a shaky breath. Mik's loving mental touch calmed him, and AJ let the images return, allowed the words to flow.

He knew it had always been just him and his mom, the two of them together in the little house that was AJ's world, though he had no memories before this one, pivotal day. He'd looked all over the house for her, dragging his tattered blanket with Pooh Bear clutched under his arm, until he pushed open the door to the bathroom.

Silly Mom. She was sleeping in the bathtub! Only Mom wouldn't wake up no matter how hard he shook her. It was time for breakfast and he was hungry, so he wandered back to the kitchen, pushed a chair against the counter and climbed up to the cabinet where Mom kept the Cheerios and his favorite plastic bowl. He was very careful when he poured the milk, and he even remembered to carry his empty bowl to the sink.

And still she slept. It was almost time for lunch when he finally put his clothes on and went to the house next door and rang the doorbell. Old Mrs. Trellini had always been nice to him, so he figured she would know how to wake up his mom.

He hadn't expected the screams. Hadn't understood the people who came and got him and took him away from everything familiar. He had no idea why he never saw his mom again, not until years later when he finally learned the truth.

Now, as the story spilled out, AJ heard his own words as if from far away, almost drowned out by the rapid thudding of his heart. He felt the gnawing pain in his gut that always came when he thought of his mother and the day everything he knew ended.

Mik's mental touch kept him grounded. Tala's warmth against his side calmed his screaming nerves and helped him hold his voice steady. He'd never spoken of this before. Not to anyone.

Only Tala and Mik knew the truth. There were no secrets in a mating bond. None at all.

"I hated her for a long time afterward." He stared at his clasped hands hanging between his knees. "The fact she took such a cowardly way out, knowing full well I'd be the one to find her. It was wrong. Just dead wrong." AJ took a deep breath. Let it out. Damn. He'd never been comfortable talking in front of people, much less spilling his guts like this.

Mik reached across Tala and wrapped his fingers around AJ's hand, adding his physical presence to the mental connection. Tala snuggled closer, plastering her small body against his side. He absorbed their love, the powerful bond the three of them shared, and drew from them both the support he'd never had as a child, as a youth, a young man.

AJ squeezed Mik's fingers and bumped lightly against Tala, but their physical connection gave him the strength to continue. He raised his head and looked at the others in the room, all of them watching him, many with eyes filled with compassion, others with curiosity. There was no condemnation. Only understanding.

"This was down in San Jose, south of San Francisco. She died in 1970, and from that time until I was eighteen, I bounced around from family to family within the foster care system. I never really had a home. About the time I'd get used to a place, feel as if the people actually cared about me, I'd get moved again and have to start all over."

He stared at his hand, still clasped tightly in Mik's big paw. Felt Tala's comforting warmth beside him, and remembered those horrible, unsettled days. "I was a cute little kid and people wanted to like me, but I was really shy, too. And, I was gay." He raised his head and smiled at Stefan. "The same way you knew you were into girls? I felt those same feelings for other boys, from the time I was maybe seven or eight years old. Even as Chanku, I still identify myself as a gay man." He glanced at Tala and grinned when he added, "Though, obviously I've become a little less discriminating."

Tala jabbed him in the side. AJ grunted and smiled, but he felt Mik's hand squeeze his and the rest of his nervousness faded away. He was among friends, sitting close to the two people he loved more than anyone in the world.

Two who loved him. He could do this. "My sexuality really became an issue in high school. I was horny all the time. I tried dating girls but it was all wrong. They wanted something I couldn't give them, but I didn't know enough to understand that my drives were normal for me. I was miserable, fully aware that the guys I lusted after weren't at all interested, and fighting off the girls at the same time. I finally graduated, but college wasn't an option and at eighteen I was on my own."

He shrugged. "By then I'd discovered sex with men, or maybe I should say that the men discovered me. I learned I had no problem at all with using my body to survive."

"How'd you end up in prison?"

It was Jazzy Blue who asked. AJ raised his head and smiled at her. He'd had a soft spot in his heart for Jazzy ever since he'd helped rescue her and her friends after one of them had shifted and killed a guy in Golden Gate Park. A guy who was attacking Tala.

"It was easier than I ever imagined," he said. "I was in the wrong place at the wrong time. I'd been picked up in the past for some minor infractions, but this time I really screwed up. The stupid thing is, I wasn't involved in the burglary, but the guys I was with had a bunch of stolen stuff in their car, and I got hauled in with them."

"And you got five years in prison for that?"

AJ hung his head. "Actually, I got a hell of a lot more, but that was after they found the loaded gun in my boot. Like I said, stupid."

"Made it damned hard for me to get him out, too." Ulrich made a sound that was more a snort than a laugh. "Thank goodness our boy didn't draw it on anyone, or he'd still be in that little eight by ten cell."

AJ flashed a grin at Ulrich. "Yeah, Boss . . . but you're good."

This time Ulrich definitely snorted.

"Anyway, I ended up in prison. It was 1987 and I was twenty years old, totally full of myself, used to using my grace and good looks to get by, and suddenly I was tossed into prison with a whole lot of very tough bastards who suddenly wanted to be my best friend. Need I say, I did not let on I was gay when I got to Folsom? Other than one rather ugly incident, my size and attitude kept me safe, but I was there for four fucking long years trying not to get myself killed or raped before Mik showed up."

Exhausted, emotionally drained by memories he generally avoided, AJ glanced to his right and caught Mik's dark gaze. The compassion in his eyes was almost AJ's undoing. He swallowed back the huge lump in his throat in order to speak. "Your turn, bud. Why don't you tell them what your road to perdition was like?"

Mik slowly shook his head. "Not nearly as dramatic as yours or most of the folks here. I grew up on a small reservation in South Dakota. My mother was Sioux, my father was one of the Mexican laborers who worked the area for a while and then moved on. My mother hung around for a while, then one day she just didn't come home. I heard later she was dead, but no one ever said exactly what happened, or even when. I mostly remember my grandfather. He's the one who raised me."

Mik studied his fingernails for a moment, searching for the right words. He felt no real emotions of any kind for his mother, but he'd hardly known her. His grandfather, on the other hand . . . "Grandfather was tough on me. He felt as if he'd failed as a father to my mother, because she had not taken on her responsibility of raising me, her only son. Instead she drank and whored around and essentially abandoned me long before she died. It became his goal in life, to raise me as a better man. He taught me the old ways. I learned much of the language and the ways of our culture. My childhood was actually pretty good compared to a lot of you guys, but I still managed to screw up."

He flashed a grin at AJ. "I didn't even need a gun to do it."

No, all he'd needed was a soft spot for a woman in

need. He was nineteen and strong from working the cattle on his grandfather's small holding. Almost six and a half feet tall, he'd finally started adding bulk to his lanky frame, and he was cocky in the way only a young man can be, thinking with his balls instead of his brain.

He was in California with his grandfather, up near the little town of Susanville in the northeast corner of the state, to check out a horse his grandfather wanted to buy. They were camped near town and Grandfather had decided to stay for a few days while he looked at more stock.

Mik had found a bar in town that wasn't too concerned with proper ID. He wasn't anywhere near legal age, but with his size and perpetually angry stare, no one ever asked for proof. He usually just ordered a soda, anyway. On the wages his grandfather paid, it was all he could afford.

Drinking wasn't what drew him back to the bar that night. No, it was the cute little blonde working swing shift.

"Like I said, I was thinking with my balls, not my brain," Mik said. "Damn, but Rosie was hot, and I was positive she'd been flirting with me." He glanced at AJ and shook his head. "Unlike you, bro, I had no problem at all screwing women. I preferred men, but I wasn't picky."

Tala grinned at him. "Obviously that hasn't changed," she said, and he knew she referred to herself.

A wave of tenderness washed over Mik, drowning out the old memories, filling his heart to the point he thought it might explode. "Sweetheart, when I picked you, I finally showed some discriminating taste. Unlike with that one . . ." He nodded toward AJ.

"Thanks, loads." AJ grunted, but his eyes twinkled as the three of them shared a very private moment. They'd all come from such shitty backgrounds, and look at them now. It was good. So damned good.

With those feelings freshly stirred, Mik realized it was

much easier to talk about his less-than-stellar youth, and the night that had sent him spiraling downward for the next few years.

And it all began the night he went back to that little bar in Susanville. Rosie had definitely caught his eye, and while he was usually pretty quiet around women, he'd had fun flirting with her. He liked the way her eyes crinkled up when she smiled at him. The way she sashayed her cute little ass around behind the bar. She wasn't much older than he was, and it might have been just the fact he was starved for someone to talk to besides his grandfather.

It was dark in the bar after the bright afternoon sunshine, and it took him a minute to adjust to the dim light and find her. He parked his ass on the bar stool and drummed his fingers on the counter to get her attention. "Hey, Rosie. How're ya doin'?"

Rosie shrugged him off, mumbled something and sort of scurried back into the shadows, like the most important thing she had to do in the world was dust the bottles behind the bar.

Where was the cute little flirt from the night before? Mik's radar clicked in and he got a chill along his spine. Something wasn't right.

"Rosie? You okay?"

She didn't answer him. Mik reached across the bar, intent on grabbing her arm to get her attention. The bartender stopped him with a meaty fist wrapped around Mik's forearm. He kept his voice low, though it was obvious Rosie heard him. "Leave her alone, kid. She's not feelin' too good. Her old man beat the crap out of her last night."

Mik sat perfectly still, unbelieving. Rosie was all of five two, maybe. He'd seen her guy, Marvin, the night before. He was almost as big as Mik, older by about ten years, with a big gut and a missing front tooth. He had to weigh a good two hundred pounds more than Rosie.

"He hit her?" Mik tugged his arm free. "Rosie?" He raised his voice. "Rosie? Turn around."

Maybe it was the command in his voice. Maybe it was the fact she was just tired of fighting, but she slowly turned and faced him.

Mik thought he might throw up. Her lip was split and so was the ridge over her left eye. Both eyes were black, the left one almost swollen shut. He clearly made out finger-shaped bruises around her pale throat. From the way she favored one side, he wondered if she might have some broken or cracked ribs.

"Fuck, Rosie." His voice was barely a whisper. "What'd that son of a bitch do to you?"

She didn't say a word, but a single tear rolled slowly down her bruised cheek before she turned back to her work.

"Did you report him? Did you call the sheriff?"

She shook her head. "Won't do no good," she said, staring at the back wall. Her voice was thick, as if she had trouble getting the words out through her split lip. He wondered if she'd gotten her teeth knocked loose as well.

"I deserved it. Marv . . . he had a right . . ."

"No man has the right to hit a woman, Rosie. No man."

She merely shrugged her thin shoulders and went back to dusting the sparkling bottles.

Frustrated and angry, Mik ordered a beer instead of a soda. He drank it, and then he had another. The bar was quiet on a week night and he was the only customer this early. Rosie didn't speak to him again. She finally disappeared into the back room and left Mik drinking all by himself. He wasn't sure how much time passed, but the empty beer bottles made a nice straight line in front of him by the time he paid his tab and left.

The walk back to his grandfather's campsite should have given him time to cool off, but the farther he got from town, the more the anger burned. He knew Rosie was due to get off work in another hour, knew the bastard she lived with had showed up the night before just as her shift ended.

Less than a quarter mile from camp, Mik turned around beside a small shed that marked the beginning of the campground. He was breathing hard, not from the walk but from anger. He saw the pale glow of lights shining over the small town and imagined the bastard showing up at the bar, hassling Rosie, maybe hitting her again. The images were so clear in his head that he almost put his fist through the wall of the shed.

He'd have been better off if he had. Instead, he headed back to town. No plan, no idea, nothing but a blazing rush of anger and the feeling that he had to do something to save Rosie from another beating.

When he walked into the bar, Marvin was there. He was already drunk, and he'd leaned across the bar and wrapped his thick fingers around Rosie's upper arm.

Mik saw it all in slow motion—the few other patrons in the bar sitting quietly, trying to ignore what was going on under their noses. The bartender reaching for the phone like he might be planning to call the cops.

Rosie, with her mouth twisted in a grimace of pain and a look of terror on her face as Marvin hauled back with his free arm, folded his hand into a fist and swung a roundhouse punch.

A punch that never landed. Mik caught Marvin's fist in his own and held him immobile. With a loud curse, Marvin turned loose of Rosie and swung at Mik.

Mik ducked, twisted the man's arm and flipped him off his feet, but Marvin moved fast for a big man. He rolled to his knees and lunged at Mik. Clipping him below the knees, he used his weight and tumbled Mik to the floor. Rosie screamed. Mik grabbed a beer bottle that rolled past him, turned and swung.

He caught the side of Marvin's jaw with the heavy bottle, heard the sickening crunch of breaking bone and followed up with a powerful punch to the man's temple.

By the time the sheriff's deputies raced through the door, Marvin was unconscious and Mik was standing over him, the beer bottle still clasped in his hand, blood pooling beneath the big man's head.

"I probably could have gotten off on self-defense if Rosie hadn't testified against me." Mik shook his head in disgust. "He'd just about killed her and she still protected him. I got charged with assault with a deadly weapon and sentenced to ten years. By the time the trial had ended and I was finally packed off to Folsom, I was all of twenty years old."

He slowly shook his head. "I don't think my grandfather ever got over the fact I ended up in jail in spite of his raising me. He understood why I'd gone back to defend Rosie, but he couldn't, for the life of him, understand how she could blame me for what happened."

"Did you kill him?" Jazzy's question hung in the air.

"No. For a long time I was sorry he lived. I blamed the fact I was going to prison on Marvin and Rosie. It took years before I realized I was the one at fault. It was their own sick relationship and their battle, but it seemed to work for them. I was wrong to interfere."

Tala wrapped her fingers around Mik's wrist. "I'm glad you interfered when Jimmy Cole was hassling me."

Mik shook his head. One of the hardest things he'd ever done was walk away from the feisty little whore in that bar in New Mexico, but with AJ's urging, he'd left Tala with her cruel and overbearing pimp when it was obvious the two of them weren't enough to help her. Not against a bar full of drunken good old boys.

"How can you say that?" He stared into her beautiful amber eyes, mesmerized as always by their sexy tilt at the corners, the intelligence and humor that defined her. "I opened my big mouth and it didn't help a bit. Cole turned you over to that pack of animals and they almost killed you."

Tala nodded, but in spite of the horror of that night, she had a soft and loving smile on her face. "Exactly, but it took almost getting killed to convince me to try and get away, and because you'd at least stepped in, I knew you'd help me if I needed help. Otherwise I never would have hidden in your car, and you never would have saved me."

Ulrich's deep voice interrupted. "Once again," he said, "by the slimmest of circumstances, another member was brought into the pack."

Tia groaned and rubbed her belly. "Well, I sure wish these new members of mine would hurry up and get here." She glanced at Luc. "Please tell me we're finally closer than seven minutes."

Luc glanced up from his wristwatch. "Actually, we're at five. The last three have been at five-minute intervals. Are you okay?"

Tia nodded. "I'm fine. I'm not feeling any pain at all. You should probably ask the rest of the women how they feel."

Mik glanced about the room, suddenly aware of the silence from the females, the sense of strain. "You're all taking her pain, aren't you?" He noticed the beads of sweat on Tala's forehead for the first time, and realized she was blocking her thoughts. "You, too?"

"Well, of course." She nuzzled his arm and kissed his shoulder. "It's not so bad when we share. Besides, the way you guys keep dropping baby hints my way, I figured I'd better check and see exactly what you were plotting for my future. I like to know what I'm getting into."

AJ nodded sagely. "Or who's getting into you?"

"You never give up, do you?" Tala jabbed her elbow lightly against his side.

He grunted and doubled over, as if in tremendous pain.

Laughter flowed about the room, teasing comments about tiny little Tala carrying a baby for one or both of her big men. She dished it out as well as she took it, and Mik sensed her growing ease with the whole idea of motherhood.

He glanced over her head and caught AJ's eye. AJ was smiling at him, and his thoughts tumbled into Mik's mind, the sense of family, the deep, abiding love he felt for Mik and Tala. There was fear, as well, the concern that she might be too small to carry a baby fathered by either one of them.

Mik shook his head. *Tala's body will know. The baby will only be as large as she can handle. Yours or mine—we'll have a baby of our own within the year. I can feel her resolve.*

AJ grinned. *I feel it, too, and it makes me hot. Are you as horny as I am?*

*Always.*

Tala's laughter flowed over both of them. *Sorry guys. Not tonight. I'm sharing labor pains so you'll have to entertain each other.*

As if that had ever been a problem. AJ caught Mik's eye again. It was time to tell the rest of their story. *My turn,* he said. *I love this memory, the one of the very first time I saw you. That was the day everything changed. It was even more profound than when I discovered I was Chanku.*

Mik nodded. He had no words. There were none to express the love he felt for AJ. For the depth of emotion that bound them, now and forever. AJ truly had saved his life.

AJ sat back in the comfortable couch and watched as Logan once again placed his hands on Tia's round belly. The room went silent as everyone waited. The sense of expectation was high.

Finally Logan nodded and stood up. "Everything's just

fine," he said. "Now that the ladies are helping you with the pains, the babies seem a lot calmer, too. When the contractions get a little closer, we'll move you upstairs to the birthing room. In the meantime, you might as well be down here where you've got your support team."

Tia laughed. "Good idea. I certainly wouldn't want to be doing this on my own."

AJ glanced at Millie and she smiled back at him. She'd done it entirely on her own.

*So did you, AJ.*

He frowned. *What do you mean? I've certainly never had a baby.*

Millie slowly shook her head. *All those years in prison? I can't imagine a lonelier place. Or a more frightening one.*

"You're right," he said, speaking softly, yet loud enough the others could hear him. "I was terrified." He glanced around the room, aware now that he had the attention of everyone here. Surprisingly, he felt comfortable with so many eyes on him, but this was about Mik as much as it was about himself. AJ glanced at his lover to steady himself even more. It was always easier when the focus was on Mik.

He explained himself to the pack. "Millie was mind-talking, commenting on how frightening and lonely prison must have been. It was. I was afraid for my life every day I was locked up, as scared of some of the guards as I was of the other prisoners." Memories washed over him. He shuddered. Took a deep breath. Then another. Then he sensed Mik close by and his fear receded.

Receded, but didn't go away. Would it ever?

"I get teased a lot by you guys about being pretty." His voice sort of cracked on the words and he felt like such a frickin' coward, but it was hard to talk about stuff like this, hard to admit the things that scared the crap out of him, even now, here, surrounded by people who loved him. He tilted his head back, took another deep breath.

Felt like he was drowning, but he finally got the words out. "Let me tell you, that's not what you want to be—pretty—when you're locked up with a few hundred of your closest and dearest friends, all of them horny and pissed and ready for a fight . . . or a fuck."

He'd dealt with that fear for four long years, living side by side with a cell mate he was afraid to turn his back on. Fearing that his secret would get out, that the others would realize he was gay and clean, and not nearly as dangerous as his size and attitude made him appear.

Then one day the guy he'd shared a cell with since his first day at Folsom made the mistake of talking back to someone bigger and meaner than he was. The other prisoner and his buddies managed to cut AJ's cell mate to ribbons with an amazing variety of homemade weapons—all of which had been concealed once again by the time guards restored order and reached the body.

As much as he'd hated the guy he roomed with for all that time, AJ felt physically ill when he thought of the way the man died, kneeling on the floor of the shower with his entrails spilling into his hands.

They eventually hauled the body out, but not until the investigation had been completed, a wide variety of weapons recovered, and the killers identified. With the whole block on lockdown, AJ had more than enough time to appreciate just how lonely a prison cell could be.

He'd spent less than a week by himself, though. Just one week, wondering who he'd be sharing his cell with next. Then he'd heard footsteps, sensed the presence of someone outside the door. The door swung open and AJ glanced up into eyes that mirrored his own.

He'd never forget that moment, the feelings that flooded him, emotions he'd all but forgotten after four long years in Folsom. He stared into the dark, haunted eyes of the huge man standing in the doorway, and felt his world unravel.

The guard, a man he recognized as new to the section, stepped through the open door. "Temple, ya got a new roomie. This is Miguel Fuentes. Fuentes, Andrew Temple."

AJ nodded and stood up. His first impression was all about size and attitude. Fuentes was a huge mountain of a man, unusually tall with broad shoulders straining his prison blues, long, shiny black hair tied back to frame a face that might have been carved from granite.

The two of them stood there a moment, sizing each other up. It took AJ a moment to realize the guy wasn't as old as he looked, and probably not nearly as mean. Dangerous, no doubt, but he was just a kid, obviously scared to death and doing his best to hide it.

In that moment, AJ recognized a kindred spirit. Some of the tension went out of him. There was something else, something he couldn't identify at first, but AJ played it cool so the guard wouldn't suspect anything out of the ordinary. Instead, AJ grunted his hello and moved aside to let the new guy into the tiny cell. The kid threw his gear on the top bunk, but he stayed out of AJ's way while they went through their introductions.

The guard watched them both with inquisitive eyes. AJ knew he studied the dynamics, wondered if the two prisoners would get along or try and kill each other the moment his back was turned. After a few moments, he nodded to both of them and left. The door clanged shut with a sense of finality AJ knew he'd never grow used to. The two of them were left alone, each of them sizing up the other.

Finally AJ shrugged and stepped back. "AJ Temple," he said.

The kid stared at him a moment. Then he nodded. "Miguel Fuentes. Mik. Just call me Mik."

"You can put your stuff over there. The top shelf's clear."

Mik nodded again and stepped by AJ. As he passed, his shoulder brushed AJ's arm.

AJ felt the connection through the cotton fabric of their prison-issue shirts and all the way to his balls. Stunned, he backed away, blinking. Mik paused in midstep, turned his head and stared at the point where their bodies had momentarily touched. When Mik raised his head, AJ looked into the young man's eyes and found the same burning curiosity he felt.

Curiosity and a sense of wonder. A soft buzzing in his head, a weight that seemed to press against his brain. Time seemed to pause as AJ stared into the kid's amber-colored eyes.

*What the fuck?*

The voice was clear and warm, filled with the same wonder, the same disbelief that held AJ in thrall. *Unbelievable.*

Mik was in his head.

Suddenly Mik stepped farther away, and clutched his small bag of belongings against his chest. He stared at AJ, looked down at his shoulder, back at AJ's arm. He said it again, silently. *What the fuck?*

AJ grinned. "My thoughts exactly." He glanced over his shoulder to make sure no one watched them. *Can you hear me? Do you hear my words in your head the way I hear yours?*

Wide-eyed, Mik nodded.

*How? I don't understand?*

"Me, either. This is just too weird." Mik sat down heavily on AJ's bunk, sort of like his big legs had just given out.

"That's an understatement." AJ rubbed his hands on his jeans. "We can't let anyone know. They'd separate us in a heartbeat." AJ paced the short distance across the cell and then spun around. "Who are you?"

The kid shrugged. "I told you. I'm Mik Fuentes. Maybe the question should be, what are you?"

AJ shook his head. There was no way to answer. "What are you in for?" He leaned against the wall like there was nothing out of the ordinary, but his heart was pounding a million miles an hour and his hands were sweating.

"ADW."

Assault with a deadly weapon. "You shoot someone?"

Mik shook his head. "Beat a guy half to death with a beer bottle for roughing up a woman."

AJ frowned. "And you got time for that?"

This time Mik actually smiled. It totally changed his appearance and transformed him from a hardened criminal into a gorgeous young man. "Turns out the woman liked getting roughed up. She testified against me. What about you?"

"I got picked up carrying a loaded weapon. Unfortunately, the guys I was riding with had a carload of stolen goods." He laughed. "Damn stupid on my part, that's for sure."

"What? Carrying?"

AJ shook his head. "Well, that too. Mostly stupid to be hanging out with guys dumb enough to get caught breaking and entering. The weapon was for protection, but try explaining that to the dude putting cuffs on you. The other guys, the ones who actually stole the crap . . . they all walked. They fingered me and, because of the gun, I'm the one doing time."

Mik grinned at him. "Sounds like your luck's as fucked as mine. We should get along just fine."

AJ sat down next to him on the bunk. "That's what scares me," he said. He stared at Mik, sizing him up. How could he possibly explain the amazing mental link he'd discovered with an absolute stranger?

The mental link, and the physical. He wasn't sure what

Mik Fuentes was feeling right now, but AJ had to clasp his hands tightly together to keep from reaching out to touch the man who would most likely be living beside him for however long their incarceration lasted.

His arousal was a living, breathing entity, pulsing between the two of them. AJ glanced down at the placket on Mik's prison-issue jeans and realized he wasn't the only one fighting a losing battle against an overwhelming sense of physical need.

Mik raised his head, glanced at AJ's groin and cocked a dark eyebrow. AJ merely groaned. Their prison cell had just become much too small, and more public than AJ had ever realized.

# Chapter 12

## AJ & Mik

AJ stood by while Mik stowed his belongings. Then, side by side, they walked to the dining hall. He tried to connect with Mik again, but there was no response. Weird. So whatever they had between them didn't happen all the time. Had he really heard Mik's thoughts?

Yes, he had. There was no denying the sound of the young man's voice in his head. If it happened once, it would happen again. He had to believe that.

There was still a connection, though. A sense of brotherhood, almost, as absurd as that sounded, but AJ felt it with every step he took. It was unusual not to feel alone and vulnerable. The sound of footsteps, the voices of the other prisoners, the smell of too many bodies in too tight an area had always left him sweating and nervous.

Tonight, he was more aware of the young man beside him than the others filling the long hallway, even without that amazing mental connection. For the moment, AJ merely wanted to feel someone beside him he could trust. He couldn't recall the last time he'd felt that way about anyone.

There was no doubt in his mind that Mik could be trusted. Walking down this sterile hallway of block and steel, he'd always felt as if there were traps waiting to be sprung. Tonight, with Mik so close, AJ felt no concerns for his own safety. Not with Mik beside him.

For the first time in his life, AJ appreciated the power of a united front, the strength of a friend.

Other prisoners moved out of their way. No one gave either of them any shit. Had the two of them somehow projected the fact they would back one another without hesitation?

Having Mik Fuentes beside him was most definitely an empowering experience. They sat across from each other on the long table. AJ kept his guard up, expecting trouble. Mik was the new kid on the block. There was almost always a test of some kind, a challenge to be met, questions to answer.

Not tonight. No one bothered the new guy. Maybe it was his size, or the subtle attitude that practically dared others to mess with him. Maybe it was the fact the two of them were obviously backing each other up, and neither of them were small men. Hell, they weren't even average. Together, they added up to a wall of muscle and attitude.

Whatever the reason, AJ wasn't going to complain. They finished their meal, nodded to a few of the older prisoners and went back to their cell.

Mik paused in the doorway. AJ saw his chest expand, almost as if he gathered strength with a deep intake of air. He let it out and stepped into the tiny cell.

Mik would adjust. Adjust or die. This small space, shared with a man he'd hated, had been AJ's home for so long, he'd forgotten what it was like to have space to himself, room to move freely.

*Freedom*. Thank God he had his dreams, or he would have killed himself long ago. He ran free when he dreamed. Alone in the darkness, the sound of his big paws thundering on the hard earth. The forest came to life for him at night, the rustling sounds of creatures in the dry grass, the deep hoot of an owl, the tiny, piercing squeaks of bats whirling overhead.

They took him away from this cell of stone and steel, away from the sounds of too many men in too small a space, away from the smells and the sense of misery that now defined his life.

His dreams either meant he was crazier than a loon, or they kept him sane. It was hard to be certain anymore, but he no longer cared, so long as they came to him each night. His dreams kept hopelessness at bay. Made it easier to deal with the specter of endless days that ran one into the other.

Now though, he was awake and the cell was his reality. He tried to see it through Mik's eyes. At least they were in the newer section of the prison with solid walls instead of bars, though the window on the door was barred, and there was really no such thing as privacy. Not when you had guards on your ass 24/7. The bunk beds were bolted to the wall on the left, there were shelves for storage, a stainless steel toilet and a tiny sink bolted to the wall. Everything was bolted down, screwed in, immovable.

Sterile.

Mik closed the door behind him. Shut his eyes when the door clanged shut. When he opened them, he looked directly at AJ. AJ felt a soft buzzing in his head and wondered if Mik was trying that weird mental thing again, but there were no words this time. No matter. It had happened once, it would happen again.

It was time for bed, and that pulsing, living thing between them, even without the mental link, was still growing stronger. Still crawling in his veins, lighting up his nerves, making his skin extra sensitive and his breath come in short, sharp puffs.

AJ refused to acknowledge it. Mik hadn't either.

How do you tell a guy you've barely met that you want

to suck his cock? That you'd do anything for the hot, wet feel of his mouth around your dick, for the scrape of teeth, the swirl of a mobile tongue?

AJ would have laughed if he hadn't felt like crying. He'd never wanted so badly, desired as much. Body shaking with need, he turned away from Mik, went to the sink and washed up for the night. Why was he so damned exhausted? His head hurt and his body ached, but he figured it must be the stress, the weird day, the strange connection to the new cell mate.

Finally, he lay in his bunk, almost preternaturally aware of the young man lying above him. They'd talked about their weird mind link, the fact they couldn't do it at will, but it still didn't make any sense.

Now, with nothing better to do than beat his own meat, AJ pulled his boner out of his sweatpants. He wrapped his fingers around his thick erection and slowly stroked the hard length.

His fingers slipped with great familiarity over his heavily veined shaft and his mind wandered over the events of the afternoon. It had been one fucking bizarre day. There was no other way to describe it.

Mik had been quiet all evening, curled into himself as if he couldn't take another change in his life. AJ remembered that feeling, the overwhelming sense of loss when he'd first been locked up. For the first time in his life, he couldn't make decisions about himself. He couldn't go outside when he wanted, couldn't eat when or what he wanted.

Couldn't fuck when he wanted. That was the hardest thing, the celibacy. He'd be damned if he'd end up some other con's fuckbuddy, but fighting off the unwanted attention his unwelcome looks always attracted had left AJ beat down and exhausted after so many years.

Now though, for the first time in forever, he'd found someone he desired, someone who somehow had connected with him on an impossible level. Without really planning it, once again he searched out Mik's thoughts.

This time he found them.

More than words, he found impressions, sensations, an underlying sense of dismay. AJ knew immediately that Mik had his fist wrapped around his own cock, but the young man's thoughts, far from arousal and the pure, carnal pleasure of bringing himself to completion, were a tangle of fears and sadness, of almost unrelenting terror at his circumstances and the horrible sense of failure for having disappointed his beloved grandfather.

While his big fist automatically stroked his cock, his thoughts were as far from the physical pleasure he might have enjoyed as they could possibly be. AJ sensed that Mik's act of masturbation was purely for the comfort of the familiar, not for any physical release.

The misery in Mik's mind almost broke AJ's heart. Surprised by how much he cared, desperate to ease Mik's pain, he focused his thoughts on the young man above him, sending him the compassion, the caring and support he'd never been able to feel for anyone else in his life. Soothing, encouraging, calming the terrified boy in the body of a giant, he cloaked Mik in a sense of peace, and, for what it was worth, his love.

As he lay there in his bunk, AJ realized he'd never felt so vulnerable in his life. He was laying himself bare to a stranger, offering up a side of himself he hardly recognized.

A small glimmer of recognition filtered into AJ's thoughts. A sense of communion, of brotherhood. A connection. Mik not only took what he offered, he returned it tenfold in the only way he knew how. Stroking his erection, he shared the sensation of his hand around his cock. Shared the tension in his balls, the low ache in his gut, the curl of heat rolling across his spine as his arousal grew.

With it, he shared the pain in his heart.

Fascinated and aroused, AJ returned the favor. Silently stroking himself to completion, his hand moving in perfect rhythm with Mik's, simultaneously giving pleasure, taking pleasure, wrapping the sensations over and around one another until the act was no longer a solitary experience. Instead it was as close to true lovemaking as AJ had ever experienced.

This sharing took the simple, lonely act of masturbation well beyond the goal of beating off for a sense of relief and a chance to sleep through the night. It was a connection almost as deep and profound as if they'd been skin to skin, their bodies touching, the slick and sweaty connection heightened by an emotional link more powerful than AJ had ever experienced.

More powerful than the words they'd shared earlier today. This link encompassed all those things words couldn't address—the fear, the sense of vulnerability only a large, physically imposing man can feel when his life is no longer his to control.

Today Mik suffered what AJ had already experienced—the loss of self when a number became more important than a name, the humiliation of having his body studied and categorized, each scar and mole noted, each identifying mark catalogued. Gloved hands invading, eyes mocking, bright lights illuminating every fear and weakness he'd ever experienced.

It couldn't be any worse. Right now, what AJ and Mik shared, somehow made it better, healed the painful scars, sealed away the overwhelming shame and embarrassment of all that had happened, all the evil that befell either of them in this place that was the result of their own damned stupidity.

AJ had no one to blame but himself.

Mik acknowledged the same.

Now, the shared touch of hands, the knowledge they

breathed as one, experienced as one, that their disparate hearts had somehow found the same rhythm, that their blood pulsed through their veins at the same frenetic speed, took this sometimes prurient and often self-indulgent act to a higher level.

When AJ stroked himself, he knew Mik felt his callused palm sliding over hot skin and solid muscle, felt the brush of his roughened fingertip as it slipped through the warm liquid drops spilling from his slit. When Mik cupped his sac and rolled the solid orbs between his fingers, AJ groaned in pleasure.

There were no words in this link. No voices clamoring, no audible sighs. There was nothing beyond the pure, carnal sensation of big hands grasping even bigger cocks and the knowledge that the experience they shared went far beyond the reality of the act.

When AJ finally reached his peak, when he turned himself loose with the final short, frantic strokes that took him over the edge, he knew he didn't fly alone. And when the final pulsing burst of his seed had spilled out over his hand and covered his fingers, when the ache in his balls still remembered that brief sense of connection with the man just a few feet away, AJ Temple turned his face into his pillow and wept.

That night, when he dreamed of the wolf, he no longer ran alone.

Silence filled the great room. AJ had been aware of Tia panting her way through a couple more contractions as he spoke, but even the sound of her labor hadn't been enough to take him away from his story. Once he'd started talking, the words had just spilled out of him, things he probably had no right to discuss, things the others probably didn't even want to know.

Talk about acting out of character! Embarrassed now,

he ducked his head, but the tight grasp of Mik's hand on his brought him back.

He turned his head and gazed first into Tala's tearful amber eyes, and then raised his head to look at Mik. The big guy's face was damp with tears, but he was smiling at AJ as if he were the only person in the room.

"I remember that night," Mik said, slowly shaking his head. His voice sounded thick, as if his words were choked by the same emotions thickening AJ's voice.

"I will never forget what it felt like, lying there in that narrow bunk with the sounds of the prison all around, terrified of my future, holding on to my dick like it was my only friend in the world. Then, out of nowhere, you were there. You filled my head with nothing more than good feelings. No words of wisdom or warnings of dire things to come. Just pure, clean, compassionate feelings. Where I'd seen nothing to live for, you gave me hope. The strength to survive what, at the time, felt like a death sentence. If I didn't love you for a million other reasons, I'd love you for that alone."

AJ couldn't speak. Instead, he nodded and squeezed Mik's hand. Then, as if they'd planned it, both men leaned down and kissed Tala's cheeks. Mik was the first to raise his head. He looked directly at AJ when he spoke.

And every set of eyes in the room focused on Mik.

"I didn't think there could be a worse day than the one when I was arrested for beating the shit out of Marvin Skerrit." Mik glanced at AJ and then forced himself to gaze out across the room, into the eyes of his packmates. "I was wrong."

The shackles cut into his wrists and left bruises around his ankles, but it was even worse when they stripped him of everything—the chains and his pants and even the eagle feather Grandfather had woven into his hair to give him courage. Naked and shivering, he'd stood there like a damned bull at auction while he was inspected from one end to the other.

He was property now. Property of the State of California, and not a damned person in this room was going to let him forget it. His body was no longer his own. Every mark, every crease and fold and personal place belonged to the state. These people, as agents of the state, had every right to do as they wished.

They wished to do a hell of a lot more than he thought they should, and his humiliation was complete.

He closed his eyes and endured. Told himself he could handle whatever anyone did to him. All they could touch was his surface, that part of Miguel Fuentes that was open to the world. They could not reach his inner spirit. He held it close to his heart, tight within his soul, and would never let that be touched by anyone.

On that fateful day, while they noted and catalogued each imperfection on his big body, he held tightly to the wolf.

The creature of his dreams had not abandoned him. His totem, his own private spirit guide sustained him even now as he stood silently for inspection.

When it was over and he'd finally had a few moments alone to get dressed, Mik knew what it was to be violated. What had been done to him was nothing short of rape. The sense of the impersonal, intrusive touch of latex covered hands, the cold air caressing shivering skin—all of that stayed with him beneath the clothes he wore.

*Violated. Unclean. Unworthy.* The words followed him, repeated with each step he took. The prison blues were stiff and uncomfortable and he missed his worn Levis and his favorite black T-shirt with the ripped off sleeves. He glanced up at the monochromatic tiles lining the ceiling and wished for the wide blue skies of his South Dakota home. He'd not been back there for a year, not since he'd been arrested.

There'd been no money for bail, and the defense attorney the state assigned to his case had done her best, but she'd not been able to get the charges reduced.

He felt badly that she'd cried when he thanked her. She did all she could with what she had to work with, but there was no self-defense involved. The fact Rosie lied on the witness stand and said Mik had come on to her had bothered him, at first, but he'd done the deed. He'd beat the crap out of a weaker man. As Grandfather said, when you break the law, you must pay.

It wasn't the white man's law he was talking about, either. Mik understood that, but it didn't make it any easier. Had anything in his fucked-up existence ever been easy? Sometimes he felt as if his life was totally out of his control, like he was a damned chess piece on a huge board, being shoved this way and that for the pleasure of some evil and inhuman deity.

One of the old ones his grandfather spoke of with such reverence? He hoped not. He wanted to think they cared more about him. He had, after all, prayed to them for months, now. Hoped against hope they would come to him, hold him up and save him. His wolf had stayed with him, but he hadn't helped. Maybe there was no help.

Now, as he put one foot in front of the other, Mik realized how foolish he'd been to hope. No one cared. His grandfather was an old man who prayed to old gods without any power. There was no power that could help him, not in this world, which made him doubt whether or not there was another world beyond this one. That *happy hunting ground* Grandfather talked about was just another fairy tale, and as he walked the long hallway to the prison cell that would be his home for many years to come, he couldn't help but think he was walking to his death.

No matter, should it come today or ten years from now, Mik couldn't see himself ever running free again. Thank goodness he had his dreams. They'd stripped him of his dignity, but they hadn't touched his soul. Tonight, no matter how hopeless he might feel, he knew he'd run as the wolf.

The guard said something Mik didn't catch, but they were stopped in front of a metal door that looked just like every other metal door along the hall. Mik stood perfectly still, his heart thundering in his chest, while the guard knocked and then, without waiting, opened the door wide.

Mik raised his head, unwilling to look like a victim going to an execution, even though that's exactly how he felt. He blinked as he met the gaze of the man inside the cell. Blinked again when he realized he stared into eyes exactly like his own.

Andrew Temple stood up when the guard said his name and waited quietly as Mik was introduced. His gaze never left Mik's face. He was tall, as tall as Mik and so beautiful he didn't seem real. Feeling as if he faced an angel of the dark side, Mik met the man's steady stare and tried not to lower his eyes.

It wasn't as difficult as he'd thought. There was something about Temple that seemed to calm his raging case of nerves. Unwilling to trust himself or his unusual perceptions about a man he didn't know, Mik began to relax in spite of himself.

Then the brief introductions ended, the guard left and the door clanged shut behind him.

He flinched as if he'd been shot and his head jerked around at the sound. Mik and Temple stared at the closed door for a moment. Then Temple seemed to shake off whatever spell the clanging door held for him and nodded to Mik. "AJ Temple."

Mik stared at him for a moment, feeling awkward and unsure of himself. He barely remembered to speak, to tell AJ to call him Mik, not Miguel. When he stepped by AJ to put his things away, their bodies inadvertently brushed together, and everything changed. A fiery shock from the point where they'd accidently made contact spread from his shoulder to his brain by way of his balls.

There was a strange buzzing in his head, a sense of connection he couldn't explain. Mik stared at his shoulder. *What the fuck?*

AJ's voice sounded in his head. Crystal clear, the word as smooth as glass. *Unbelievable.*

Mik stared at AJ. Again, he thought, *What the fuck?* Then he sat down on the edge of AJ's bunk before he fell on his ass.

"Like AJ said, later, when we tried to communicate with mindtalking, we couldn't read each other. Not until that night." Mik shot a heated glance at AJ and knew he was every bit as hard as Mik was right now. Merely thinking about that first night was enough to get both of them hot.

"We finally figured out, in the beginning, anyway, we could only converse that way under intense emotion," AJ added. "Or if we were really horny. We never had trouble, after that night, sharing our experiences when we brought ourselves to climax."

"AJ?"

He raised his head and smiled at Jazzy. She looked sleepy, but too interested in everything to leave.

"Did you and Mik ever manage to make love while you were in prison? I mean, actually do it together, or were you always doing it on your own but in each other's heads?"

Mik laughed. "I learned very quickly that with AJ, where there's a will, there's a way."

AJ grinned at Jazzy. "Does that answer your question?"

She shook her head, wide awake now, and shot a sassy grin back at him. "Not when I really want the details."

AJ turned to Mik and shrugged. "You're doing so well . . ."

Mik snorted. "Like I did so well that first time?"

Nodding, AJ settled back against Tala. "You did great that first time, Mik. I've never forgotten that night."

Mik stared at AJ for a long time as the memories washed through him. He blinked back the quick burn of tears, the immediate rush of arousal. "Me, either," he said. "I'll never forget."

*Fuck! What the . . . ? Mik, look out!*

The blade ripped through AJ's shirt before Mik realized they were even under attack. It came so fast and hard, he still couldn't believe AJ managed to twist out of the way before the big guy could stab him with the damned shank.

One minute they'd been walking across the exercise yard and the next thing AJ's warning was ringing in his ears, only it was in his head and Mik was turning, slipping into a crouch with his back against his buddy, both of them ready for whatever was coming at them.

He still remembered the dry heat rippling off the paving stones, the way the air shimmered in the hot California sun. They'd all been foul tempered during the heat wave, bodies sweaty and tempers hot, but this was different.

The stink of fear and filth practically gagged him. It was coming off the six big men that had Mik and AJ surrounded. Unarmed, Mik faced the three on his side. The one guy that had gone for AJ still held a big steel shank in one fist. The others appeared unarmed, but he knew that could change in a heartbeat.

AJ's thoughts slipped into his head. One guy facing AJ had a homemade set of brass knuckles wrapped around his fist. There was no time to look and see if the guard was watching, no time to plan any type of defense, but Mik knew AJ had his back.

That knowledge alone gave him the strength he needed.

The strength to straighten up and stare at the big guy with the shank. Stare at him calmly, without fear. "What's goin' on Raul? You and your guys got a problem with AJ?"

He sensed their confusion, the fact they really didn't have a plan.

"Got no problem with you, Fuentes. Move aside."

"I don't think I can do that, Raul." Mik kept his gaze glued to the other man's. He could tell the guy was high, though what he was using was a mystery. You could get any drugs you wanted in the joint, and it was obvious Raul had gotten something with one hell of a kick.

He was one scary dude even without the dope. He wasn't all that tall, but his chest was wide and muscular, his thick arms covered with tats showing his gang affiliation. The other guys with him were just as powerful and marked the same.

Mik held his position. "Say it, man. Why're you after AJ?"

"Don't like him. Don't need him here." Raul shuffled from one foot to the other. His buddies were beginning to shift their eyes from side to side and look around, probably wondering what the boss had gotten them into this time.

Mik shrugged. His confidence grew. "Don't hurt him, man. I know you can. There's six of you, two of us, but I'm not going down easy. Neither is AJ. Is it worth it?" He glanced in the direction of the guard tower.

Guards were watching. Not doing anything to stop the situation. Probably wondering how it would all play out, who'd end up dead.

Of course, by now Mik and AJ and the six surrounding them had the attention of everyone in the yard. Mik sent a quick thought to AJ. *We don't end this fast, it could get real ugly.*

AJ's laugh echoed in his head. *You mean it's not ugly now?*

"Break it up down there. Now." The guard's amplified voice caught everyone by surprise, including Mik. He'd been ready to go down fighting.

At that moment, it hit him. He realized he'd do anything to save AJ, even if it meant killing—or being killed. Anything.

The knowledge left him stunned, even as the ones circling him and AJ held their positions, ignoring the guard a heartbeat longer. Then, with a nod from Raul, the group broke up. They all drifted away, leaving Mik and AJ unharmed.

A small incident. Not something of great importance in the overall scheme of things, yet it was a crossroads for Mik that left him shaken and confused.

For the first time, he'd allowed his feelings for AJ to surface. Feelings he'd managed to bury so deep he'd even hidden them from himself. They were cell mates, that's all. Friends. Close friends, nothing more, right? So they shared the same weird dreams—the wolves and the forest and all that shit, and they liked to beat off together at night. So what?

They stayed in their own bunks. They didn't touch.

Simple guy stuff, or so he'd been telling himself.

Damn. He was so full of shit.

# Chapter 13

## Mik & AJ

*Damn, Fuentes. You're so full of shit.*

He couldn't shut that voice down for anything. Mik tried to shake it off, the sense of destiny that lingered after the event in the exercise yard. Lingered through the rest of the afternoon, the evening meal. The feeling grew, the gut-level sense that if he didn't take his relationship with AJ to the next level, he was missing his only chance at what had to be the most important thing in his life.

The problem was, he didn't know what it was he was missing. He didn't have any idea what the next step was—or maybe it was just that he didn't have the balls to admit it. What he did know, deep in his gut, was the fact he had to take a chance at something important that had always been just out of reach.

He was acting like a complete jerk. He knew AJ was worried about him, but he didn't bug Mik with any questions or anything. AJ was like that. Accepting him no matter what kind of an ass he was. There weren't many men who could be that understanding. No one, as far as Mik could recall. No one like AJ anywhere.

He was only a few years older in actual years, but so far ahead of Mik in knowledge, in self-control. He had a sense of himself that Mik envied. He wished he could be as confident, as self-assured as AJ always seemed to be.

AJ crawled into his bunk first while Mik was still washing at the small sink. Killing time, more like it. Avoiding the confession he was almost ready to make. It was hot in the cell in spite of the forced air. He'd pulled his heavy, waist-length hair back with a leather tie so at least it was off his neck, and stripped down to just his boxers. It didn't help. He was still hot, still sweating when he finally headed toward the bunks. Conflicted, not really sure exactly what he felt or what he wanted to do or say, Mik turned out the light and reached for his top bunk.

Maybe he could get the words out in the dark. Him on the top bunk, AJ on the lower, the anonymity of space between them making it easier to say the words in his heart.

AJ's fingers brushed his bare leg, touched just above his knee and slipped higher to rest on the front of his thigh. A shiver of arousal raced along Mik's spine.

"Thanks, Mik."

Mik paused and stared down between his outstretched arms. He focused on AJ's fingers, pale against his dark skin.

"For what?"

"For taking my back. You could have ended up dead today."

Mik shrugged and tilted his head. He looked directly into AJ's dark amber eyes. "So could you."

AJ nodded. "Easily, if you hadn't been there. Raul and I had a problem a few years ago. He was high today, probably thought about it, decided he was still pissed. Whatever. It wasn't your fight."

Mik smiled. The tension flowed smoothly out of his body. For the first time today, hell, in a long time, everything came together. "Yes," he said. "It was. Don't you understand? The prick tried to kill you. No one tries to kill someone I . . ." He looked away, still unable to voice what was in his heart . . . filling his mind with a choir of a thousand voices.

"Someone you what, Mik?"

AJ's soft question hung in the air between them. Mik thought of a million things in that brief moment and realized none of them meant as much to him as the man whose fingers still rested on his thigh.

"Someone I love. Stupid, isn't it?" He slowly turned and sank down on the edge of AJ's bunk. He couldn't look at AJ, not now that he'd opened his big mouth, so he stared at his clasped hands hanging between his knees instead. "I'm in love with you, man, and I have no idea if you even swing that way. I wasn't sure if that's how I was wired, except that when I met you, it all sort of fell into place. It was like I finally figured out something I'd known all along, ya know?"

AJ wrapped his fingers around Mik's joined hands and he squeezed. "I love you, too, Mik. I couldn't say anything. Didn't know what to say, to be honest, but you're the only reason I keep going in this place. The only reason."

Mik was glad the light was so dim. He hoped AJ couldn't see that he was fighting back tears. You didn't cry here. You couldn't show that kind of weakness and survive, but it was good. So fucking good to know he didn't have these feelings all by himself.

AJ slipped to one side and pulled the sheet back. He was naked beneath the light cover, and Mik didn't hesitate. He stepped out of his cotton boxers, crawled into the narrow bunk and wrapped his arms around AJ and held him close. Their bodies connected from pectorals to thighs, knees to toes. As hot as it was, Mik broke out in shivery chills. He didn't care about the heat or the fact they were both sweating buckets in the hot cell.

All he cared about was being close, holding AJ in his

arms. He hadn't allowed himself to want this, because it was too damned perfect. Good things didn't happen for Miguel Fuentes.

This was good. So fucking good, the way their skin felt where they touched, all slick and sweaty, and the soft puffs of AJ's breath against his shoulder. He wanted to stay here and sleep here, close like this. It was early, not quite nine o'clock, and there wouldn't be another bed count until midnight, which meant he could hold AJ close for hours without risk of discovery.

Mik allowed himself to relax until he was enveloped in the musky scent of clean sweat and warm male. Quietly, gently, with an unfamiliar but exhilarating sense of reverence, Mik used his fingertips to discover more of AJ. The smooth swell of his shoulder, the taut muscles along his flank, the coarse hair at the backs of his thighs.

AJ did the same, gently touching and exploring. There was none of the groping Mik had experienced with other men. This was lovemaking, pure and simple. Exploration. Gentleness.

It had been much too long since anyone had touched him gently.

AJ's fingertips trailing across his chest tickled and made his heart race. Mik bit back a groan when AJ leaned close and sucked one of his nipples between his lips and tongued the pebbly surface. The sharp nip of AJ's teeth sent an electric shock directly to Mik's balls.

His penis was already engorged, but now it lengthened and swelled even more until the thick head pressed against his belly, trapped close beside AJ's. Mik reached down and wrapped his fingers around AJ's shaft, touching it, really feeling it for the first time. The soft skin covering the solid length of muscle was exactly what he'd experienced each night, only it had all been in his head.

The same girth. The heat, the slick bead of moisture leaking from the slit at the apex, the improbable length, all of it exactly the same, yet different. Connecting both physically and mentally took every touch, every breath, every heartbeat to an entirely new level of sensation.

They lay like that for a while, stroking each other, touching, tasting, realizing just how perfectly their minds had allowed them to share this experience, yet understanding, at the same time, what they had missed. Mik's arousal grew, not in a rush of fire and strength, but at a slower, steadier pace, a constantly intensifying passion expanding beyond mere lust.

Expanding beyond physical desire and carnal hunger. He wanted more without knowing what it was, needed more, but it wasn't something he knew to ask, even of someone he loved.

AJ took the first step. He reached behind him and grabbed something off a small shelf beside the bunk. He rolled partly over and handed a tube of lip balm to Mik. Put it in his palm and wrapped Mik's fingers around it. Mik was still wondering what it was for when AJ leaned close, spread his fingers across the back of Mik's head to hold him still, and kissed him on the mouth.

It was the first time Mik had ever kissed another man. The first time he'd parted his lips and suckled on another man's tongue. There was something unimaginably sensual about the gentle pressure of AJ's fingers against his skull, the warmth of his mouth, the dampness on his lips.

AJ's five o'clock shadow scratched the tender skin above Mik's upper lip and their teeth clicked when they met. The soft slide of AJ's lips grew more pressing as he deepened the kiss. He searched the inner recesses of Mik's mouth, slipping inside so that their tongues danced, thrusting and parrying, stroking deep, then withdrawing to lick at wet lips and sharp teeth. As their mouths met, AJ thrust his hips forward. Hipbones clashed, pubic hair tangled together and the hard length of his penis rubbed over Mik's swollen shaft.

Mik's heart wanted to beat out of his chest. It was a struggle keeping his breathing as quiet as he could, not moving so much that the bed squeaked or rattled. There was so little privacy in this place. No way in hell did he want to draw any attention to what they were doing.

What they were about to do.

He held that small tube in his hand as he and AJ explored each other's mouths. Finally, it was AJ who pulled away and rested his forehead against Mik's.

"It's not lube." He whispered, but Mik still heard the smile in his words. "But it's going to have to do. I have a feeling it's the only way you're going to get that beast of yours inside me. It's been awhile."

Mik hadn't been certain. He'd hoped. God, how he'd hoped. If it was at all possible, his cock got even bigger, but he didn't waste another minute. Mik squeezed half the tube of greasy lip balm into AJ's hand and the other half onto his own fingertips. AJ stroked Mik's shaft, coating him with the slick oil. Then he rolled over on his belly and sighed as Mik spread the rest of the stuff over AJ's puckered asshole.

Mik palmed AJ's taut buttocks, tracing the hard muscles and then slipping along the cleft between his cheeks. He trailed one finger down the sweaty crease, found the tight ring of muscle and pressed gently against it with one greasy fingertip. He grinned when AJ groaned softly, and almost laughed aloud when he finally shoved his face into his pillow to muffle any sound.

Mik pressed harder, felt AJ's sphincter give. He slipped his middle finger through the tight opening. The narrow ring of muscle constricted around his first knuckle. He pushed harder.

AJ pressed back against him. Mik added a second finger, slowly pumping in and out, and then a third as the taut muscle softened. AJ held perfectly still so the bed wouldn't squeak. The area beneath Mik's bunk was tight, especially for two big men, but Mik slid down a bit, pulled AJ's hips close to his groin and managed to get the crown of his cock against the cleft in AJ's buttocks.

He dragged the thick length of his cock along AJ's sweat-slick cleavage before stopping with his glans pressed firmly against his puckered hole. Slowly, with steady pressure, he pushed forward, breaching the softened muscle. AJ groaned into the pillow as Mik slowly shoved the full length of his cock all the way inside AJ.

He held perfectly still as AJ took deep, steady breaths. Mik was engulfed in heat and moisture. Powerful muscles rippled along his length and AJ's slick inner walls were tighter than any woman's sheath and a million times hotter than his own fist could ever hope to be.

The connection went far beyond any physical sensation he'd ever known, beyond any emotion he'd ever experienced. Buried deep inside AJ, Mik savored each sensation. The rhythmic pulse of powerful muscles clinging to his shaft, the curled hairs of his groin against AJ's smooth buttocks. The strange, yet unbelievably erotic connection of their balls pressed close together.

Mik slipped one hand over AJ's flank and wrapped his fingers around his erect cock. Skin like silk sliding over an iron shaft filled his grasp. He squeezed, released. Stroked the full length a couple of times and then stopped as AJ buried another low groan in the pillow.

Both men lay perfectly still, lost in the amazing connection they'd finally achieved. Mik shivered, almost overwhelmed by the intensity of the moment—of AJ's hot flesh pulsing with life and passion in the palm of his hand. He was connected now as he'd only dreamed—his cock buried deep inside the one he loved, his fingers tightly wrapped around his thick shaft.

Mik experienced the moment as a spiritual awakening—bodies united, minds open and waiting.

Then, as Mik slowly began to move in and out of AJ's

tight passage, his head filled with images and his body responded to the amazing sensations pouring from AJ's mind, until they were cloaked in the shared reality of two men fucking—a single experience times two.

Mik felt the thick penetration as he drove deep inside AJ as if a cock filled his own bowel. He shared the rippling muscles contracting around his shaft, the wet heat drawing him deep and gave that sensation to AJ.

It took only a few thrusts before AJ's cock jerked in Mik's hand and filled his palm with thick streams of ejaculate, before Mik's hips forged deep and hard and he finally experienced the release he'd been afraid to imagine until now.

Their shared orgasm seemed to go on forever. Moving in slow motion, concealing sounds from anyone who might be just outside their door, they lay together long after the final thrust, the last tortured breath, the final pulsing spasm of ejaculation. The heat of the summer night closed in around them, their bodies dripped sweat and still they lay, connected as intimately as two men can ever be.

Mik had lost track of time and the fear of discovery gave him the courage to carefully slip free of AJ's body. He'd expected awkwardness when they separated.

There was none.

He wondered if AJ would look at him differently.

He did, but his eyes were filled with love, his face tender, his thoughts wide open and caring.

They made love throughout the night, watching for guards but relaxed, now, feeling like kids at a slumber party sneaking around as they explored one another's bodies, fascinated and enthralled by each other's touch and taste and scent. Every touch was new. Every experience fresh, but when morning came, Mik realized something even more unexpected than their amazing lovemaking had happened during the night.

The mental link that had escaped them so often since they'd met, the one that surfaced only when they were threatened or aroused, now appeared to be firmly lodged in their minds. AJ's thoughts filtered into Mik's mind. His thoughts were an open book to AJ.

When morning sounds warned them the day was at hand, they cleaned up as best they could, dressed and prepared for the day ahead. Without discussing it, each of them threw up a wall to block the other. Too much had happened and the risk of discovery was much too great.

No one could know their new reality. Their relationship was theirs and theirs alone, the only private thing either of them owned behind the block and cinder walls.

That and the wolf. They shared the wolf, for whatever reason. Why it had come to them they didn't know, but the shared dreams had to mean something. Did mean something.

Mik shot a wink at AJ. Then he turned his back on his lover. The two of them walked down the hall to breakfast, not speaking, not sharing a thought or a smile. Mik refused to think about the past night. Refused to acknowledge anything that had happened between them, even though he knew it would happen again.

Just as he knew the wolf would come.

They ran together now, in their dreams. Last night, their wolves mated beneath a starlit sky even after Mik and AJ had finally, regretfully drawn apart and slept in separate bunks.

Their wolves had hunted together and brought down game. They'd fed from the same kill.

Now they mated in reality. Two men or two wolves. Did it really matter? No, not as long as they could be together. Mik knew without a doubt it would happen again tonight.

He couldn't wait. He couldn't think about it. Couldn't admit it or even hold that dream in his heart, because it was good. So damned good, and it scared the shit out of him.

Where before he'd had nothing, now there was everything to lose. He glanced at the man walking quietly beside him as they headed to the chow hall and knew that if he lost AJ Temple, he would most assuredly lose his life.

Mik glanced up, blinking as he pulled himself out of his story, and looked at Jazzy. She watched him with an odd little half smile on her full lips, and he wondered what she was thinking.

What any of them thought, because everyone was watching him, waiting for the rest of the story, he guessed. Then Tia gasped and the moment was lost as she began to pant with her next contraction. Luc knelt in front of her with his hand on the curve of her belly as she worked her way through it. Mik felt Tala's slow, steady breaths beside him and knew that she breathed with Tia.

Knew she shared her friend's pain. Women amazed him. They were tough, and no one was tougher than a Chanku alpha bitch. He raised his head and glanced at AJ, caught him grinning back at him. Obviously he'd heard Mik's thought, because he was nodding in agreement.

Luc twisted away from Tia and glanced over at Logan, who still lay with his head in Jazzy's lap. Logan opened one eye when Luc said, "Four minutes. They're every four minutes now."

"Getting closer," Logan said. He closed his eyes.

AJ burst out laughing. "That's all the good doctor has to say? 'Getting closer?'"

This time Logan didn't even open his eyes. "Yep," he said, and snuggled against Jazzy.

Anton stood up and stretched. "I'm going to make a fresh pot of coffee. Anyone else want some?"

Hands went up around the room. "Okay," he said. "Two pots." He wandered into the kitchen while Keisha and Xandi went in to check on the babies. A few of the others, Tia among them, got up to stretch and move around.

Within a few minutes, though, Anton was back, setting two pots of strong coffee on the sideboard. Keisha and Xandi returned together and settled back into their seats. AJ got coffee for the three of them. By the time Mik had his cup and was settled back beside Tala, almost everyone else was back in their chairs or stretched out on the floor. Obviously no one wanted to miss anything.

Ulrich knelt in front of Tia. "Are you okay, sweetie? Do you need anything for pain?"

Tia kissed Ulrich on the cheek and smiled gently. "I'm fine, Dad. There's no pain, not when it's shared. I'm just anxious for it to be over. Relax."

Ulrich grunted and stood up. "I'm gonna kill Luc," he muttered.

"Dad!" Tia's outrage had everyone laughing, including Luc, who ducked dramatically as Ulrich passed by.

"You'd better duck," he said, but Mik noticed a definite quirk to his lips when he said it. Ric's bluster reminded him of the day, so long ago, when AJ first met the big detective.

He raised his head and caught AJ's attention. "Your story or mine?"

AJ grinned. "Mine," he said. "Definitely mine."

He took a sip of his coffee and settled back in the chair. His left arm was looped over Tala's shoulders and rested on Mik's, linking the three of them.

"Things went along remarkably well for Mik and me," he said. "We managed to keep our relationship secret, and after the problem in the exercise yard with Raul, no one else hassled us. I don't think they liked the idea of having to fight two of us, and we were always together."

"Except for that one day," Mik added. One fateful day,

when once again, everything in his world—and AJ's—changed forever.

AJ was pretty disgusted when the warden called him in. He'd made the mistake a couple years earlier of letting the guy know he could fix the copy machine, which was a damned stupid thing to admit because the thing was always jamming or needing new toner or just acting up. For whatever reason, it hadn't been an issue before Mik, but now it meant they were separated while AJ worked on the damned machine.

Mik was doing his regular job in the laundry. AJ figured he'd be okay for the short time it would take him to fix the copier. They didn't like to be separated, not since they'd established the fact they were a team, that they worked well together.

It made them feel a lot more vulnerable when they were apart. In many ways, it turned whoever showed up alone into a target. That was the downside of one of a team.

When AJ showed up at the main office, there was another man meeting with the warden, a big guy with prematurely gray hair. He was broad-shouldered and held himself as if he might be ex-military, but he was deep in conversation with the warden and hardly raised his head when AJ walked through the office.

AJ nodded to him and walked on past the two men. He went straight to the next room where the copy machine was. The warden followed him. AJ turned and stood at attention, uncomfortable to think he'd been singled out. It was a lot safer when you got away with blending into the surroundings.

"Temple, I want you to meet Ulrich Mason. He was a detective with the San Francisco Police Department."

Curious, AJ nodded. When Mason held his hand out, AJ stared at it a moment too long. No one shook hands in prison, not when it meant the risk of getting pulled off balance and attacked. Mason's hand didn't waver, the warden never moved, and AJ finally, tentatively shook hands with him. He raised his head to meet the man's steady gaze, and his breath caught in his throat.

It was like looking into Mik's eyes. Or his own.

"I'll be in the other room." The warden shot a stern glance at AJ and left, closing the door behind him.

Totally caught off guard, AJ took a step back. "What the . . ."

"Relax." Mason smiled at him and leaned against the desk. He folded his arms across his broad chest and gazed candidly at AJ. "I asked the warden to give me a few minutes alone with you. We've been friends a long time. He trusts me."

"I don't," AJ said. He folded his arms across his chest and stared at Mason.

The guy just laughed. "You shouldn't. I can be a sneaky bastard when I want to. The thing is, I saw you out in the exercise yard a couple weeks ago and recognized something special in you. Special enough that I checked to see if I could get your sentence shortened, or maybe even set aside." He paused and slowly looked AJ up and down. "You interested in getting out of here?"

"You're shittin' me, right?" Either this guy was nuts, or he wanted something illegal. And no matter what it was, AJ realized he couldn't leave Mik. "What's the deal?"

"I'm no longer with the SFPD. I run a very exclusive agency. We do some work for the government, a lot of stuff under the radar. I'll be honest with you and say there are only two of us now. The reason for that is because I've only found one other man with the qualifications I require. You, however, appear to have what I need."

"Not interested."

Mason raised one bushy eyebrow. "What I'm proposing isn't illegal. I can get your sentence wiped from the records—legally. A few words from me and you can walk out of here a free man, and you're saying you're not interested?"

AJ nodded, but at the same time he sensed a pressure in his skull. The same kind of pressure he felt when he and Mik used their minds to communicate. Could this man . . . ?

Impossible.

But so was telepathy. He pushed at Mason, tried to communicate. Nothing, but that didn't mean . . . "You said you've investigated me," AJ said. "Have you checked out my cell mate? Miguel Fuentes?"

Mason straightened up. His eyebrows came together as he frowned. "No. Should I?"

"I think you should. And then I'd definitely like to talk to you again."

Mason smiled at him, tipped an imaginary hat, and left the room. AJ watched him go, kicking himself and hoping like hell he was right.

Within the month, both AJ and Mik walked through the gates of Folsom Prison as free men, their records wiped clean.

"What was it like?" Manda's soft question caught AJ by surprise. She so rarely spoke up. "How did it feel when you were finally free?"

Mik answered before AJ had a chance. "I cried," he said. "I walked out of that prison and Ulrich and Luc met us in front with the Chevy Blazer. I remember climbing into the backseat and looking back at the prison gates, and I started to cry."

AJ shot him a grin. "He got me going, and the two of us were sitting back there blubbering all over each other while Luc and Ric sat up in front, probably wondering what kind of lunatics they'd just hired."

"Oh, I knew what I'd hired," Ric said. "Of course, neither one of you had a clue what you were getting into."

"We found out soon enough. AJ thought it had something to do with our mindtalking, but it was a hell of a lot more."

"We figured that out about the time Ric dropped his pants and shifted." AJ shook his head. "Damn, I hate it when they do that."

Mik laughed. "He got his point across, we took his honkin' big pills, and two weeks later AJ and I shifted within hours of each other. Luc took us up to the place in Lassen where we could learn how to run on four legs instead of two, but to answer your question, Manda, it was an amazing experience, from the moment we walked out of Folsom as free men. A lot better than your first days of freedom."

Manda shrugged. "I didn't consider myself free until long after my first shift. I was as much a prisoner of my body as I was the cage in the lab, even when I lived in that little apartment in upstate New York. Even after Bay rescued me and I shifted, I was a prisoner to my memories."

She gazed up at Baylor, and the love in her eyes made AJ's heart ache. "I wasn't free until I could go to Baylor as a whole woman and make love with him. Then, the night I met Millie—Mom—for the first time . . . that was the night I was truly free. We ran together as wolves. Me, Baylor, Millie, and Ulrich, Jake and Shannon. Ran as wolves, hunted as wolves, howled at the night sky. That's what I remember when I think of freedom."

"I have to agree," Mik said. He might have been answering Manda, but his eyes were on AJ. "The night we mated as wolves I finally understood freedom."

AJ nodded. As crazy as it sounded, Mik was right. The night he'd forever tied himself to another man, the night he and Mik bonded and swore to always be together was the first time in his life he truly understood the meaning of living free.

# Chapter 14

"Luc!"

Wide-eyed and shaking, Tia half rose from her chair. Panting, she gripped Luc's hand until her knuckles turned white. Logan jerked awake from his sprawl on the couch and Jazzy's lap and rushed to Tia. She panted, but it was obvious the pain and her emotional distress with this particular contraction were intense.

Anton glanced around the room and noticed that all of the women sat perfectly still, their faces empty of expression as they concentrated on trying to hold Tia's pain under control. Keisha sat as still as the others. Beads of sweat glistened on her forehead.

Anton searched for Tia's pain, curious as to what the women experienced. The power behind it startled him, the intensity painfully cramped the muscles across his abdomen and stabbed into his testicles. He backed away with a quick glance at Keisha to make sure she was all right.

The contraction appeared to have ended. Keisha raised an eyebrow and grinned at Anton as he turned away to watch Logan with Tia.

Logan held both palms pressed to Tia's abdomen. His eyes were closed. After a moment he slanted a look in

Adam's direction. Anton intercepted the private communication without even stopping to consider whether he was violating anyone's privacy.

Logan's words echoed in Anton's mind. *One of the babies is showing some distress. I don't want to frighten anyone, especially Tia. Meet us in the clinic as soon as you can get away without letting anyone know where you're going.*

*I'll be there.*

Logan raised his head and smiled at Tia. "I think it's about time for you to get into a gown and get comfortable. We're definitely getting closer. What do ya say? Let's move this show to the clinic." He continued to smile as he rose to his feet. Relaxed. In control. "That invite's just for Luc and Tia for now, folks. Let me get her settled before the support team shows up."

He turned and glanced at Anton. It was impossible to read Logan's inscrutable expression, but his mental words seemed as calm and relaxed as he appeared. Every bit the professional.

*I know you were eavesdropping, Anton. Can you send Millie, Lisa, and Keisha to the clinic in just a bit? No more . . . I don't want a crowd, but I want the women closest to her there for Tia.*

Anton sat back and smiled. He'd been caught . . . and forgiven. He merely nodded as Luc and Logan helped Tia out of the room. Adam caught Anton's eye. Anton nodded and then he turned toward Stefan.

Before Stefan could react, Anton stood up, pulled Stefan to his feet and kissed him full on the mouth. Wide-eyed, Stefan didn't question him a bit. He put his arms around Anton and kissed him back. His lips were surprisingly soft.

Well aware that every eye in the room was on them, Anton wrapped his long fingers across the back of Stefan's head and held him in place for his kiss. It really wasn't necessary. Stefan made absolutely no move to pull away, no matter how surprised he might be by Anton's bold move.

Anton's mouth moved slowly over Stefan's. His tongue probed the seam of Stefan's lips, gained entrance and teased the inner recesses of his mouth. What had begun as merely a ploy to divert attention took on a life of its own.

Stefan's thoughts drifted into Anton's mind and he shared the taste and texture of the one he'd loved long before he'd ever admitted to himself he could feel such powerful emotions for another man. Now that love was something each of them relied upon, each of them shared, one with the other.

When Anton finally ended the kiss, both of them were flushed and aroused . . . just like everyone else in the room. Smiling sheepishly, Anton took a long, shuddering breath and inhaled the musky, provocative scent of sex. His. Stefan's . . . the others.

He sensed the way Stefan's thoughts spun, roiling with an overload of sexual stimulation and confusing questions. It was not Anton's way to publicly claim another. Not as he'd done just now. He'd always been and still was, by nature, much more circumspect, more private with his sexual needs and desires, but now he licked his swollen lips and tasted Stefan.

*That was amazing,* Stefan said, *but it tells me something's wrong. What's happened?*

Anton tightened his barriers and narrowed the direction of his thoughts so that no one else would overhear. *I wanted Adam to be able to leave the room without anyone noticing. It worked better than I'd hoped.*

*You could say that.* Stefan's quiet humor tickled Anton's senses before he suddenly grew serious. *What's wrong? Where did he go?*

*Upstairs to the clinic. All is not well with Tia. Logan doesn't want Ulrich or any of the others to worry.* Anton leaned close once more and kissed Stefan lightly on the mouth. Then, with a slight smile on his face, he returned to his chair.

There was an audible sigh in the room. Anton settled comfortably in his leather recliner beside Stefan's. "I imagine you're all wondering what that was about," he said, steepling his fingers in front of his chin and glancing about the room.

Jake Trent laughed. "I was going to tell you to get a room, but then I decided I'd rather watch."

Shannon elbowed him. "You'd rather be right there in the middle of things, don't you mean?"

"Actually, I was thinking of Mik and AJ and all they went through before they finally discovered their birthright. The fact that they knew there was an unusual connection between them, long before they knew they were Chanku. It reminded me how much I love my own packmate . . ." He glanced toward Stefan, and added softly, "How very much I love him. Stefan and I aren't bonded, though we might as well be, as close as we are. I was thinking of how surprised I was when I first met the members of the San Francisco pack and discovered they had a mated pair who were of the same sex."

He shot a glance at Tala and laughed. "Of course, then Tala came along and totally skewered all my conjecture."

"I did that on purpose," she said, snuggling close to both her big men and smiling broadly. "They were much too complacent, just the two of them. I figured they needed me."

"We needed you more than you needed us." Mik leaned over and kissed Tala's cheek. "Don't ever think otherwise." He raised his head.

Anton caught him with a single glance. He included AJ in his tightly focused comment. *Guys, there's a slight problem for Tia. We don't want to alarm anyone unnecessarily, and Logan doesn't want anyone disturbing them in the clinic. Do you mind telling about the night you bonded? I know it's a private moment, but . . .*

Mik, bless the Goddess, never missed a beat.

"We certainly didn't know we were breaking ground when we decided to do a mating bond. It merely felt like the natural progression to our relationship." He turned toward AJ, but he included Tala in his smile. "Of course, we didn't know we were breaking ground when we did a three-way bond, either."

Tala grabbed both their hands. "See? I knew you boys were trendsetters the minute I laid eyes on you."

Mik chuckled when he leaned back with his arm across Tala's shoulders. AJ rested his arm over Mik's, completing the link. "Setting trends really had nothing to do with it. Once Luc explained the mating bond to us, at least what little he knew of it which wasn't a hell of a lot, that was all I could think of."

AJ nodded. "I was the same way. I think I needed something like that to focus on, something solid. Everything had happened so fast."

"We went from cell mates at Folsom to free men, to suddenly discovering we had the ability to shift into wolves. My head was spinning," Mik said. Sometimes it still seemed unreal, so many years later.

"Not only that, as two gay men, we'd lived in the shadows as far as our sexuality went. Here we were, hired by a pretty cool investigative firm and given an apartment to share because it was a known and accepted fact we were lovers."

"Exactly," Mik said. "Luc not only didn't question our sexuality, he occasionally joined us." He glanced at Ulrich. "We tried to get the boss to come play, but he kept his distance."

Ulrich looked like he was going to say something, but he glanced up as Millie, Keisha, and Lisa stood.

"Logan's invited us to the clinic," Millie said. She leaned over and kissed his cheek. "Just the three of us. I think we're the first shift."

"Call me when she gets close," he said. He watched the women leave the room, and then turned and focused on Mik. He sighed, and for once his age actually showed. Obviously he was concerned about Tia.

"The boss occasionally thought quite seriously about joining all of you, but if you'll recall, I had a teenaged daughter at home at the time. I had to behave."

"I wondered if that was it." Mik grinned at AJ. "We didn't behave at all. We never even considered the fact that what we intended to do—a mating bond—was at all unusual. It was right for us."

"I've never once regretted it." AJ's soft words resonated on an almost spiritual level with Mik.

He'd never forget the night. The magic. The sense that what they did went beyond anything either of them had ever done before.

The full moon hung just above the treetops, a harvest moon casting sharp shadows across the broad meadow as it rose higher in the midnight sky. Luc sat off to one side, tongue lolling, ears pricked forward while Mik and AJ tumbled like pups in the thick grass.

There'd never been a more perfect moment. Mik had never felt the depth of love he felt tonight, at this precise moment, for the man, the wolf, that nipped at his heels and chased him through the cool night air.

The day had come together perfectly, from the lazy sex they'd shared that morning to the second, rowdy playtime that included Luc and the whole top floor of the cabin.

After a day of napping and screwing and even a couple of laid-back games of chess, they'd shifted just after sundown and hit the woods running. They'd hunted, and then the three of them had bathed in the perfect woodland pool that lay beneath a ghostly shroud of steam. Heated by underground hot springs, the water soothed tired muscles and left them feeling cleansed of more than just the blood and dirt from the kill.

Mik felt as if he'd finally shed the last of the prison stink from his skin. He'd not be going back to Folsom. No one was going to come in the middle of the night and tell him it was all a huge mistake, that he never should have been released.

He wasn't going to awaken and discover that a lifetime of dreams had all been a monumental joke some unknown entity had played on him—mind games to screw with what little sanity he had.

No, it was real. He felt it as deep as the marrow in his bones, in the rush of blood through his veins, in the spiritual sense of something greater than even the wolf. With his shift had come knowledge of the Goddess. The one Luc occasionally swore to, swore at, swore on.

He'd wondered at Luc's use of the feminine term—*Goddess*. Once he shifted, Mik understood. She existed. She was real, a powerful entity with some sort of stake in AJ and Mik's well-being. A personal, loving interest.

And when he thought of AJ, when he looked at him with all the love in his heart, Mik knew the Goddess blessed their relationship. Just as she would bless their union.

If not for her, he might never have considered it that night, but the moon was full and there was a sense of magic mingled with the silvery light that bathed them. Love filled him until he thought he might explode if he didn't set it free. With his heart pounding in his chest, Mik turned to AJ. Without hesitation, he opened his heart and his mind.

And he'd found the courage, with the Goddess's blessing, to ask the question that had haunted him throughout so many days and nights. A question with only one acceptable answer.

He stalked across the open meadow and stopped directly in front of his lover. Stared directly into his beautiful amber eyes and laid his heart out on the ground between them, bare and unprotected. It was the hardest thing he'd ever done in his life, yet they were the easiest, most natural words he'd ever spoken.

*I love you, Andrew Jackson Temple. I will always love you. I want you as my mate, my bonded mate. Here. Tonight. If you'll have me.*

AJ sat up and stared at Mik, glanced back at Luc and then at Mik again. *Can we do that? Mate as wolves? Bond as a pair?*

*Why not?* Mik turned to Luc. *Is there a reason we can't?*

If Luc had been human, he would have shrugged. As a wolf he merely tilted his head and stared from one set of amber eyes to the other. *Not that I know of. If you can work out the logistics.* He trotted across the meadow and sat between the two. *All I know about the mating bond is what Ulrich has told me, that two people who love each other can link at the height of orgasm. Every secret they've ever had, everything they've ever wanted or dreamed or done becomes an open book to their partner. It takes unimaginable trust to share everything. Do you guys have that?*

AJ turned to Mik. *I trust him with my secrets as completely as I trust him with my life. I love him more than I ever imagined loving anyone.*

*I feel the same.* Mik shivered. He could have sworn the moonlight bathed the two of them in magic.

Luc dipped his head in a very human gesture. *I'm going back. I'll leave you two to figure out how the hell you're going to do this. I wish you both luck.*

He turned and trotted down the trail that led to the cabin. Mik watched him go. He stared at the moonlit trail long after Luc had disappeared into the shadows. Then he turned to AJ. *Are you certain?*

*More certain than I've ever been of anything else in my life.*

It hadn't been difficult at all, though AJ still managed to turn it into a game when he nipped Mik's flank and took off running. When Mik cornered him in a small meadow not far from the hot spring, when he mounted his partner and drove deep inside AJ with his slick wolven cock, the sensations both of them experienced went from physical to the full range of emotions in a heartbeat.

Aroused beyond belief, Mik's hips pumped furiously as he drove his cock deep inside AJ's virgin wolven passage. Snarling and baring his teeth, AJ braced all four legs and held his ground, but his arousal spilled out over Mik.

Each of them caught in the pure passion of their mating, ruled entirely by the bestial lusts their human sides so often controlled. But as Mik's orgasm neared, as AJ's cock swelled and escaped his sheath, their minds linked.

Moonlight couldn't explain the brilliant shaft of light that pierced Mik's thoughts, the sense that what happened this night was more important than anything he'd ever done in his life. His arousal continued to grow and expand as the link intensified.

Was it the sanctity of their mating? The fact it was all so new because they'd never fucked as wolves before? Was it the sense they'd broken every rule, laughed in the face of convention . . . or was it simply the fact they loved?

They'd linked before during sex, but never with such intensity, such clarity. Mik found himself engulfed in unfamiliar memories, in AJ's fears and hopes, his dreams and his successes, his failures and his nightmares.

For every memory Mik absorbed, he knew, on some deeper level, that AJ found the same in him, a parallel existence between two young boys who were forced, much too quickly, to became men.

Mik's cock swelled and locked him tightly to his mate as he spurted jets of hot ejaculate deep inside. As Mik climaxed, AJ came as well, hips jerking as he found his own release while still tied to Mik.

Exhausted, panting, the two of them collapsed to the ground. Mik's mind was still caught deep in AJ's thoughts. Still slipping in and out of memories, riding the brilliant synapses of thought and desire. He was filled with questions, with pride in his mate, and with a sense that finally, after so many years wandering, he had found his home.

"It was, without a doubt, the most intense experience I'd ever had. Spiritual, in a way. Something much more than merely the two of us together, fucking in the moonlight." Frowning, Mik turned to AJ, struggling to find the words.

Nodding in agreement, AJ spoke hesitantly, as if he was still working the concept through in his mind. "It was sex, but it wasn't. You guys have all bonded, you've each got a mate, so you know what your bonding link was like. For us, for two guys who had never expected to find real love, it was an amazing experience. Uplifting, yet intimidating, too." He glanced at Mik and actually blushed. "I hadn't realized how complete the sharing of our memories would be. That was . . . difficult."

"AJ was worried what I'd think about him when I learned a few things." Mik glanced at AJ out of the corner of his eye.

"It's okay. We have no secrets here," AJ said, but he stared down at his feet when he said it.

Oliver spoke from across the room. "You're talking about the bondage, aren't you? The night Mei and Tala wanted to tie you guys up—you didn't want any part of it."

AJ raised his head. "You're too damned perceptive for your own good, Ollie."

"It's Oliver," he said, but he was smiling. Encouraging AJ.

"What I hadn't told Mik was that my first year at Folsom, I was caught by a group of guys who bound me and gang-raped me. I didn't think I'd live through it. It took me a long time to get past what happened. When we bonded, when I realized Mik knew everything that had happened, I was afraid it would affect how he felt about me." He raised his head and smiled at Mei. "I should have had more faith in my mate. If anything, I think finally talking about it with him has made our bond stronger. I'm still not crazy about Mei's kinky sex games, but I'm getting better."

"He's much better," Mei said. "Any time you need more of Mei and Tala's therapy, you just let us know."

"I'll do that."

Mik's story about their bonding and AJ's admission seemed to open the rest of them up. Mik leaned back in his seat, his arm still over Tala's shoulders, his hand still resting on AJ, and let the warmth of family flow over him. When he turned his head and smiled at AJ, they both realized Tala had drifted off to sleep between them.

Without Tia's contractions to work through, she'd finally given in to exhaustion and fallen sound asleep.

Tia rested. Her eyes were closed and her always-curly hair was plastered to her face in damp tangles when Adam slipped quietly into the clinic. Millie, Keisha, and Lisa sat at the foot of Tia's bed. Luc paced nervously at the far end of the room.

"There you are!" Luc raised his head as Adam crossed the room to Tia. "Logan thinks there might be a problem, but he's not sure what it is. Nothing shows up on the ultrasound, but . . . shit, man. See what you can find out."

He brushed Tia's hair back from her face. Her eyelashes fluttered, but she slept now, between the contractions.

Adam nodded and took the stool next to Tia's bed. He glanced up at Logan, who was studying the readouts on a small screen.

"Everything the machinery is telling me says labor is fine, the babies are fine . . ." Logan shook his head. "Her cervix is effaced, she's dilating, but . . . crap! When I go inside, mindwalking like you do, there's a definite sense of anxiety, almost as if one of the babies is trying to tell me something, but I can't figure out what it is. You're better at this than I am. I want your opinion."

"Mindwalking?" Adam raised an eyebrow at Logan.

"What else are you gonna call it?"

Adam shrugged and carefully pulled Tia's loose gown aside, baring her huge abdomen. Long white striations glistened against her tightly stretched caramel skin. A dark line ran from her pubic bone to her navel and from the shape of her belly it was obvious the babies had dropped lower in her pelvic region in preparation for birth. Gently Adam pressed both his hands on either side of the dark line bisecting her gravid belly. Closing his eyes, he relaxed and allowed his consciousness to slip carefully into Tia.

He passed through skin cells and a thin layer of fat. Sensed the strong wall of her uterus as it prepared for another contraction. He passed beyond the uterine wall and found the tough membrane that contained the uppermost baby girl. She lay calmly in her torn amniotic sac. Most of the fluid had drained out from the earlier tear, but she was still a somewhat nervous and expectant, yet healthy little girl. Adam didn't attempt a mental link, since all seemed perfectly all right. Exploring further, his consciousness followed the umbilical cord. It led to a single placenta that nourished both babies.

The discovery made him smile. Tia hadn't made a mistake. She'd released a single egg, not two. The division that created two babies from a single egg had occurred after Tia and Luc's mating. This was definitely proof of Camille's hand . . . or the work of the Goddess.

Adam slipped through the clear amniotic membrane to check the second little girl. The sense of well-being ended the moment he entered her space. This sac had not yet ruptured, but pink tinged what should have been a clear fluid.

Blood was leaking somewhere. A quick search didn't give away the source. Adam focused on the baby.

Anxious and afraid, the little girl was obviously aware of something not right. Adam tried to link, but her mind swirled with confused images and fears. He sent soothing thoughts her way, calming her, offering his help, projecting love and peace and a sense of well-being.

Slowly the sense of terror eased. The images in his mind coalesced into a single, graphic visual of what terrified the unborn girl.

The union between her umbilical cord and the placenta had begun to separate. The tiny rupture was leaking blood. Each contraction weakened the connection and threatened her life.

Adam's heart begin to race. Immediately he calmed himself. He had to think rationally, but there was no way she could survive delivery. Unless something was done, and done quickly, this perfect little girl would bleed to death either before or during her birth.

Swallowing his own fears, Adam touched her mind with his. She was amazingly lucid now, her terror tightly constrained.

*I'm here to help you, little one,* he said. As his words entered her mind, the baby shocked him by opening her eyes and looking right at him, as if she could actually see him even though he was nothing more than a burst of mental energy.

*I know.*

Two words. Two very simple words, yet the telepathic

voice was as powerful, as well formed as if he conversed with his mate. Then the baby's large gray eyes blinked slowly and closed once again.

Adam knew he would do whatever was in his power to save her life.

Adam blinked owlishly and sat back from the bed.

"What's going on?" Luc kept his voice low. He didn't want to wake Tia or disturb the women who kept her pain at bay, but he had to know. He'd never been so frightened in his life. Not only was Tia in danger, his unborn daughters appeared to be at risk, as well. "What did you see?"

Adam, as always, seemed remarkably calm. Thank the Goddess someone was, because Luc felt as if his heart might beat right out of his chest.

"There's a problem, but I think we can fix things if we hurry." Adam rubbed his fingers across his brow, frowning, obviously processing everything he'd just learned. "First of all, Logan, I imagine you're aware there's one placenta, two amniotic sacs."

Logan nodded. "Okay. That confirms what we got on the sonogram. What's wrong?"

"The umbilical cord for the posterior twin is tearing loose from the placenta. It hasn't ruptured yet, but each contraction appears to put more strain on the area where it connects. There's a tiny amount of blood in the amniotic fluid. It looks like only one sac ruptured, hence the soaked carpet in the great room, but that baby is fine. She just wants out. It's the other one we need to worry about. The connection between the umbilical cord and placenta appears to be too weak to survive a normal, vaginal delivery."

Luc's skin went hot and then cold. He turned and gazed at Tia. Exhausted, she slept, blissfully unaware of the danger.

"What can you do?"

"I looked at the point of rupture and it's not going to be possible to repair it. The cord's shorter than usual, and that's probably what's causing the tear." Adam sighed. He looked at Logan, obviously sharing everything he had seen.

After a moment, Logan nodded. "Luc, we need to do a caesarian, and we should do it as soon as we can. The risk to the baby is too great to allow a vaginal delivery. Wake Tia. She needs to know what's going on."

Luc grabbed Logan's wrist. "Can you do that here? In this little clinic?" He glanced around at the comfortable room Anton had built for deliveries. It looked more like a bedroom than a hospital, but that's exactly what it had been in the beginning.

A bedroom.

Logan smiled. "The clinic's got all the equipment we need, and Adam and I have the skills. We'll move Tia into the room next to this one. It's a complete surgery. Anton saw to it that we got the best of everything." He turned his arm within Luc's grasp and wrapped his fingers around Luc's wrist.

"I'm good, Luc. I was a good surgeon before I discovered I was Chanku. I haven't lost those skills. If anything, they've improved because my senses are sharper, my reactions faster and more precise. I promise I won't let anything happen to Tia or your little girls. With Adam here to assist, they're all in excellent hands."

"Everything will be fine." Keisha's voice projected a sense of calm no one could ignore. "However, we need to bring Ulrich up here. Tia's father should be with her. I also think we should let everyone know what's going on. The pack is a valuable source of strength. A powerful source we'd be foolish to ignore."

She stood up, rested her fingers lightly on Luc's shoulder and smiled at him. "Luc, trust me. Trust Logan. Everything will be fine. Tia is in excellent hands, not only the good doctor, but Adam, as well. She is surrounded by love and the strength of the pack. They have never once let any of us down. They certainly won't now. The Goddess is with you, Luc."

"What about pain?" Shit, there was no anesthesiologist, no way to . . . "Crap, Logan . . . you have to cut her open! You . . ."

"Luc. Stop it." Keisha's firm command sliced through Luc's panic. He jerked his head around and glared at her.

Keisha drew herself up and glared right back at him. "There will be no pain. The other women and I will see to that. We can do this, but we need to be calm for Tia and you need to trust Logan. He's good at what he does."

The tone of her voice left no room for argument. She leaned over and kissed his cheek, straightened and turned to leave. "And so are we," she added. Then she headed out the door to find Ulrich and gather the pack.

# Chapter 15

Anton sensed his mate before she entered the room. He glanced up as Keisha paused in the doorway of the room where the pack gathered. Everyone was still here, still teasing Mik and AJ and enjoying the chance to gather together for a happy occasion, not a scary one.

He sighed. From the stress radiating from his mate, Anton had a feeling that was about to change.

He raised his head and smiled at her. Keisha's amber eyes practically glowed with love. Would he ever get enough of her?

She shook her head. *No, my love. I see you and my body responds. I feel your heat from my heart to my core. If you were inside me now, you would feel my muscles clenching in a slow and needy rhythm. I will always want you, and I will never have enough.*

With a provocative sway, she slowly walked across the room and paused in front of him, standing between his knees. He rested his palms on the smooth swell of her hips and let her heat invade him.

Oblivious to the curious looks of the others in the room, Keisha leaned over and placed both palms on his shoulders, tilted her head and fit her mouth to his.

Perfect. Absolutely perfect. He groaned softly against

her mouth and took the kiss deeper. His tongue parted her lips, slipped over their lush fullness, brushed her teeth, tangled with her tongue. She suckled at him, drawing his tongue into her mouth, and he wished they could go on like this forever.

But they couldn't. She'd come bearing news and they had no business indulging themselves like this. Breaking the kiss, Keisha straightened up and turned away from Anton. She addressed everyone in the room. "I hate to interrupt, folks. I've just come from the clinic. Logan says it's not an emergency, but there's a problem with one of the babies, and he's preparing Tia for a C-section."

Ulrich leapt to his feet and started for the door. "Is she okay?"

Keisha nodded. Anton sensed the calm she shared with Ulrich. It was an honest emotion. Considering the situation, it should have surprised him, but nothing about Keisha would ever surprise him. She was right, though. They really did have the best care in the world for Tia and her babies.

"Tia's fine," she said. "She understands the need for the surgery and they're getting her prepped now. Ulrich, I'm sure she and Luc would like to have you close by. Millie and Lisa are with her and everything's under control."

Ulrich left the room. Keisha explained what was going on in the little clinic upstairs. "Adam will assist Logan and I'm going back to help control her pain. Xandi? I want you to come with me. We figure that having three women who've already experienced birth, along with Logan and Adam doing their thing, should make the surgery pain free for Tia and the babies."

Keisha grabbed Xandi's hand and tugged her to her feet. Everyone in the room focused on Keisha. Anton felt their energy, their loving concern wrapped around her like a warm blanket, as Keisha turned once more and smiled at everyone.

"Logan's asked that all of you consciously send strength. Concentrate on the babies, on their health as well as Tia's. Logan's not worried, but he knows he'd be a fool not to take advantage of the linked power of this group."

She leaned over and kissed Anton again. Then she kissed Stefan. *Stay here and keep things as calm and as positive as you can. It's pretty dicey for one of the babies. Luc's scared to death, so it's good Ulrich is with them. I checked on Lily and Alex and they're still sound asleep. They should be down for the rest of the night.*

*If you need me,* Anton said, *I can be there within seconds.*

*I know.* Keisha squeezed his hand, flashed a smile at the group and left the room with Xandi.

Anton turned to Stefan with a grim expression on his face. *We need to shift. All of us. We'll go into the meadow and link. The Goddess is stronger there, and so is our magic.*

"Luc, I am so scared."

Logan and Adam had moved Tia into the surgery and Logan was preparing for the operation. Tia reached for her mate's hand and he tightened his trembling fingers around hers. Fat lot of good that did. Now they were both shaking. She forced a smile. "You're not supposed to be scared, silly. You're supposed to comfort me."

"I'm so sorry, sweetheart. I love you so much." He leaned close and kissed her.

She kissed him back and felt a great surge of power, a sense of calm like she'd not felt for hours, but it wasn't from Luc's kiss. It was so much more.

The pack had gathered. Their energy seemed to enfold her. Tia was bathed in a sea of love and well-being. Her labor pains were totally under control from the combined energy of Keisha, Millie, Lisa, and Xandi and they were ready to handle the pain of surgery as well. The contraction that was beginning to build grew and tightened the muscles of her abdomen, but there was no sense of anxiety from her babies.

Just like that, Tia's nervousness disappeared.

Luc brushed her hair away from her face and she realized he hadn't sensed the gathering of power. It was all directed at Tia . . . at Tia and the two little girls she carried.

Luc's eyes sparkled with unshed tears. "I didn't realize the risk. If I'd thought there was any danger to you, I never would have asked for babies."

She smiled at Luc, at the serious expression and the fear in his eyes, and she knew she and her babies were going to be fine. Teasing, she said, "It's a little late for that now, big guy."

Luc didn't seem to appreciate her attempt at humor. Tia glanced up as her father stepped quietly into the room. "Hi, Dad. You look as bad as Luc. Don't worry. I've got the power of the pack behind me." She waved a hand at Millie, Lisa, Keisha, and Xandi. "I've got the Fearsome Foursome dealing with the pain, and Logan and Adam ready to deliver your granddaughters. Adam checked on me just a minute ago. The cord's still attached and the bleeding isn't any worse. Everything's going to be fine."

"Fearsome Foursome?" Xandi laughed and high-fived Keisha. "I think I like that."

Ulrich leaned over and kissed Tia. "I know, sweetie. Damn, this reminds me of the night you were born. I was scared spitless, but your mom was just as cool and collected as she could be. Just the way you are now. We didn't have the pack, then. We just had the nurses. You showed up before the doctor even arrived."

Tia touched her dad's hand, needing the connection. "No one's showing up until Logan does his thing."

Logan stepped back into the room. He wore blue scrubs and had a mask over his face. His hands were gloved. Adam was right behind him, dressed and scrubbed exactly the same.

Tia got the giggles. "You look like Tweedledee and Tweedledum."

Logan's eyes crinkled above his sterile mask. "No, Tia. I look like a doctor, and thanks to you, I finally get to act like one. Everyone out of the way, except Luc, and Luc, you need to wash your hands really clean and take your place on the stool behind Tia. Ric . . . ladies, I want you either in the next room, or if you're going to stay, take a seat in the chairs against that wall. Anyone passes out, they're on their own."

Logan turned in the direction of the back meadow, the place where he knew the pack waited. He sensed the power gathering there, sensed it here, now, in this room. He connected with Anton. Felt the leader's calming strength surrounding him.

*It's time, Anton. I'm making the incision now.*

Luc took his seat behind Tia and held both her hands in his. Keisha, Millie, Xandi, and Lisa closed their eyes and linked hands. Adam positioned the drapes and sterile cloths. With a prayer to the Goddess, Logan lifted his scalpel.

Moonlight filtered through the trees and left slivers of silver light across the large meadow. The night was cool, the air fresh with the taste of early spring.

Fifteen wolves gathered in the moonlight. Their eyes glittered with green fire in the moon's reflection, their minds connected with a single purpose as they sensed the pressure in the heart and mind of Logan Pierce.

He was maintaining an aura of calm for Tia and Luc, for the others in the surgery with him, but Anton felt Logan's fear, his worry that he wouldn't be fast enough to save the little girl whose distress projected a palpable sense of disquiet.

Anton sat as one of the circle—no more, no less. He gazed from one powerful wolf to the next, absorbing the myriad emotions and thoughts swirling among them. He'd never felt such pride in his Chanku packmates before—and he couldn't help but recall the first meeting with the San Francisco pack just a few short years ago.

They'd met here for the first time as wolves, shortly after Ulrich was kidnapped. Even though they came asking for Anton's help, the few males who arrived had still met Anton and Stefan with stiff-legged pride and all their alpha-male attitude intact. They'd eventually gotten past all of that, though it hadn't been easy to control their feral nature when they were in their wolven form.

This time, though, they'd come together as wolves with a common goal, something he'd never asked of them before. Subduing their feral nature, digging into their hearts and drawing forth whatever power they had. All of them, gathered together with a united purpose, their singular focus on saving their own.

Anton felt a subtle pressure to move to the center of the circle. He stood slowly, gazed around him, curious as he attempted to understand the feeling directing him to walk to the middle and sit, ears forward, eyes on the rising moon.

His change in position quickly made sense. The power surrounding him grew. It pulsed as a thing alive with amazing strength. Wolven eyes glowed with an unearthly green light and the energy took on a physical presence, a phosphorescent aura surrounding each beast in the circle then reaching out to touch Anton, joining all of them in green light.

It shimmered there in the meadow, about a foot off the ground, shaped like the spokes of a wheel with Anton as the hub.

As the focal point, Anton absorbed the energy, the mental strength, the power intrinsic to the beast. Somehow he knew to combine it with his own, and it was the right thing to do, when he called on the Goddess, on the natural power of the moonlit night and the ancient forest around them.

He called on all these sources of strength, added them to the reservoir building within him and directed it to Logan, to Adam and Luc and Tia, to the ones repressing Tia's pain.

He bathed the two little girls in the warmth and strength of fifteen powerful minds, steadied their hearts, prepared their lungs. Calmed the surgeon's hands.

Then, almost as an afterthought, Anton linked with Adam. Caught in the powerful vortex of Adam's mind-walking power, Anton secretly hitched a ride and traveled through skin and muscle, moving at the cellular level until he was inside Tia's womb.

Astonished, he realized he was witness to the miracle of new life before birth. He viewed Lucien's daughters through the veil of their amniotic sacs, perfect little girls with their mother's patrician features, waiting impatiently for birth. He sensed the sharp cut of the scalpel, the steady hand of the surgeon.

Surprisingly, Tia felt no pain. None at all. Between the power of the four women here in the room and the strength of the pack, Anton knew she was aware of the pressure of the incision, but she had no discomfort. None. *Amazing.*

Yet all was not well. Logan wasn't moving quickly enough. Adam slipped through the clear wall of the amniotic sac still filled with fluid. Blood pulsed where the thick umbilical cord connected to the placenta, staining the fluid a darker red.

The cord was tearing loose.

This perfect little girl could still bleed to death before she was safely delivered. As if everything moved in slow motion, Anton saw the pulse of blood spurting out faster, stronger, right at the point where cord and placenta joined.

There was no time to think, no time to concur with Adam, the one who "fixed things." Drawing every ounce of energy he could take from the wolves gathered in the circle about him, his mind still locked with the unsuspecting mindwalker, Anton focused a blinding pulse of pure energy precisely at the point that was tearing. The beam of energy cauterized the cells and fused the damaged area back together.

*Anton? Was that you? Are you with me?*

Adam's voice. Anton acknowledged his presence, along with the joined power from the others.

*Thank you. I wasn't sure how to stop the bleeding without harming the baby. We'll have her out in a second. Logan's lifting the anterior baby free now.*

Anton sensed new life as one little girl drew her first breath. Then the second one was lifted from Tia's womb, the cord clamped and cut. The baby cried and gasped for air.

Both babies were alive, both healthy and breathing. Through Adam's eyes, Anton witnessed the tears streaming down Luc's cheeks as the new father held one perfect little girl. Then Adam turned to Ulrich, and Anton, still seeing through Adam's eyes, saw Ulrich cuddling the second identical twin in his arms.

Two perfect little girls, just as Camille had promised. Still with Adam, Anton watched as Logan carefully stitched the incision closed, a horizontal slice low on Tia's belly. He'd closed her uterus already and the stitches he made now were tiny and precise. There'd hardly be a scar when she healed.

Feeling like a voyeur now, rather than a participant, Anton slipped his consciousness free of Adam's mind and returned to the circle. Then he shared what he'd seen, shared the emotions he'd experienced, the miracles he'd witnessed. When he had given the good news to everyone here, when he'd thanked them for all they had done, he shifted.

The others shifted as well. Anton turned to Stefan and drew his friend into his arms. Only then, when he knew that all was well, that Tia and both her babies were safe, did he allow the pent-up fear and anxiety free. Holding tightly to Stefan, surrounded by the love and strength of his pack, Anton wept.

This time, thank the Goddess, they were tears of joy.

Late morning sun filtered through the blinds of the guestroom where Tia and Luc and their new family had been moved. Luc dozed in an overstuffed rocker with one tiny little girl asleep on his shoulder. Tala held the other while Tia slept.

"I can't believe how little she is." She glanced at Mik standing silently beside her. "I know five pounds is a healthy size for a twin born early, but just look!" She lifted the baby's hand with her forefinger, spreading all five tiny little fingers wide. "So perfect and yet so small and helpless. It's kind of scary when you think of it."

"This whole thing has been scary." Mik's low voice rumbled in her ear. "Her labor and the emergency C-section, the fact one of the babies could have died. I dunno, sweetheart. As much as I thought I wanted a baby, I'm not sure if I want to put you through that."

AJ nodded. "I couldn't stand it if something were to happen to you. Did you see Luc? He was a wreck. Worried about his mate, about their babies. What a nightmare."

Tala kept her gaze fixed on the beautiful baby in her arms, but her thoughts flew all over the map. What was it with these guys? Pressure for months to convince her to have a baby, and now, when she finally had this little one in her arms and her hormones were screaming it was time to get a move on *now,* not tomorrow but right now, her guys were suddenly freaking out on her?

Tia's eyes fluttered open and she smiled up at Tala.

"Here. Looking for this little lady?" She handed the baby to Tia and felt an amazing tug that started in her heart and went straight to her womb.

No way was she letting Mik and AJ change their minds.

"Have you got names picked out yet?" Tala brushed her finger across the baby's cheek as she rooted against Tia's full breast.

Tia glanced toward Luc. "We have. Luc's holding Camille Rose, after my mom and the roses I carried when Luc and I were married." She tilted her head and kissed the baby now suckling at her breast. "This little one is going to be Shannon Olivia. Shannon's my oldest friend, and Olivia is for Oliver." She gazed at the baby a moment longer, as if mesmerized by the new life in her arms. "I get the feeling, sometimes, that Oliver hasn't got a clue how much he means to all of us." She looked up, grinning at Tala. "He's the glue, ya know? He makes things work."

"How are you ever going to tell them apart?" Mik leaned over Tala's shoulder.

"That's the strangest thing." Tia carefully unwrapped the blanket swaddling Shannon Olivia and pulled the little gown back. There, on her thigh, was a perfect little birthmark in the shape of a leopard's rosette.

"Camille doesn't have one. We're not sure, but we're wondering if, when she's finally old enough to shift, Shannon might become a leopard. We won't know, at least not right away. Of course, it might be purely coincidence . . ."

AJ and Mik both laughed. Tala shushed them.

"Anton and Stefan are going to love arguing this one," Mik said. "So far, Anton's winning. I really hope, for Stefan's sake, this is merely a coincidence."

"Right," AJ's drawl stopped at the jangled sound of very loud rock music. Luc jerked awake. Camille Rose began to cry as her daddy fumbled, one handed, for his cell phone.

"Sorry," he said, as he put it to his ear. "Forgot to turn it off."

Tala grabbed Camille Rose and walked to one side of the room so that Luc could take his call. Holding the crying infant to her shoulder, she felt the tug in her womb again, accompanied this time by a sharp ache in her breasts.

Those hormones were definitely kicking in. No matter what AJ and Mik worried about, it was definitely time to . . .

"Tala?"

Blinking, she glanced up. Mik stood beside her.

"That was a call for Pack Dynamics. There's a hostage situation just a few miles away, near Kalispell. Luc's exhausted and said he didn't want to take it, but I told him we'd handle it."

Tala merely nodded. The baby stopped crying and rooted against her shoulder. Mik's words seemed to echo in her head. Why did she have such a bad feeling about this?

"We have to hurry," AJ said. "Some guy's high on drugs and he's got his ex-girlfriend and their infant son locked in the house with him. He's threatening to torch the place. Police said he's already spread an accelerant."

The scene of the stand-off was less than an hour's drive from Anton's property. Tala drove the SUV with AJ and Mik, already in wolf form, riding in the back. She found the address using the GPS they'd installed on the dash, and pulled up beside a state trooper's car. A crowd of armed officers and newspaper reporters along with a few curiosity seekers, had gathered behind cover in front of a small log cabin partially hidden in a grove of conifers.

Two pumper trucks from the local fire department were parked off to one side, just in case things went south.

Working on automatic pilot, Tala opened the rear door and brought her team out. After a magical night, this all felt wrong to her. She hadn't had time to properly switch gears from new babies to baby in danger, but she quickly snapped collars with leashes already attached on each of the huge wolves, which gave others around them an idea she might actually be in control of the ferocious looking beasts.

A tall, serious looking state trooper approached them. "Ma'am? You from Pack Dynamics?"

"Yes," she said, nodding in his direction. She held tightly to the leashes. The smell of gasoline was strong in her sensitive nostrils. She knew it was making the guys nuts. Chemical smells this strong were actually painful, and accelerants were the hardest of all.

Maybe it was knowing the potential for danger. The wolf's natural fear of fire was difficult for even Chanku to control.

"What's going on?" She rested a hand on AJ's head. Sent soothing thoughts to Mik.

"It's a mess." The trooper frowned as he stared toward the cabin. "We'd let the bastard blow himself up, but there's an innocent young woman and a baby in there. We need to get them out, but we can't use tear gas, and we can't risk a bullet setting off a spark. He's soaked the place. Luckily the gas was turned off awhile ago so there's no pilot light. We've shut off power to the place, but anything could set it off."

"What do you want us to do?"

"There's a back entrance with shrubs growing close to the cabin. One of the guys mentioned your team, how he'd seen the wolves sneak into a place without anyone spotting them, they're that good. Can they get in? Take the guy out?"

He glanced at AJ and Mik, sitting alertly beside Tala.

"They look smart, but do they understand who the bad guy is? Will they be a danger to the women and child?"

Tala smiled and patted Mik's head. "They understand a lot more than anyone realizes. Can you keep the guy occupied at the front of the cabin?"

*How long?* she asked the guys. *How much time do you need?*

*Is there anyone watching the back side of the cabin?*

"Is there anyone around the back he might be wary of? Does he have a reason to suspect you might attempt an entry that way?"

The trooper shook his head. "No. The brush is too thick. Brambles and such. A human couldn't get through it."

*In and out in five minutes,* AJ said.

*Or less.* That was Mik.

"Five minutes. Keep him busy." Tala leaned over and removed the collars and leashes. The wolves looked directly into her eyes. She rested a hand on each one's broad head. *Be careful,* she said. *I don't want anyone hurt. We're making a baby this afternoon and there will be no excuses.*

*We need to talk about that,* Mik said.

"Now go." Tala ignored him. AJ and Mik turned and slipped into the thick brush.

The trooper watched them disappear. "They know what to do? But how?"

"They're very well trained and very smart." Tala looped the collars and leashes over her shoulder and headed toward the front of the cabin and the armed contingent surrounding the cabin. "They'll get your man."

*Shit. That guy wasn't kidding about the brambles.* AJ jerked free, but he left a thick tuft of fur from his shoulder stuck in the vicious thorns.

*Be glad we've got them.* Mik paused at the edge of the tangle of vines and stared at the back door of the cabin. It was less than five feet away. The air was heavy with the reek of gasoline fumes. The sound of a newborn crying made his hair stand on end.

He couldn't help but think of the difference in this tiny one's circumstances compared to little Camille Rose and Shannon Olivia. Life sucked, sometimes. Really sucked.

A man cursed. There was a loud smack, a woman's cry. The baby cried louder.

AJ glanced at Mik. *Now*, he said.

They reached the back door in seconds. AJ shifted, grabbed the door handle and quietly turned the latch, Thank the Goddess it was unlocked. As flimsy as the place was, he knew they could break in, but they'd lose any chance of surprise. He opened the door just the width of Mik's nose and shifted back to wolf form.

It took him barely two seconds.

There was a commotion from the front of the cabin. A curse from inside. Both wolves slipped through the open door and moved as quietly as they could across the dirty linoleum floor of the filthy kitchen.

Peering around a low wall that separated the kitchen from the front room, Mik spotted the woman huddled against the far wall. She held a baby in her arms, a newborn from the size of the small bundle wrapped in a dirty blanket.

Her hair was tangled, her face bloodied, but at least the woman was conscious and the baby crying. The front door was open, as if it had been kicked off its hinges. A man stood to one side of the large but broken front window. Bearded and ugly, with long, stringy hair and a body as big as Mik's, he waved a rifle and screamed curses at the small crowd in front of the cabin.

Mik spotted Tala hunkered down behind a wine barrel full of dead plants. *Dammit! Get down, Tala. If I can see you, he can too.*

Her head immediately disappeared as she ducked down lower.

*Shit, man. She never minds me like that.*

Mik silently chuckled. *I don't mind you like that, either. You ready?*

AJ nodded and crouched lower. *I'll take out the guy. You go for the baby. Let's hope the woman has the sense to follow, because if he gets a shot off and this place blows, it could go sky-high.*

Mik opened his mind to Tala's searching thoughts. He had to be certain he included her in everything they did from here on out. Every move they made until the job ended.

He caught her silent acknowledgment, her soft prayer for their safety.

*Be careful.* Mik gave AJ a look he hoped conveyed everything he felt. There was always a chance something could go wrong. Always.

*You too, buddy. Go!* Silent as a wraith, AJ cleared the low wall in a single leap.

Mik reached the baby a split second before AJ slammed the man hard, midchest, shoving him against the wall.

Mik wrapped powerful jaws around the baby's blanket, jerked the baby from his mother's arms, turned and leapt past AJ and the drug-crazed man as the two fought. Holding onto the tightly wrapped blanket, Mik sailed through the broken window with the screaming mother hot on his heels.

Tala jumped to her feet and shouted, "Hold your fire!"

The woman raced through the door as AJ and her ex-boyfriend tumbled to the floor in a snarling, cursing twist of arms and legs and lethal teeth.

The rifle fell from the man's grasp.

A single shot fired. Whatever it hit, struck a spark.

The fumes in the cabin exploded in a ball of fire. Mik went flat to the ground, shielding the baby with his big, furry body.

The force of the explosion threw the woman past him. She lay in the grass, unmoving as burning bits of wood and shingles landed all around. Tala raced across the yard, outpacing the state troopers. She reached Mik, dropped to her knees and grabbed the crying baby out from under him. "Where's AJ?" she screamed. She clasped the baby against her shoulder. "He didn't come out! Where is he?"

Still rattled from the force of the blast, Mik scrambled to his feet and spun around on all fours as a second explosion lifted the cabin from its foundation.

Tala ducked to the ground, protecting the baby with her body. Mik raced toward the burning cabin.

*AJ! Where are you AJ?*

Nothing! Frantic, Mik raced through smoke and burning debris and what was left of the front door. Heat seared his thick coat and smoke burned his eyes and nose. His feral nature made him cringe from the fire. He fought it and pressed forward. Flames were everywhere and the pungent stink of gasoline gagged him. Crawling on his belly, he searched through smoke and burning rubble.

A couple of feet from the door, Mik's nose brushed thick fur, a big paw. Choking in the thick smoke, he clamped his jaws around AJ's rear leg. Slowly backing up, he dragged the big wolf through the flames to the open door.

Streams of water met him. Firemen had moved close and trained their hoses on the flaming wreckage of all that was left of the cabin. Mik managed to tug AJ's comatose body as far as the doorway before two large firemen grabbed the unconscious wolf and carried him carefully away from the fire.

Mik followed, coughing and gagging. Tala wrapped her

arms around his shaggy neck and burst into tears. *AJ? Is he alive? I can't sense him.*

Gasping for air, Mik raised his head. *He's alive because he's still a wolf. Sweetie, we shift when we die, remember? Besides, he knows if he dies I'll kill him. We need to get him to Anton.*

*They're giving him oxygen. As soon as we can move him, we'll go.* Wiping her eyes with her shirttail, Tala left Mik in the yard and ran to the paramedics. One of the men held an oxygen mask against AJ's muzzle. Between deep, hacking coughs, AJ filled his lungs with air. Tala touched one paramedic's arm to get his attention. "Can you put him in the back of my SUV as soon as he's breathing okay? I need to get him to our medical people immediately."

"No problem. He's coming around." The medic glanced at Tala and grinned. "I'm assuming he won't bite me?"

Relief poured over her in waves, and she laughed at the question. "Nope," she said, feeling a whole lot better. "Only if I ask him to."

"Well . . ." The paramedic glanced at the mouthful of teeth as AJ sucked air. "That's good to know. Remind me not to piss you off."

Before Tala could reply, she felt a soft touch on her arm and spun around. Tala'd lost track of her in all the excitement, but now the young woman stood beside her, face bruised, hair hanging in sooty tangles. She held tightly to her baby and smiled through the tears and soot and blood staining her face.

"Thank you. The trooper said those are your wolves that saved us. I . . ."

One of the paramedics tried to get her to go with him, but she stopped him with a hand on his arm. "Please? They saved our lives. I've always been afraid of wolves, but these two are wonderful. Are they going to be okay? Thank you so much."

"You're welcome, and yeah, they'll be fine. That's their job." Tala touched the blanket hiding the baby. "May I see?"

The woman nodded and pulled the blanket aside. The baby boy stared up at Tala with dark, dark eyes. He couldn't be more than a couple of weeks old.

"He's beautiful. I'm so glad he's safe. And you, too." The baby smiled at her. Tala felt the now familiar clench in her womb as the paramedic led the woman away.

*Damn you, AJ. You'd better be okay.*

Mik walked over and sat beside her, nuzzling her belly. AJ coughed.

And once again, Tala burst into tears.

# Chapter 16

Logan listened carefully to AJ's chest through his stethoscope and then straightened up. He'd already checked both AJ and Mik, but AJ had spent more time in the heat and smoke. Tala was almost certain that was the only reason he wanted to listen again.

At least she hoped that was the only reason.

"Your lungs sound clear, but I can't tell if you have any damage from the heat. Shifting cleared your lungs of all the smoke, but if you notice any breathing difficulties . . ."

AJ laughed. "Tell you. I got it." He grabbed his T-shirt and slipped it over his head.

"Keep the burns lightly covered. I imagine they'll heal up in a day or two. They're not that serious. Hopefully not too painful."

"Not too bad. Beats the alternative." AJ glanced at Mik. There was a large bandage taped over his shoulder, and another on the back of his neck. *Thanks, Bud.*

*You're not kidding.* Tala felt her throat get tight again. If Mik hadn't gone back into the fire for AJ, hadn't found him when he did, there was no telling what might have happened. As it was, both her guys were safe. The woman was okay, her baby unharmed.

The ex-boyfriend was dead. No great loss there, as far

as Tala could tell. Any jerk willing to harm his own child . . . she glanced at her guys. They would be such perfect fathers. Any child of theirs would grow up knowing he or she was loved, protected, wanted.

She yawned. It was either that or start crying again. Her heat had started just hours ago and it always made her sleepy and weepy. The circumstances over the past couple of days hadn't helped her at all. "We all need some sleep," she said. "We've been up for over twenty-four hours and I'm absolutely beat."

The guys nodded and silently followed her out of the clinic, down the stairs, and along the hallway that led to their room. Luckily they didn't see anyone. As exhausted as she felt, Tala didn't feel capable of talking to anyone.

As depressed as she felt right now, she doubted she could carry on any kind of a conversation without tears. She wondered what the guys were thinking, if they'd changed their minds on making a baby.

That was all she could think of, all she wanted, but after what happened with Tia and the twins, and now the mess this afternoon, they'd probably never want a child. Damn.

Mik opened the door to their room. Tala and AJ followed. She kept going straight into the bathroom and turned on the shower. She wasn't the least bit surprised when both men followed, carefully removing the bandages Logan had just applied.

"Should you take those off?" She didn't look at either guy. She couldn't, not as fragile as she felt.

Mik leaned close and kissed her. "It'll be fine. I can't stand the stink on me."

AJ leaned over and kissed Mik's cheek. "I can't stand the stink on you, either. Let's hose off and get some sleep."

It was still light when they all crawled into the big bed together. Mik threw an arm over Tala's waist and pulled her close against his chest. AJ snuggled her from behind.

She felt the thick length of his partially tumescent cock riding in the crease of her butt. Mik's shaft nestled softly against her belly.

There was no talk of sex, no mention of babies, but for now, it didn't matter. Surrounded by the men she loved, Tala drifted into sleep.

Long shadows shrouded the room when Tala awoke, though it wasn't entirely dark out yet. The three of them hadn't moved a bit, but AJ's cock was now fully erect and the broad mushroom head pressed between her legs and rode softly over her clit. Mik's cock felt like a baseball bat, rising up against her belly. Still half asleep, Tala undulated her hips against her men and opened her eyes.

Mik's amber eyes glittered in the dusky light. His teeth gleamed against his dark skin. "I was hoping you'd wake up." He leaned close and kissed her. His tongue licked the crease between her closed lips and slipped inside the moment they parted. She felt AJ moving behind her. He grabbed his thick shaft in his hand, slowly rubbed the broad head of his cock between her legs, parted the damp folds of her pussy and pressed forward.

She groaned into Mik's mouth as her body softened, became pliant and adjusted to AJ's sensual invasion. She felt the thick, hot length of his penis sliding through her grasping sheath as he slowly filled her. There was a slight bump as he hit the mouth of her womb, and then the tip moved beyond her cervix and stretched her inner walls to their max. She tilted her hips, helping him press as deep as he possibly could, as far as her body would allow. The amazing sense of fullness made all her inner muscles clench and ripple along his length.

Once buried, AJ held perfectly still. Mik continued making love to her mouth as his hands roamed over her breasts. He plucked at her sensitive nipples and his cock pressed, hot and heavy, against her belly.

Then he rolled over, slipping away from Tala and coming in behind AJ. *I thought I lost you today,* was all he said, but Tala felt the pain in those few words. She'd felt the same fear when the gun fired, when the cabin exploded.

When she'd reached for AJ's mind and found nothing. Not even a sense of him in her thoughts, and she was terrified he might be dead. Then, for a moment she'd been certain she'd lost both of them when the blast knocked Mik to the ground.

He'd thrown his body over the baby and hadn't flinched when burning chunks of roof and walls landed on and around him. But Mik was strong and he kept the baby safe. Still shaken from the force of the blast, he'd turned back into the fire and he'd saved AJ's life.

There was no way AJ should have survived both blasts, but he had.

He should have been killed in the fire, but he was alive.

Thanks to Mik.

Both of them, alive and well and making love to her now as if nothing horrible had happened today.

Thank the Goddess.

But something terrible had happened. This had been too close, had happened too fast, and Tala knew that, but for a few seconds and a lot of luck, she might be sleeping alone tonight, without her men.

Without the ones who loved her. The men she loved above all others. The more she thought of how close they'd come, the more her chest ached, the tears threatened. Then AJ began to move, slowly and surely inside her. He opened his mind and Tala knew that Mik filled him, that the three of them were connected now, as they always were. Mentally and physically, by a love that went beyond anything Tala had ever known.

This was more than she'd ever expected or ever

dreamed. AJ slid one hand over her hip and found the sensitive bundle of nerves at the apex of her thighs. He softly brushed his fingers back and forth over the hard little nub, finding the same rhythm Mik moved to as he filled AJ, as AJ filled Tala.

They'd loved like this before, so many times, but tonight it was magic. Tonight Tala took their love with the grim knowledge it all might have ended today, and the thought tore at her heart and ripped a painful sob from deep in her chest.

AJ understood. So did Mik, and together they took Tala higher, further than she expected. Her body shivered on the edge of orgasm. Surrounded by her men, she lay beneath AJ with his big body covering hers, his chest pressed against her back, his huge length filling her receptive core. Behind him, Mik practically flowed over them both, his long cascade of hair a curtain that brushed Tala's hips and the sides of her breasts as he slowly rolled his hips back and forth in time with AJ's sensual dance.

Overwhelmed by life, by the knowledge they had come too close to death today, Tala wept. AJ dropped kisses along her spine. Mik's love flowed over her like honey as he climbed closer to orgasm, closer to taking the three of them with him over the edge.

It was perfect. It was miraculous.

And she'd almost lost them both.

But she hadn't, and they loved her, and she still wanted their baby, risk be damned. She wanted a bit of AJ, of Mik, growing inside her. That warm little body, those perfect little fingers . . . AJ's smile. Mik's beautiful eyes. Their courage, their honor, their boundless capacity to love.

Tala wanted their babies nursing at her breasts.

*You never know what tomorrow will bring,* she said, speaking almost as much to herself as the men who loved her. *You can't live in fear. You can't worry that something bad will happen. If you do, you're giving up on the best part of life. Do you think Luc regrets those two little girls? That Tia wishes she hadn't had the babies?*

Mik shuddered and thrust his hips forward as climax gripped him. AJ cried out and drove deep, and the hot jets of his seed took Tala over the edge. Sobbing, shivering, she arched against AJ and her tight vaginal muscles rippled and clenched around his spasming cock.

Their minds linked, the sensations of one swirling and mingling with those of the other until the three of them finally collapsed in a heap of arms and legs and spent bodies.

Tala felt their love, their devotion to her and to one another, yet still she sensed the slightest hesitation, their fear for her. They'd come too close to losing one of their own today.

They weren't willing to risk her life, no matter what she might want.

At least that's what they thought. But the decision was Tala's after all. As the alpha bitch, her desires outweighed their fear, and she let them know how she felt as easily as she could. She rolled beneath their sprawled bodies and held her hands up, cupping AJ's chin in one palm, Mik's in the other.

*All I ask is that you love me,* she said. *Love me now and forever. Worry if you must, but tonight we run as wolves.*

Tala and the guys showered again and joined everyone for a relaxed dinner. Tia arrived, moving slowly and carefully, but she walked to the dining room on her own while Luc and Lisa carried her little girls. Camille Rose and Shannon Olivia—already shortened to Cami and Shay—slept soundly while they were praised and kissed and passed from one set of loving arms to another.

Everything seemed different tonight, and it wasn't merely from their brush with death earlier today. People were more relaxed. More like a family. Tala gazed around at the familiar faces and realized the things they'd learned about each other during the long night of Tia's labor had brought all of them closer.

It was a good feeling. A comfortable, safe feeling. She glanced at Mik and he smiled at her. He'd hardly moved away from AJ's side all evening, but at least he was relaxed, laughing now and teasing the man he loved.

Everyone was still here, though it appeared most of the guests would be leaving in the morning. Ulrich and Millie needed to get back to the wolf sanctuary, and Shannon, Jake, Manda, and Bay were planning a leisurely trip home to Maine that would take them into Canada and around the northern shores of the Great Lakes.

Tinker and Lisa would stay on until Tia was ready to travel so they could share the driving on the way home. Tala and the guys would be heading south to San Francisco in the morning. There was work to be done, and they were needed to cover the office until Luc was ready to go back into the field.

Tala sat with Lisa, Mei, and Eve and the four of them shared glasses of wine. Their conversation turned to their own unhappy childhoods, the years they'd spent growing up in Florida.

Tala sipped her Chardonnay and gestured at Mei and Eve. "You guys were in foster homes just a few blocks from where Lisa, Baylor, and I lived. We might have crossed paths when we were kids."

"I know." Mei glanced across the room at Oliver and Anton. "I wonder if we were there at the same time as Anton? It's weird, you know, the fact we were in such a small area of the country, yet all Chanku."

Stefan sat down on the arm of Lisa's chair. "Don't tell me were back to the fate versus coincidence thing. I told Anton I wouldn't argue with him anymore."

Tala laughed. "Well, you've got to admit, it's very interesting that seven of us all came from the same small part of the country. There have to be more Chanku there. I think we need to find out."

Anton raised his head. "Find out what?"

"Why Florida, specifically Tampa." Tala stood up. "You can have my seat and see if you can figure out why so many Chanku came from there, and whether or not we should be looking for more."

She stepped aside as Anton slipped into the chair she'd just vacated. Mei grabbed her hand. "Where're you going?"

Tala slanted a seductive smile at her guys. "Me'n the boys are going to run tonight. We've got a long drive ahead of us tomorrow, so I figured we'd better get some exercise tonight."

"Have fun." Mei waved her off.

Tala walked over to the big sliding glass door and opened it to the cool April evening. She didn't even look to see if Mik and AJ followed her or not.

She knew they'd come.

She was right.

Tala left her comfy sweats lying in a heap on the deck, shifted and cleared the railing in a single leap. Mik and AJ were right behind her, racing her into the dark woods.

The air was crisp and clear with the scent of new grass and damp moss and the sense of new life forming. Buds on the deciduous trees were swollen and ready to burst, the fiddlehead ferns were just breaking through soil where nothing but snow had recently covered the ground.

Ripe with her heat, Tala practically flew over the now-familiar trail, racing the two large wolves that flanked her on either side. They'd not said a word, but she felt their love like a physical touch.

Just as she sensed their fear, the concern that was so much a part of them. They were big and hard, their temperaments strong and unyielding—powerful, remorseless men who could be as cruel and ruthless as life called on them to be.

Yet they loved without reservation. Loved with tenderness, with joy, with the same powerful feelings that drove them in every other aspect of their lives. They loved one another as much as they loved their woman. They didn't always understand her, but that didn't diffuse the powerful love they felt for her.

She knew they would do anything in their power to make her happy, and that included giving her a baby. Even if it terrified them. Even though each man, in his own way and for his own reasons, had serious reservations, they would do whatever she wanted of them, whatever she asked.

Tala locked both AJ and Mik out of her mind while she savored the decision she'd reached.

Tia had done it, though not on purpose. Why couldn't she? Well, for one reason, it wasn't easy to concentrate on the logistics of procreation when her body was thrumming with need, when she felt feminine and needy and so ready to mate.

Tala's mind was spinning and her body was ready when they halted their run in a small meadow bathed in silvery moonlight. Both males stalked her, hackles raised, teeth bared and glinting in the silvery light. She recognized the fact her heat brought out their feral nature. She doubted they would fight over her, not two men who loved one another as much as they did, but she didn't intend to risk it.

Planting her feet, she faced them, unafraid of either size or ferocious appearance. Raising her head, she looked into eyes as bright as her own.

*I want you to take me tonight. Me alone. Not each other. I want your seed in me, all of it, all those little critters swimming together. I can't choose which of you fathers our first child, but I can give each of you an equal chance. If we leave it up to fate to choose . . .*

*Are you sure? There's a risk . . .* AJ glanced at Mik when he cautioned her.

Tala shrugged. Such a human gesture, she thought. *There's always a risk. Life is a risk we all take. I'm not afraid.*

Mik nudged AJ forward. He glanced over his shoulder at Mik, who was obviously aroused. AJ's amber eyes gleamed. *You're certain?*

Mik dipped his muzzle and stepped back, giving Tala and AJ room. AJ whirled around and raked her back with his front paw. She felt the sharp claws through her thick coat. The pain sent her arousal spiking and she planted all four feet.

He mounted her quickly, pierced her swollen sheath with a single hard thrust of his slick wolven cock. She felt his penetration, the thick slide of the knot that would tie them together during climax.

His hips jerked in short, sharp thrusts. Tala dug her sharp nails into the turf to hold herself in place, reveling in the sense of AJ's strong body, his powerful thrusts. They rarely did this—sex between just two of them. This was good, so good, even though she missed Mik. Missed the connection the three of them made when their bodies were linked, their minds . . . so quickly, orgasm swept over her. Thoughts dissipated and her front legs collapsed under AJ's weight. They rolled to the ground, still tied. She felt the pulse and flow of his seed forced deep inside her womb.

The egg was there. She sensed it as a separate entity and wondered if she would know when it was fertilized. *If* it was fertilized.

Nothing happened. There was no sense of anything special occurring. Nothing beyond the fact she had just mated with one of the men she loved.

A man she'd almost lost today.

She wouldn't go there. Couldn't. He was safe and they

were making a baby and she would think of the future, not the past.

Long minutes later, AJ slipped free of her tight sheath. He stood up, shook himself and glanced first at Mik, and then back at Tala.

*I love you. I will always love you.*

AJ's thoughts filled her mind as Mik trotted across the meadow and sniffed her vulva. She dripped with AJ's seed and her own juices. Her passage was swollen and tender from sex and her heat. Her body jerked involuntarily when Mik's tongue gently laved her.

Then, shamelessly, Tala rolled to her back and spread her legs. Mik's head came up and she could have sworn his eyes were twinkling. He dipped his head again and licked her. She sensed Mik's arousal, his feral need. The power of his passion enveloped her in his musky scent, and her sensitive nostrils flared.

His tongue drove deep, bathing her, healing her. Tala's ears flattened to her skull and she whimpered. Her womb clenched and she knew Mik prepared her, readied her body for his. She rolled over and rose to all four feet, shook herself as if she'd just climbed out of a creek. Shocked by her body's response to Mik's tender ministrations, she wanted him. Now.

Already she ached with need. There was no foreplay, no reason to delay. She turned and looked over her shoulder at the beautiful wolf behind her. Droplets of moisture sparkled in the stiff whiskers along his muzzle. He stood with one foreleg raised, his haunches quivering, eyes narrowed.

Tala growled and bared her teeth.

Mik lunged forward. His huge jaws caught the thick ruff of fur at her neck and he clamped down, hard. Tala twisted her body, but she wasn't fast enough to avoid the clasp of his forelegs, the sharp jerk of his powerful hind legs.

The unbelievable joy of penetration as he drove into her, filling her with his cock. Sharp and slick, it slipped easily through her softened folds. Mik's spine twisted, his hips thrust forward, hard and fast, and Tala yipped in shock and surprise as the big wolf slammed into her.

He growled and jerked at the loose skin on her neck, anchoring himself with tightly grasping forelegs and the power of his strong jaws. Tala dug in her claws and braced her body, taking all that Mik gave her. He was deep, the tip of his penis connecting with her womb on every forward thrust, forcing its way through tightly grasping muscles until the thick bulb at its base slipped through her vaginal opening and locked them together.

She felt the hot spurts of ejaculate, the millions of tiny sperm filling her this time with a purpose.

And once again, Tala released an egg.

She loved them both equally, Mik and AJ. Loved them enough for this, that each of them should have a child of her womb, a baby to love and care for.

She dipped her head until her nose almost touched the green grass. Her body shivered and her legs quivered beneath Mik's impressive weight. Finally, as she felt the rhythmic jerks deep inside begin to slow, her front legs gave out and she toppled to the turf with Mik still locked inside.

AJ had been lying in the grass nearby, watching. He got up now and wandered over to the two of them, leaned close and sniffed Tala's face, her belly, the place where their bodies still connected.

Then he shifted and sat cross-legged beside them, naked in the chill night air. "You've done it now, sweetie. You popped out two, didn't you?"

Mik shifted. "She did what?" He glared at the wolf.

Tala shifted. She shoved her dark hair back from her eyes and grinned at both her men. "I did exactly what I planned to do. With both of you. We . . ." She cast a glance first at AJ and then Mik. "Together, the three of us just made a couple of babies. Babies who should arrive in around nine months."

Neither man said a word. The silence that followed unnerved her. Shaken, Tala looked from Mik to AJ and back at Mik. Had she totally misread her men? Dear Goddess, had she made a terrible mistake?

AJ swallowed, blinking. He raised his head, but he didn't look at Tala. Instead, he gazed directly into Mik's dark eyes. Eyes that glistened with tears. "December," he said. His voice cracked and he cleared his throat. "Unless they come early, we should have our babies in December. You and me, Mik. We're going to be daddies."

Mik nodded. He took a deep breath and reached for AJ. They clasped hands. Both men reached for Tala. She felt her smaller hands engulfed in their huge mitts, felt the power of their love surrounding her like a warm, protective blanket.

There were no words. No need to discuss what they'd done or question what had happened. Nothing any of them could say that would make this moment more perfect. They sat there for a long time, the three of them linked more powerfully than they'd ever connected before, hands and hearts united, sitting cross-legged like kids in the springtime grass without saying a word.

Hearts filled with love. Emotions spilling over and turning to dreams. A future to anticipate, one built on a past so contradictory and impossible there was no risk of repeating their bizarre beginnings.

Tala shivered and smiled at both her men. She had no idea where the knowledge came from, but she knew without any doubt, she carried new life.

Heart full of love and laughter, she shifted, raised her muzzle to the nighttime sky and howled. The long, clear note hadn't yet faded when Mik and AJ joined her song. Satisfied she'd sent her message of hope, Tala turned away and trotted down the well-worn trail to the house. Mik and AJ followed close behind, guarding her flanks. Seeing her safely back home.

The house was dark and quiet when AJ led Mik and Tala through the open door into the great room. They'd slipped into the clothing left on the deck and turned to go toward their room at the far end of the long hallway.

AJ stopped them and nodded toward Anton's study, where a light still glowed. As wound up as he felt from the events of the day and hours just past, there was no way he was going to fall asleep right away, and if Anton was still awake . . .

*I'm going with you.*

*Me, too.*

*So much for sleep.* AJ shrugged and headed toward the pale light. He stuck his head around the open door.

Anton looked up from the maps spread across his desk and waved the three of them into his study. "What are you guys still doing awake?"

AJ glanced at Mik, Mik grinned at AJ and the two of them focused on Tala.

She blushed. "We, uh . . ."

Anton's grin lit up his whole face. "I see. I predict a population explosion come December."

Tala planted her hands on her hips. "C'mon, Anton. Two babies does not a population explosion make."

Anton sat back in his chair and folded his hands behind his head. "Well, it does when you multiply that by Tinker and Lisa, and Adam and Eve, and those are the only ones I know of at this point."

"Two, each?" AJ cleared his throat. "Are you sure?"

"I don't know how many they're having, but if all went according to plan, they're having at least one apiece." He glanced around the office. "I may need to open a preschool."

He leaned forward then and, changing the subject entirely, pointed to a spot on the map. "Tala, you grew up near Tampa. Was it around here?"

Frowning, she leaned over the desk. "No, we were actually south of Tampa, down near here." She followed a main route with her finger and finally stopped and tapped a spot. "Here, near a big park. Why?"

"I think that's the same park Mei was found in. Where she was abandoned as a newborn. It's also very close to the area where Eve was born, and not all that far from the place where the circus I worked for overwintered, where Oliver showed up when he came into the country from Barbados. I'm not sure what it is, but there's something about the area that has produced or attracted an unusual number of Chanku. I intend to find out why."

Before anyone had time to respond, Keisha slipped quietly into the room. Her hair was tousled as if from sleep and she was wrapped in a pale blue silk robe. Anton's eyes lit up the moment he saw her.

She glanced at Tala, her eyes went wide and she laughed, a low, throaty sound that skittered along AJ's nerves. "You, too? My goodness. We may need to enlarge the clinic!"

"You can tell?" Tala glanced down at her flat stomach.

"Not you, sweetie. The guys. They're absolutely bursting with that 'I'm gonna be a daddy' look. You might not recognize it in your own men, but take a look at Tinker and Adam tomorrow. It's got to be the testosterone, but they can't seem to help themselves."

She leaned over and planted a kiss on Mik's cheek and then one on AJ. His skin heated with what he knew had to be a blush, but Keisha just chuckled and moved on to Anton. She glanced at the map of Florida and shook her head. "Can't let it go, can you m'love?"

Anton slowly folded the map closed. "Did you expect me to?"

Keisha shook her head and took his hand. "Of course not. If there're questions, I think you're programmed to find the answers. Now come to bed. Your mate needs you."

Anton took Keisha's hand without hesitation, and followed her to the door. He glanced back on his way out. "Turn the lights out, would you?" Then he and his mate disappeared down the dark hallway toward their wing of the house.

"How does she do that?" Tala crossed her arms over her chest and stared at the spot where Keisha and Anton had paused on their way out of the room.

"Do what?" Mik wrapped an arm around Tala and herded her toward the door.

"Get him to do exactly what she wants, when she wants." She glanced at AJ. "Why don't I have that kind of control over you two?"

AJ flipped off the light and stopped dead in his tracks. He stared through the gloom at Tala. "You're kidding, right?

Mik just shook his head. "Don't tell her, bro. I don't want her to know what she . . ."

"You say jump, we jump and ask how high," AJ groused. "You say you want babies, even if we're not really sure, and . . ."

"Wham," Mik said, laughing. "We've got babies—and yes, that's plural—on the way. And you want to know how Keisha does it? I want to know how you do it!"

She was still grumbling as they walked her back to their room, all five foot nothing of the most amazing woman either man had ever known. Mik looked up and grinned at him and the love in Mik's eyes almost stopped AJ in his tracks. He caught his breath and smiled at Mik, but his heart felt so full he thought it might burst.

Not bad, he thought as the three of them entered their room together. Not bad at all.

If you enjoy Kate Douglas's super-erotic WOLF TALES novels and her "Chanku" novellas in the SEXY BEAST anthologies, you're in for a different but equally delicious treat as she makes her debut in paranormal romance!

# DEMONFIRE

*Don't miss it!*

A Zebra mass-market paperback on sale in March 2010.
Turn the page for a special early preview . . .

# Chapter 1

*Sunday Night*

He struggled out of the darkness, confused, disoriented . . . recalling fire and pain and the soothing voices of men he couldn't see. Voices promising everlasting life, a chance to move beyond hell, beyond all he'd ever known. He remembered his final, fateful decision to take a chance, to search for something else.

For life beyond the hell that was Abyss.

A search that brought him full circle, back to a world of pain—to this world, wherever it might be. He frowned and tried to focus. This body was unfamiliar, the skin unprotected by scales or bone. He'd never been so helpless, so vulnerable.

His chest burned. The demon's fireshot, while not immediately fatal, would have deadly consequences. Hot blood flowed sluggishly from wounds across his ribs and spread over the filthy stone floor beneath his naked hip. The burn on his chest felt as if it were filled with acid. Struggling for each breath, he raised his head and stared into the glaring yellow eyes of an impossible creature holding him at bay.

Four sharp spears affixed to a long pole were aimed directly at his chest. The thing had already stabbed him once, and the bleeding holes in his side hurt like the blazes.

With a heartfelt groan, Dax tried to rise, but he had no strength left.

He fell back against the cold stones and his world faded once more to black.

"You're effing kidding me! I leave for one frickin' weekend and all hell breaks loose. You're positive? Old Mrs. Abernathy really thinks it ate her cat?" Eddy Marks took another sip of her iced caffé mocha whip and stared at Ginny. "Lord, I hope my father hasn't heard about it. He'll blame it on the Lemurians."

Ginny laughed so hard she almost snorted her latte. "Your dad's not still hung up on that silly legend, is he? Like there's really an advanced society of humanoids living inside Mount Shasta? I don't think so."

"Don't try and tell Dad they don't exist. He's convinced he actually saw one of their golden castles in the moonlight. Of course, it was gone by morning." Eddy frowned at Ginny and changed the subject. She was admittedly touchy about her dad's gullible nature. "Mrs. Abernathy's not serious, is she?"

"I dunno." Ginny shook her head. "She was really upset. Enough that she called nine-one-nine. I was on dispatch at Shascom that shift and took the call. They sent an officer out because she was hysterical, not because they actually believed Mr. Pollard's ceramic garden gnome ate Twinkles." Ginny ran her finger around the inside of her cup, chasing the last drops of her iced latte. "I heard there was an awful lot of blood on her back deck, along with tufts of suspiciously Twinkles-colored hair."

"Probably a coyote or a fox." Eddy finished the last of her drink and wished she'd had a shot of brandy to add to it. It would have been the perfect finish to the first brief vacation she'd had in months—two glorious days hiking and camping on Mount Shasta with only her dog for company . . . and not a single killer garden gnome in sight.

She grinned at Ginny. "Killer gnomes aren't usually a major threat around here."

Ginny laughed. "Generally, no. Lemurians either, in spite of what your dad and half the tourists think, but for once Eddy, don't be such a stick in the mud. Let your imagination go a little."

"What? And start spouting off about Lemurians? I don't think so. Someone has to be the grown-up! So what else happened while I was out communing with nature?"

"Well . . . it might have been the full moon, but there was a report that the one remaining stone gargoyle launched itself off the northwest corner of the old library building, circled the downtown area and flew away into the night. And . . ." Ginny paused dramatically, "another that the bronze statue of General Humphreys and his horse trotted out the park. The statue is gone. I didn't check on the gargoyle, but I went down to see the statue. It's not there. Looks like it walked right off the pedestal. That thing weighs over two tons." She set her empty cup down, folded her arms and, with one dark eyebrow raised, stared at Eddy.

"A big bronze statue like that would bring in a pretty penny at the recyclers. Somebody probably hauled it off with a truck, but it's a great visual, isn't it?" Eddy leaned back in her chair. "I can just see that big horse with the general, sword held high and covered in pigeon poop, trotting along Front Street. Maybe a little detour through the cemetery."

"Is it worth a story by ace reporter Edwina Marks?"

Eddy glanced at her. "Do not call me Edwina." She ran her finger through the condensation on the scarred wooden tabletop before looking up at Ginny and grinning. "Maybe a column about weird rumors and how they get started. I'll cite you as Ground Zero, but I doubt it's cutting edge enough for the front page of the *Record*."

Ginny grabbed her purse and pulled out a lipstick. "Yeah, like that rag's going to cover real news?"

"Hey, we do our best and we stay away from the tabloid stuff . . . you know, the garbage you like to read?" Laughing, Eddy stood up. "Well, I'm always complaining that nothing exciting ever happens around here. I guess flying gargoyles, runaway statues, and killer gnomes are better than nothing." She tossed some change on the table for a tip and waved at the girl working behind the counter. "Gotta go, Gin. I need to get home. Have to let Bumper out."

"Bumper? Who's that? Don't tell me you brought home another homeless mutt from the shelter."

"And if I did?"

Ginny waved the lipstick at her like a pointer. "Eddy, the last time you had to give up a fostered pup, you bawled for a week. Why do you do this to yourself?"

She'd be lucky if she only bawled for a week when it was time for Bumper to leave. They'd bonded almost immediately, but she really didn't want a dog. Not for keeps. "They were gonna put her down if no one took her," she mumbled.

Ginny shook her head. "Don't say I didn't warn you. One of these days you're going to take in a stray that'll really break your heart."

Eddy heard Bumper when she was still half a block from home. She'd only left the dog inside the house while she went to town for coffee, but it appeared the walls weren't thick enough to mute her deep-throated growling and barking.

Thank goodness it wasn't nine yet. Any later and she'd probably have one of the neighbors filing a complaint. Eddy picked up her pace and ran the last hundred yards home, digging for her house keys as she raced up the front walk. "Bumper, you idiot. I only left you for an hour. I hope you haven't been going on like this the whole time I've been gone."

She got the key in the lock and swung the front door

open. Bumper didn't even pause to greet her. Instead, she practically knocked Eddy on her butt as she raced out the front door, skidded through the open gate to the side yard and disappeared around the back of the house.

"Shit. Stupid dog." Eddy threw her keys in her bag, slung her purse over her shoulder and took off after the dog. It was almost completely dark away from the street light and Eddy stumbled on one of the uneven paving stones by the gate. Bumper's deep bark turned absolutely frantic, accompanied by the added racket from her clawing and scratching at the wooden door to Eddy's potting shed.

"If you've got a skunk cornered in there, you stupid dog, I swear I'm taking you back to the shelter."

Bumper stopped barking, now that she knew she had Eddy's attention. She whined and sniffed at the door, still scratching at the rough wood. Eddy fumbled in her bag for her keychain and the miniature flashlight hanging from the ring. The beam was next to worthless, but better than nothing.

She scooted Bumper out of the way with her leg and unlatched the door just enough to peer in through a crack. Bumper whapped her nose against Eddy's leg. Shoving frantically with her broad head, she tried to force her way inside.

"Get back." Eddy glared at the dog. Bumper flattened her ears against her curly head and immediately backed off, looking as pathetic as she had last week at the shelter when Eddy'd realized she couldn't leave a blond pit bull crossed with a standard poodle to the whims of fate.

She aimed her tiny flashlight through the narrow opening. Blinked. Told herself she was really glad she'd been drinking coffee and not that brandy she'd wanted tonight, because otherwise she wouldn't believe what she saw.

Maybe Mrs. Abernathy wasn't nuts after all. Eddy grabbed a shovel leaning against the outside wall of the shed and threw the door open wide.

The garden gnome that should have been stationed in

the rose garden out in front held a pitchfork in its stubby little hands like a weapon, ready to stab what appeared to be a person lying in the shadows. When the door creaked open, the gnome turned its head, glared at Eddy through yellow eyes, bared unbelievably sharp teeth, and screamed at her like an avenging banshee.

Bumper's claws scrabbled against the stone pathway. Eddy swung the shovel. The crunch of metal connecting with ceramic seemed unnaturally loud. The scream stopped as the garden gnome shattered into a thousand pieces. The pitchfork clattered to the ground and a dark, evil smelling mist gathered in the air above the pile of dust. It swirled a moment and then suddenly whooshed over Eddy's shoulder and out the open door.

A tiny blue light pulsed and flickered, followed the mist as far as the doorway, and then returned to hover over the figure in the shadows. Bumper paused long enough to sniff the remnants of the garden gnome and growl, before turning her attention to whatever lay on the stone floor. Eddy stared at the shovel in her hands and took one deep breath after another. This was not happening. She *had not seen* a garden gnome in attack mode.

One with glowing yellow eyes and razor-sharp teeth.

*Impossible.*

Heart pounding, arms and legs shaking, she slowly pivoted in place and focused on whoever it was that Bumper seemed so pleased to see.

The mutt whined, but her curly tail was wagging a million miles a minute. She'd been right about the gnome. Eddy figured she'd have to trust the dog's instincts about who or whatever had found such dubious sanctuary in her potting shed.

Eddy squinted and tried to focus on the flickering light that flitted in the air over Bumper's head, but it was jerking around so quickly she couldn't tell what it was. She still had her key ring clutched in her fingers. She wasn't quite ready to put the shovel down, but she managed to shine the narrow beam of light toward the lump on the floor.

Green light reflected back from Bumper's eyes. Eddy swung wider with the flashlight. She saw a muscular arm, a thick shoulder, and the broad expanse of a masculine chest. Blood trickled from four perfectly spaced pitchfork-sized holes across the man's ribs and pooled beneath his body. There appeared to be a deep wound on his chest, though it wasn't bleeding.

In fact, it looked almost as if it had been cauterized. A burn? Eddy swept the light over his full length. Her eyes grew wider with each inch of skin she exposed. He was marked with a colorful tattoo that ran from his thigh, across his groin to his chest, but other than the art, he was naked. Very naked, all the way from his long, narrow feet, up those perfectly formed, hairy legs to . . . Eddy quickly jerked the light back toward his head.

When she reached his face, the narrow beam glinted off dark eyes looking directly into hers. Beautiful, soul-searching dark brown eyes shrouded in thick, black lashes. He was gorgeous. Even with a smear of dirt across one cheek and several days' growth of dark beard, he looked as if he should be on the cover of *People* as the sexiest man alive.

Breathing hard, her body still shaking from the adrenaline coursing through her system, Eddy dragged herself back to the situation at hand. Whatever it was. He hadn't said a word. She'd thought he was unconscious. He wasn't. He was injured . . . not necessarily helpless. She squatted down beside him, and reassured by Bumper's acceptance and the fact the man didn't look strong enough to sit up, much less harm her, Eddy set the shovel aside.

She touched his shoulder and grimaced at the deep wound on his chest, the bloody stab wounds in his side. Made a point not to look below his waist. "What happened? Are you okay? Well, obviously not with all those injuries." Rattled, she took a deep breath. "Who are you?"

He blinked and turned his head. She quickly tilted the light away from his eyes. "I'm sorry. I . . ."

He shook his head. His voice was deep and sort of raspy. "No. It's all right." He glanced up at the flickering light dancing over head, frowned and then nodded.

She could tell he was in pain, but he took a deep breath and turned his focus back to Eddy.

"I am Dax. Thank you."

"I'm Eddy. Eddy Marks." Why she'd felt compelled to give her full name made no sense. None of this did. She couldn't place his accent and he wasn't from around here. She would have recognized any of the locals. She started to rise. "I'll call nine-one-one. You're injured."

His arm snaked out and he grabbed her forearm, trapping her with surprising strength. "No. No one. Don't call anyone."

Eddy looked down at the broad hand, the powerful fingers wrapped entirely around her arm, just below her elbow. She should have been terrified. Should have been screaming in fear, but something in those eyes, in the expression on his face . . .

Immediately, he loosened his grasp. "I'm sorry. Please forgive me, but no one must know I'm here. If you can't help me, please let me leave. I have so little time . . ." He tried to prop himself up on one arm, but his body trembled with the effort.

Eddy rubbed her arm. It tingled where he'd touched her. "What's going on? How'd you get here? Where are you clothes?"

The flickering light came closer, hovered just in front of his chest, pulsed with a brillant blue glow that spread out in a pale arc until it touched him, appeared to soak into his flesh, and then dimmed. Before Eddy could figure out what she was seeing, Dax took a deep breath. He seemed to gather strength—from the blue light?

He shoved himself upright, glanced at the light and nodded. "Thank you, Willow."

Then he stood up, as if his injuries didn't affect him at all. Obviously, neither did the fact he wasn't wearing a stitch of clothes. Towering over Eddy, he held out his hand to help her to her feet. "I will go now. I'm sorry to have . . ."

Eddy swallowed. She looked up at him as he fumbled for words, realized she was almost eye level with his . . . *oh crap!* She jerked her head to one side and stared at his hand for a moment. Shifted her eyes and blinked at the blue light, now hovering in the air not six inches from her face. What in the hell was going on?

Slowly, she looked back at Dax, placed her hand in his and, with a slight tug from him, rose to her feet. The light followed her. "What is that thing?" Tilting her head, she focused on the bit of fluff glowing in the air between them, and let out a whoosh of breath.

"Holy Moses." It was a woman. A tiny, flickering fairy-like woman with gossamer wings and long blond hair. "It's frickin' Tinkerbelle!" Eddy turned and stared at Dax. "That's impossible."

He shrugged. "So are garden gnomes armed with pitch-forks. At least in your world. So am I, for that matter."

Eddy snapped her gaze away from the flickering fairy and stared at Dax. "What do you mean, you're impossible? Why? Who are you? What are you?"

Again, he shrugged. "I'm a mercenary, now. A hired soldier, if you will. However, before the Edenites found me, before they gave me this body, I was a demon. Cast out of Abyss, but a demon nonetheless."

He knew she was bursting with questions, but she'd taken him inside her home, given him a pair of soft gray pants with a drawstring at the waist and brewed some sort of hot, dark liquid that smelled much better than it tasted.

She handed him a cup, then as she left the room, she told him to sit.

He sat, despite the sense of urgency and the pain. The snake tattoo seemed to ripple against his skin, crawling across his thigh, over his groin and belly to the spot where the head rested above his human heart. He felt the heat from the demon's fireshot beside the serpent's head burning deeper with each breath he took. Exhaustion warred with the need to move, to begin the hunt. In spite of Willow's gift of healing energy, he felt as if could sleep for at least a month. Instead, he waited for the woman, for Eddy Marks. He sipped from the steaming cup while she opened and closed drawers in an adjoining room and mumbled unintelligible words to herself.

The four-legged creature stayed with him. Eddy called it "damned dog," but she'd also said its name was Bumper and that it was a female. The animal appeared to be intelligent, though Dax hadn't figured out how to communicate with her yet. She was certainly odd looking with her bullet-shaped head, powerful jaws and curly blond coat.

"Sorry to take so long. I had to hunt for the first aid kit."

The woman carried a box filled with rolls of bandages and jars and tubes of what must be medicine. He wished his mind were clearer, but he was still growing used to this body, to the way the brain worked. It was so unlike his own. This mind had memories of things like bandages and dogs and the names for the various pieces of furniture he saw, but too much in his head felt foggy. Too much was still trapped in the thinking process of demonkind, of kill or be killed. Eat or be eaten.

All that was absolutely clear was the mission, and he was woefully behind on that.

Of course, he hadn't expected to encounter a demon-powered gargoyle armed with fire just seconds after his arrival through the vortex. Nor had he expected the power of the demons already here. Eddy had no idea she had truly saved more than his life.

So much more was at stake. So many lives.

Her soft voice was laced with steel when it burst into his meandering thoughts. "First things first," she said. "And don't lie to me. I'm trusting you for some weird reason when I know damned well I should call the authorities. So tell me, who are you, really? Who did this to you? How'd you get this burn?"

Blinking, he raised his head. She knelt in front of him. Her short dark hair was tousled and her chocolaty brown eyes stared at him with concern and some other emotion he couldn't quite identify. Thank goodness there was no sign of fear. He didn't want her to fear him, though she'd be better off if she did.

He shook his head. He still couldn't believe that blasted demon had gotten the drop on him. "I really am demonkind. From Abyss. The wound on my chest? It was the gargoyle. He surprised me. I wasn't expecting him, especially armed with the fire."

She blinked and gave him a long, narrow-eyed stare. "Hookay. If you say so." She took a damp cloth and wiped around the burn on his chest. The cool water felt good.

Her soft hands felt even better. Her touch seemed to spark what could only be genetic, instinctive memories to this body he inhabited. He felt as if his mind was clearing. Maybe this world would finally start to make sense.

She tilted her head and studied the burned and bloody wound. "That's the second reference to a gargoyle I've heard tonight," she said, looking at his chest, not his face. "They're not generally part of the typical conversation around here."

Shocked, he grabbed her wrist. She jerked her head around and stared at his fingers. He let go. "I'm sorry. I didn't mean to startle you. Have you seen it? The gargoyle? Do you know where it is?"

She stared at him a moment, and then sprayed something on the wound that took away the pain. She covered it with a soft, flesh-colored bandage before she answered him. "No," she said, shaking her head, concentrating on the bandage. "Not recently."

Her short dark hair floated against the sharp line of her jaw. He fought a surprisingly powerful need to touch the shimmering strands. He'd never once run his fingers through a woman's hair. Of course, he couldn't remember having fingers. He'd never had any form beyond his demon self of mist and scales, sharp claws, and sharper fangs.

She flattened all four corners of the bandage and looked up at him. He wished he were better at reading human expressions. Hers was a mystery to him.

"Last time I saw it," she said, "it was perched on the corner of the library building where it belonged, but I heard it flew away. It's made of stone and most definitely not alive, which means it shouldn't be flying anywhere. What's going on? And what are you, really? You can't be serious about . . ." She glanced away, shook her head again and then touched the left side of his chest, just above the first puncture wound. "Turn around so I can take care of these cuts over your ribs."

He turned and stared at the fireplace across the room. After a moment he focused on a beautiful carved stone owl, sitting on the brick hearth. The owl's eyes seemed to watch him, but he sensed no life in the creature. It was better to concentrate on the bird than the woman.

Her gentle touch was almost worse than the pain from the injuries. It reminded him of things he wanted, things he'd never have.

He was, after all, still a demon. A fallen demon, but nonetheless, not even close to human. Not at all the man he appeared to be. This form was his for one short week.

His avatar.

Seven days he'd been given. Seven days to save the town

of Evergreen and all its inhabitants. If he failed, if demonkind succeeded in this, their first major foray into Earth's dimension, other towns could fall. Other worlds. All of Earth, all of Eden.

Seven days.

Impossible . . . and he'd already wasted one of them.

He would have laughed if he didn't feel like turning around and heading back to Abyss—except Abyss was closed to him. With only the most preposterous of luck, he might end up in Eden, though he doubted that would happen no matter how he did on his mission. The promises had been vague, after all.

So why, he wondered, had he agreed to this stupid plan?

"I asked you, what's going on? I'm assuming you know how my cheesy little WalMart garden gnome suddenly grew teeth and turned killer. Try the truth this time. With details that make sense."

He jerked his head around and stared at her, understanding more of his new reality as each moment passed, as the memories and life of this body's prior owner integrated with his demon soul.

Eddy sat back on her heels and her dark eyes flashed with as much frustrated anger as curiosity.

He glanced down at his side. There were clean, white bandages over each of the wounds from the demon's weapon. The big burn on his chest was cleaned and covered. The entire length of his tattoo pulsed with evil energy, but if he ignored that, he really did feel better.

Stronger.

He sensed Willow's presence and finally spotted her sitting amongst a collection of glass figurines on a small bookcase. Could demons enter glass? He wasn't sure, but at least Willow would warn him in time. He caught the woman's unwavering stare with his own. She waited more patiently than he deserved for his answer. "I always tell the truth," he said. "The problem is, will you believe me?"

She nodded and stood up. "I'll try." She stalked out of the room. He heard water running. A moment later she returned, grabbed his cup and her own and left again. This time, when she handed him the warm mug of coffee, he knew what to expect.

He savored the aroma while she settled herself on the end of the couch, as far from him as she could get, yet still have room to sit.

She was close enough for him to pick up the perfume from the soap she'd used to wash her hands, the warm essence of her skin, the scent that was all hers.

He shrugged off the unusual sensations her nearness gave him. Then he took a sip of his coffee, replacing Eddy's scent with the rich aroma of the drink. He couldn't seem to do anything about his powerful awareness of her. Of this body's reaction to her presence, her scent, to every move she made.

He could try to ignore her, but he didn't want to. No, not at all. It probably wouldn't work, anyway.

She curled her bare feet under herself and leaned against the back of the couch, facing him. He turned and sat much the same way, facing her.

Bumper looked from one of them to the other, barked once and jumped up on the couch, filling the gap between them. She turned around a couple of times and lay down with a loud, contented sigh. Her fuzzy butt rested on Dax's bare foot, her chin was on the woman's ankle.

"Bumper likes you." She stroked the silly looking beast's head with her long, slim fingers. "If she didn't approve, you wouldn't be sitting here."

Dax smiled, vaguely aware that it was an entirely new facial expression for him. Of course, everything he did now, everything he felt and said, was new. "Then I guess I'm very glad Bumper approves. Thank you for battling the demon, for taking care of my injuries. You saved my life."

She stared at him for a long, steady moment, as if digesting his statement. There was still no fear in her.

She would be safer if she was afraid.

"You're welcome," she said. "Now please explain. Tell me about the garden gnome. What was it, really?"

He steepled his fingers in front of his face and rested his chin on the forefingers. Had the one who first owned this body found comfort in such a position? No matter. It was his body now, for however long he could keep it alive, and resting his chin this way pleased him. "The small statue was inhabited by a demon from the world of Abyss. They've broken through into Earth's dimension, but the only form they have here is spirit—that dark, stinking mist you saw after you shattered the creature was the demon's essence. They need an avatar, something made of the earth . . . ceramic, stone, metal. Nothing alive. The avatar gives form and shape, the demon provides the life."

She nodded her head, slowly, as if digesting his words. "If I hadn't seen it . . . good Lord . . . I still can't believe I saw what I saw out there." She glanced around the room. "Where's that little fairy? The one you called Willow?"

"She's actually a will o' the wisp, not a fairy. She's a protector of sorts. She gathers energy out of the air and shares it with me. Helps me understand this unfamiliar world, this body. Right now, she's sitting on your bookcase. I think she likes being surrounded by all the little figurines on the top shelf." He looked over his shoulder at Willow. Her light pulsed bright blue for a second. Then, once again, she disappeared among the tiny glass statuettes.

Eddy shook her head. She laughed, but it sounded forced, like she was strangling. Mostly, her voice was low, sort of soft and mellow. It fit her.

"I'm generally pretty pragmatic, unlike my father who believes every wild story he hears. I can tell it's going to be really hard for me to deal with all this. Just point to Willow as a reminder that the impossible is sometimes possible . . . you know, when I look at you like I think you're lying."

"I promise to do that." He smiled over the edge of his cup and took a sip of the dark brew. She'd said it would perk him up, whatever that meant. He did feel more alert. He hoped it wasn't because danger was lurking nearby. He still didn't understand all this body's instincts.

"You said you were a demon, but you look perfectly human. What exactly do you mean?"

"Exactly that. I'm a demon from the world of Abyss. It exists in a dimension apart from yours, but I was sent here by people from another world, one called Eden that's in yet another dimension. The two worlds never touch, never interact. They exist, complete yet apart, entirely dependent on the balance that holds them apart as much as it connects them."

"So what does that make Earth?"

He stared at his cup of coffee a moment, picturing the three worlds as he imagined them. "Earth is the fulcrum," he said, raising his eyes to study her reaction. "Eden on the one side is a world of light filled with people who are inherently good. Abyss, on the other, is a world of darkness, a land of fire and ice populated by creatures who personify evil. Earth is in the center, holding them apart, keeping them in perpetual balance . . . or, at least, that's the way it's supposed to work. The way it's always worked in the past."

Her brows knotted over her dark eyes and she looked confused, but at least she was still listening. Dax ran his fingers through Bumper's curly coat. The dog was a hard-muscled, frilly contradiction—she had a powerful body with strong jaws, yet she was covered in a curly blond coat that made her look utterly ridiculous. Dax couldn't imagine anyone creating an animal like Bumper on purpose, yet somehow the combination worked.

Sort of like Earth. "Your world is mostly populated by

a mixture of different kinds of humans—some who will always try to do the right thing as well as those who are set on doing something evil. The best of you and the worst of you are balanced by the vast majority who are sort of like this dog of yours, a blend of both good and bad, beautiful and ugly." He laughed. "Smart and stupid. Somehow, it all works and, on the whole, humans get along and live their lives."

She snorted. He grinned at her. "Well, most of the time, anyway."

Shaking her head, she set her cup down. "I beg to differ with you, but people don't get along that well. There are wars going on all over the world, people are starving and dying, we have to worry about terrorists blowing things up, and . . ."

"I know. That's why I'm here. Evil has grown too powerful on your world. It's giving demonkind a foothold. Balance has reached a tipping point. It's slipping over to the side of darkness. The people of Eden recognized the danger, but they're incapable of fighting. Their nature doesn't allow it. They can, however, hire fallen demons to fight their battles."

She ignored his reference to himself and instead asked the one question Dax didn't want to answer.

"What happens if the balance slips too far?"

He didn't want to think about that. Couldn't allow himself to consider failure. Bumper raised her head, stared beyond Dax, and growled. Dax looked down at the dog, but he spoke to Eddy. "Then the demons of Abyss take over. If Evergreen falls to the demons, they gain a powerful foothold in your world. If this town falls, others may follow. The fear is that all of Earth will fall to darkness and demons will rule. There's a risk that eventually, even Eden will be overrun."

"Dax? I think you need to turn around."

He snapped his head up at the quaver in her voice and

Eddy's terrified gaze. He spun around on the couch and his feet hit the floor just as the stone owl by the fireplace stretched its gray wings and clicked its sharp beak, as if testing to make sure things worked.

Willow shot up from the bookcase so fast she left a trail of blue sparkles in the air behind her. Dax leapt to his feet, pulled in the energy Willow sent him and pointed both hands at the owl, fingertips spread wide.

Fire burst from his fingers in long, twin spikes of pure power. He caught the owl as it prepared to take flight, trapped the creature in a blazing sphere of heat and light and blew it right through the wire screen and into the fireplace.

Eddy screamed. The creature screamed louder, sounding eerily like the garden gnome Eddy had flattened. The cry cut off the moment the flaming owl hit the back of the firebox and shattered. A dark wisp, stinking of sulfur, coalesced in front of the broken pieces, but before it could race up the flue to freedom, Dax called on Willow's power once again.

This time a blast of icy air caught the amorphous mass of darkness, freezing it before it could make its escape. It hovered a moment, quivering in midair, then fell to the hearth and shattered into a thousand tiny pieces of black ice.

Dax hit the ice with a burst of flame. The pieces sizzled and disappeared in puffs of steam.

He took a deep breath and turned away from the mess. Eddy sat on the end of the couch, with Bumper caught in her shaking arms. Both of them gaped, wide-eyed, at the fireplace. Before Dax could assure Eddy that everything was all right, at least for now, she raised her head and stared at him.

"Okay." Her voice cracked and she took a deep breath. "I take back what I said. You won't need to point to Willow for proof. I promise to believe anything you tell me. Explain, please, what the hell just happened?"